All
Time
Lowe

~Full Bifta Books~

DEDICATION

To a gentleman and an angel,
Francis and Isabel Jones.

Susan–simply the best.

Where does reality end and
imagination begin? SR

1987

JANUARY
Flotation of British Airways.
Terry Waite, special envoy, was kidnapped in Beirut.

FEBRUARY
The General Synod votes to allow the ordination of women.

MARCH
MS Herald of Free Enterprise capsizes, killing 193 people.
The value of the pound was at a five-year high.
Vincent van Gogh's painting, Sunflowers, sells for £24,750,000.

APRIL
MPs vote against the restoration of the death penalty.

MAY
Andrew Murray, a tennis player, was born.

JUNE
Margaret Thatcher secures a third term in Parliament with a reduced majority.
Peter Beardsley, an England striker, was the most expensive player transfer at £1.9 million.

JULY
Rick Astley's - Never Gonna Give You Up was released.

AUGUST
Moors murderer Ian Brady claims to have committed a further five murders.
One person a day in Great Britain is reported to be dying of AIDS.

SEPTEMBER
Ford completes the takeover of Aston Martin.

OCTOBER
IKEA opens its first British store in Warrington.
Great Storm batters south-east England.
Black Monday - Wall Street crash.

NOVEMBER
In King's Cross, London, an underground fire kills 31 people.

DECEMBER
Channel Tunnel construction initiated

ONE

15th May 1988 – Hotel Poolside. Spain.

If ever there was a moment in life when you questioned your sanity, then this was it for Mary. Earlier, she had heard an insane voice echoing in her ear; unnervingly, it had started again. The troubling squeaky inflexion sent a chill down her spine, pervading the very essence of her being. Could alcohol be the problem? Too many margaritas on an empty stomach at that time of the morning was foolhardy. She dismissed the insanity plea and searched her mind for a clear, logical answer. Any answer would be good. However, her neural pathways were malfunctioning.

A bothersome fly landed on the bridge of her sunglasses. She swished it away. Ever persistent, it lifted and landed on her face. "What is it with you? Now go away... shoo."

"You say something to me?" A poolside waiter stood nearby, ready to serve another cocktail.

Shading her eyes from the glare of the early summer sun, she gazed upon a sun-kissed Adonis in white shorts and a Hawaiian shirt. Any thoughts of voices abated. "No, sorry, I didn't mean you." How could she tell him she was venting her feelings on a fly? He would think she was off her head or maybe even a psycho.

The waiter placed the cocktail within easy reach. "I hear you say, 'what is it with you?' and I theenk I am... how you say, wrongdoing."

Not so long ago, his swarthy good looks would have bowled her over. However, with a change in her personal circumstances, her life was now fulfilled and complete.

Even so, that wasn't always the case. At secondary school, her shy, retiring nature made it difficult for her to relate to others. Teased and tormented, she quickly learnt that keeping to herself was less complicated, less challenging. Being persecuted by bullies and needing to deal with the situation full-scale was her worst nightmare. However, the most significant cause of her disquiet was brought about by bashful interaction with the opposite sex. It turned her into a quivering wreck. By far the worst for Mary was the embarrassing, uncontrollable blush, inching up from her neck and covering her cheeks. Of course, insensitive people pointing and staring made her humiliation worse. Then the flush would persist and turn blotchy, adding to her mortification. At that moment, it was as if she were under the microscope for all to see, exposed, defenceless and stupid. Given time, she learnt to cope with the problem by being outspoken and challenging. This distinctive form of defence didn't come easy, but once she realised its potential, Mary used it with devastating effect. People were disinclined to make fun of such a ballsy female who would bite their heads off as soon as look at them.

She engaged the waiter in conversation. "I haven't seen you here before. Do you work at the hotel all the time?" She chided herself for using what sounded like a corny chat-up line.

"No, how you say, I am party timer. Some days I learn English in Colegio in Alicante. If I have time, I work in shop with Papa."

Mary couldn't resist a smile at his innocence. "What sort of shop does your dad have?"

"He sell mmm... things from Spain. Somebody say me it is

tourist tat, and another he say tourist crap. What is meaning—tourist tat and tourist crap?"

She didn't have the heart to tell him the truth; he seemed so naive. With feelings for his innocence, she searched her mind for a diplomatic answer. "I'm not sure; maybe you should ask your teacher."

"I want how you say, be better."

Noticing his nametag, she continued the conversation. "Your English is very good, Pepe."

"Thank you. We say *"muy amable"* — very kind."

She held out her hand. "Nice to meet you, Pepe. My name is Mary."

"*No... Es el nombre.*" In his excitement, he forgot his English, "I am sorry. It is name of my mama."

She caught sight of him looking at her ample cleavage. The feeling of being sexy made her feel good. Over the years, her self-image had taken quite a battering, owing to a bad relationship. Nevertheless, her lack of confidence was steadily changing in favour of a more optimistic, self-assured Mary. Despite the rigours of having two children and a stressful life, Mary still had an exquisite figure, which was more to do with a fast metabolism than a sensible diet. Many women would have given their eyeteeth for such a toned, perfect body.

"I've never known a Pepe before. It is such a lovely name."

"My name is... mmm, I theenk for your Joseph."

"It's short for Joseph? Well, I never knew that."

"Yes, it is shorty name."

"And do you like the work here, Pepe?"

"Yes, it is good, I... mmm, practice English and meet happy people. It is, how you say... mmm, brill. I learn brill from people in otel." Pepe smiled with satisfaction, confident that his communication skills were improving. He pointed to postcards on the lounger. "You writing a posty card from Spain?"

She put a hand to her mouth to suppress a smile. "Yes, I'm writing to my Mum and two children in England. They've never been to Spain, so I'm telling them all about it. It's my first time here as well."

"Why you not gone to Spain before?"

"Oh, many reasons. Money is the obvious one, but also a death in the family..." She stopped, realising she was discussing her personal life with a stranger. Mary changed tack. "Well, anyway, it's nice to be here in this lovely country, Pepe." She smiled at him, putting on a brave face over the sadness; even so, it lurked just below the surface. "I... I just wanted to get away." She faltered, in danger of breaking down, maybe even revealing secrets she had tried so hard to pigeonhole. Her sudden adverse change in emotion with the mention of death shocked Mary. She thought the sadness was long gone.

Guests nearby called for Pepe's attention, saving her from further embarrassment. He looked towards the pool area.

"Excuse, I must go, *muchas* peoples want me, but I am seeing you again." With a flourish, napkin over his arm, tray at shoulder height, he hastened to the other guests in need of refreshment. "*Hasta luego, señora Mary.*"

Pepe beamed a smile as he scurried over to the poolside. "Yes, holiday people, what can I get you for?"

Lying back on the sun lounger, determined to calm her agitated mind, Mary closed her eyes. The soporific effect of the alcohol edged her towards a world of warmth, comfort and distant sounds. All was peace and tranquillity, except that a tickle on her nose interrupted her dream-like state. Eyes closed, she rubbed her nose. The tickle went away. Unknown to Mary, the nuisance fly was back. What happened next completely freaked her out. A chilling voice, more forceful than before, echoed in her ear. "Give me the money, bitch."

"What the bloody hell?" shrieked Mary. Freaked out, she leapt to her feet, staring at nearby guests as if in some way they were responsible for the troublesome words. Nothing seemed to make sense. Did she imagine it? Did she, in truth, hear a voice?

"Are you all right, dear?" enquired a lady sitting nearby, eager to find out why Mary had leapt off the lounger, uttering, 'What the bloody Hell?'

Mary realised her behaviour must have seemed odd. She searched her mind for an answer. "Oh, just cramp." As if to confirm her fib, she reached down to massage the back of her leg. "Always troubles me when I lie for long; it hurts like hell."

"You should drink tonic water; it's good for cramp. I drink it all the time."

"Really, I didn't know that," said Mary, rubbing her leg, feeling confident that her ruse had worked.

As she sat down on the lounger, Mary tried to make sense of the strange happenings. I've got to pull myself together, she thought, but how the hell do I deal with a voice in my ear and just one ear, come to think of it? It's such a weird squeaky voice; it's in my head, yet it isn't. She beamed a reassuring smile at the nosey lady.

Hang on a minute, my friend Jean, her husband hears voices. Turning it over in her mind, she tried to get a handle on the bizarre happenings. Yeah, but he has a mental illness and has to take tablets. Oh no, am I a nutcase? This isn't good.

She felt the urge to get up and pace about, but thought better of it. Sitting tight, she continued the frenetic search of her mind. I'm sure I'm not... what's that word, hall... hallucinated? Yes, that's it, hallucinated. No, I'm right. Maureen said, If you hear voices and question, 'Am I mad?' then you're not. Was that what she said? Exasperation took hold; she shook her head in frustration. Oh, I don't know.

Mary reached for the cocktail and took a much-needed medicinal slurp. Deep in thought, she held the glass in front of her eyes. Could it really be that simple, she speculated, too many margaritas? Mary racked her brain, waiting for a reply – nothing was forthcoming. Why not shout Pepe over and order a coffee? No, that's stupid. How can a cup of coffee stop voices? If it is the margaritas, then... oh my God, maybe someone's spiked the drinks.

Paranoia took hold. She scanned the immediate area for the culprit. No, not him, he's too old. No, not him, too young. Now wait a minute; look at him. What a weird, pervy-looking thing *he* is. Ugh... Oh, my God, he's looking at me.

Reaching for her book, Mary raised it to face height, blocking the weirdo's eye contact. Hang on a minute; what am I thinking about? This is crazy. They only spike your drink when they want to abduct you and have their wicked way with you. That couldn't happen here, could it? Mary tried to calm her manic thoughts. She reached into her bag for suntan lotion, hoping a pampering session could mellow her mind. She took a sneaky look at the weirdo as she applied lotion. He was no longer watching her. All the same, she couldn't trust him; she'd seen his sort before.

Lying back, Mary gazed up at white, wispy clouds in a beautiful, blue sky. A light, warm breeze caressed her body. Palm leaves floated in and out of her field of vision, hypnotically lulling her to sleep.

Unknown to Mary, an unusual number of flies had settled on her parasol, drawing the attention of hotel guests. Although flies, *per se,* are considered harmless, sheer numbers always caused revulsion. The weirdo, acting as a Good Samaritan, headed over to Mary to warn her of the impending menace as it closed in. Guests around the pool distanced themselves from the strange gathering of flies and headed to the bar.

"Hello!" said the weirdo as he tried to stir Mary from her sleep. Glancing up at the flies, he shuddered in disgust. They crawled beneath the parasol, emitting a frenzied, surreal sound. His gut instinct was to run from the teeming, repulsive sight. Yet, he held his ground. Unable to wake Mary from her alcohol-induced nap, he shook her arm, "Hello! Excuse me... Hello!" Mary came to and recognised the man in an instant. She squealed. The man shrieked with fright.

"Get away from me, you perv!"

All he could think about was apologising. However, he realised that it sounded as if he was apologising for being a perv when, in reality, he was apologising for disturbing her. Fellow guests looked on with concern. The flies, with military precision, continued down the parasol support pole, gaining on Mary.

Screaming, part of the body's response to fright, also attracted help, and so Mary shrieked with gusto, turning heads all around the pool. Members of staff ran to her aid. Only then did she notice the flies in huge, seething numbers as they hopped onto her sun lounger table. From here, they were just feet away. With a combination of shock and horror, she squealed even louder.

No one had ever seen such a hideous amount of flies as they infested the area of the surrounding poolside. This was an extraordinary occurrence, and many a Spaniard looking on made the sign of the cross and uttered 'Dios Mio' – 'My God'.

To calm a very distressed Mary, Pepe moved her sun lounger away from the area of concern near to the pool attendant's station. Another member of staff lifted the offending parasol out of its base, closed it up and hastened away. People stood watching the events unfold, parted like a wave, distancing themselves from the parasol of flies.

Peace slowly returned to the poolside. Bathers, who had vacated the area because of the unsettling kerfuffle, drifted back to the poolside, resuming where they had left off, although they kept a cautious eye on the proceedings.

To foster a sense of normality, staff members walked around the poolside, chatting and handing out small bowls of fruit salad and sweets. They reassured their guests that all was well and, more importantly, all was now under control. Even a member of the hotel's management moved around the area, smiling and shrugging the incident off as a freak of nature.

Nevertheless, from a vantage point high up in the palm trees, more flies mustered and watched. A swarming, heaving mass of little black devils, preparing to do their damnedest, bided their time.

Then, *en masse*, swooping down, they landed on a terrified, very hysterical Mary. As they settled on her skin, they nipped with agonising intensity. One bite would have been a nuisance, but multiplied by hundreds, the pain was excruciating. The seething, buzzing mass were on a mission with no compromise. They crawled on her face and body, biting with such intensity that her skin became red, blistered and painful. Despite frantic movements to shoo the flies away, they refused to leave.

Mary squealed with such harrowing intensity that she retched. The flies crawled in her ears, mouth and nostrils, intent on invading her body through any orifice available, and they were succeeding. It all became too much for her to handle. Spinning around and moving relentlessly, she overbalanced and fell to the ground with a sickening thud. Blood oozed from a cut on her head, exciting the flies all the more.

To shocked onlookers, Mary lay motionless – unconscious. Nobody knew why this strange, abnormal behaviour in flies should be happening, and it was happening entirely to one person. It was as if the doors of damnation had swung open, releasing Satan's little devils to do their worst on a poor, unsuspecting soul.

Mary lay where she fell, her face frozen in a terrifying rictus. An allergic reaction took hold of her body. Death was but minutes away.

TWO

Thursday, 15th October 1987.
Seven Months Earlier.

Thursday afternoon gave way to a weather depression over the Bay of Biscay. Guidance from weather prediction models at the time suggested that severe weather would extend as far as the English Channel and southern coastal England. In the early hours of Friday, 16th October, with force eleven gales, the depression paid no heed to weather predictions and made its way to Cornwall. Unabated, it tracked north-east to the Midlands and moved towards the Wash, causing widespread destruction and mayhem. Many people died, houses were damaged, and thousands of trees were felled. The national grid suffered extensive damage, leaving many without power for days. The storm that wasn't meant to be cost insurance companies an estimated £2 billion. To many, it seemed a bad omen, heralding the great financial crash of 1987.

Monday, 26th October 1987.

Seated at the head of the conference table, Quentin St John gazed out of the investment bank window over rooftops to the horizon and beyond. Seagulls soared in the late October sky as onshore winds buffeted and tested their flying skills. No longer focused on the job in hand, Quentin conjured up thoughts of the West Country, where he had spent many happy days with his parents on their annual holiday, though it was very different then. According to Quentin, nowadays there is too much commercialisation, which has spoiled the Cornwall he knew and loved. Above all, his pet hate was the annoying kiss me quick mentality (referring to hats worn at seaside resorts). Yet, despite the changes, Cornwall still held so much for him. He recalled the beauty and serenity of the county, the rugged coastline with its azure-blue sea, isolated coves, and golden sand. Closing his eyes, he felt the warmth of the sun on his face, the sound and smell of the ocean; he was transported back in time. Contentment suffused his body with immense pleasure. Quentin often relived the daydream, especially in testing and trying times at work. The fantasy helped him rise above the challenges of the day – seemingly made it more bearable.

Life was changing in the world of finance, and not for the better. Work had become more demanding. Clients expected more for their money. Management had set the bar higher.

The conference room door opened, and staff filed in, ending Quentin's wave of nostalgia. He looked at blank faces and tried to enliven them.

"Come in. Please take a seat." In a few minutes, he would have to deliver troubling news to the staff. A phrase ran through his mind, 'cometh the hour, cometh the man.' Decisions had been taken; it was up to him to put the plan into action. He gathered his thoughts as he stood to address the staff. There was little need to bring the meeting to order; stony silence prevailed, unnerving him completely.

"I know you're all aware of the catastrophe in the city last Monday," said Quentin. "And I'm sure you want to know how the events will impact your jobs and our investment bank here in Southport." He took a moment. "Last week in the UK, we were cursed with the infamous Black Monday, which followed the Wall Street Crash. As a result, £50 billion was wiped off the value of shares on the London Stock Exchange. The London FTSE fell 11 per cent on Monday, with further declines of 12 per cent on Tuesday and 6 per cent on Thursday. It reached an all-time low in the City, which hasn't happened before, certainly not in my time in the banking world. People have compared this with the crash of 1929. I was a child then, but reading about it, that crash was born out of different circumstances. Some of you will know that it led to the start of the ten-year great depression. What we face today is undeniably different from the 1929 crash. With skilful handling by the new government, particularly from Chancellor Nigel Lawson, we in the banking world hope it will be dealt with swiftly, bringing about a return to normality. I don't want to give the impression of complacency; the result of *this* crash has had a catastrophic effect on the money institutions of Great Britain and our investment bank."

Staff sat motionless, taking in every word, caught up in the moment's intensity. They believed things were serious, but attending the conference room for a meeting with the manager confirmed how serious all the rumours were.

"There have been rumours circulating as to whether continuation of this branch in such financially hard times is assured. I don't like speculation. I think it leads to uncertainty, discontentment and a poor work ethic, so I want to put the record straight. There are two things I need to say. First, I have been in lengthy discussions with head office and can tell you that our bank is safe from any talk of closure. It will continue in its capacity for the foreseeable future." He looked around the room. There was a palpable sigh of relief. "Second, and I am sorry to have to say this, management had already decided that they wanted to shed several staff jobs. So, there are redundancies in the pipeline for our branch." Relief turned to uncertainty as the staff took in the devastating news. Having delivered the worst news possible, he tried to put a positive spin on the proceedings. "Nevertheless, it is hoped the redundancies will be minimal and voluntary. Those near to retirement would be first to be considered for redundancy." With the gravitas of a priest conducting a church service, he held his hands out to imbue calm. "There are still a lot of details to be worked out, and redundancies are a long way off. Even if there hadn't been a crash, head office was looking to reorganise. So, there we are; now you have the up-to-date news."

Quentin paused momentarily; he noticed one of his longest-serving secretaries in a state of shock, comforted by a colleague. She felt sure she would be one of the unlucky few to be encouraged to take early retirement. His heart sank, but, as a seasoned manager, he held his feelings in check. Taking a gold fob watch from his waistcoat pocket, a present from his wife Eleanor for his 50ᵗʰ birthday, he appeared to check the time. It was a habit he employed when needing to steady and ground himself. Like a mantra, he read the inscription on the watch casing. *To my darling Quentin – Amo Et.* Closing the fob watch and placing it back in his waistcoat pocket, he looked around the room.

"Now I can assure you none of us are happy with this news. However, it is a sign of the times. The bank is determined to turn its fortunes around and put us back on the road to profitability. So we must all try to pull together to secure our future." He stared at troubled faces. "I want to assure you I will do all in my power to keep your jobs here at the bank; even so, it will be an uphill struggle. Now, it has been quite a shock for you all and a lot to take in, so we will leave it there." He tried to give a reassuring smile, but it didn't come. "Okay, thank you for your time, drive carefully, and I'll see you tomorrow bright and early."

As members stood to leave, Quentin caught the eye of James, the deputy manager. "James, hang back a minute, please. I need to speak to you."

The boardroom door closed. Quentin loosened his collar and tie, leaned back in his chair and emitted a pent-up sigh.

James was the first to speak. "Not good, sir."

"No, not good at all, James. We'll be okay; however, I fear for other members of staff." There was an awkward pause in the conversation as Quentin dealt with his emotions. The tearful secretary weighed heavily on his mind. Being the harbinger of doom didn't sit well with him.

"Any other branches affected, sir?"

"Between you and me, yes, many. Management are streamlining the whole service. The buzzword is rationalising; God, how I hate all of this." Thoroughly depressed, Quentin headed for the filing cabinet, opened the drawer and took out whisky and two glasses. "Drink?"

"Thank you, sir." James had something to say but was reticent owing to its sensitive nature. "If you don't mind me saying so, sir, you've been looking exhausted these past few days."

Quentin sat down with the whiskies, pushing a glass to James. The first drink of the day kept its promise; alcohol coursed around his body, mellowing his mind.

"Yes. I haven't been sleeping too well. I think it's the worry of this – this debacle." Exasperation showed in his demeanour; even so, he sat on it. "Do you know, James, when I came into this profession, it was a job for life. Everybody pulled their weight; things ran without a hitch; everyone was happy. Now the powers that be chase profit as if it were their only..."

The phone rang, disturbing Quentin's flow; his face

contorted with frustration as he listened. "Not now!" He slammed the phone down with annoyance.

James imagined the poor secretary at the other end of the phone, shocked and surprised at the boss's out-of-character behaviour. Maybe she sat staring at the receiver, unsure if she had really heard the tirade from the boss.

Quentin had never been one for rudeness, let alone raising his voice. It amazed everyone at the bank that he was such a polite and pleasant boss. They all loved and respected him for his gentle yet firm manner.

Breaking the awkward silence, James proffered some well-meaning advice. "I have a nightcap and a sleeping pill every night, and I sleep like a top, ready for anything the following day, or the boss has to throw at me." He smiled with concern.

"You're a good lad, James. I don't know what I'd do without you."

"Thank you, sir. I like the work and staff here very much. You've always been good to me and given me free rein, and it's allowed me to develop my skills and gain confidence as your deputy."

"You do know, don't you, that, when I retire as manager, you would be number one?"

James tried to look sufficiently surprised. "That's good of you to say so, sir. I always hoped, although never presumed."

"That's what I like about you, James, diplomacy. You can't teach it; it's in the blood. Unlike these..." his tone changed, "youngsters, who come into the profession no more than kids, barely old enough to shave, and they want to tell you how to run the business. The world's gone mad, James, I don't mind telling you, and I don't know how it's all going to turn out."

"Indeed," James was at a loss. "But, with your management, we'll all get through this, won't we?"

The lack of response spoke volumes; Quentin shrugged and moved on to other matters. "James, I need to talk to you about next week."

"Oh, that's right; you have a week's holiday booked?"

"This fiasco with the market has come at a bad time, James, and I am seriously considering cancelling the holiday."

"Do you think that is necessary, sir? I'm aware of the situation and well-informed. You have kept me in the loop, and additionally, we have contingency plans in place should there be a further hiccup in the market."

"Next week is our silver wedding anniversary."

"Oh, congratulations, sir."

"Thank you. I wanted to surprise Eleanor with something special and planned on taking her to Cornwall for a week. I want to spoil her and make the most of our anniversary celebration."

"I'm sure she would like that," James smiled. "Seriously, it won't be a problem. I can look after the bank for a week without any difficulties. Besides, if what you say were true about me being next in line, it would be good for me to steer the ship for a while; it's the least I could do for you on such a momentous occasion. Please go, everything will be fine."

"Thank you, James, I find that very reassuring; even so, I insist on giving you the phone number for the hotel in Bude, in case there is a problem."

"If it makes you feel happier, then fine, but I won't need it."

"Well, then, that's it," said Quentin, in a better frame of mind. "We can meet over the next few days and troubleshoot the unexpected. Oh, just one more thing before we conclude. I will write a personal cheque for £2,000 tomorrow. If you could oversee that for me, I would be most grateful."

"Yes, of course, sir."

Quentin held his glass in the air. "One more for the road?"

THREE

Eureka moments happen in a variety of ways, such as brainstorming, evaluating, or just talking with friends, as you develop ideas. Such a moment came to Gary as an answer to all his financial problems, or so he thought. Over a pint, he and his friends mused on the old chestnut of making a personal fortune. Trevor, a wag, tried a wind-up on Gary over the right-to-buy scheme for council houses, popular in the 80s. The right to buy allowed council house tenants to purchase their property from the local government at a preferential rate.

"You've got a council house, haven't you, Gary?" said Trevor, giving his mates a wink, hoping they would join in with the ruse.

"Oh, aye, yeah. Don't pay the rent, though," said Gary, quite proud of the fact. He was a work-shy individual who sponged off the state and was typical of his ilk, with a 'why should I work' attitude, even though his partner, Mary, worked hard to make ends meet.

"Doesn't matter, if you've rented the house for years, the council will let you buy it. It means money in your pocket, Gaz; you'll be quids in."

"Money," said Gary, cutting through his alcoholic haze, powering up his brain cells. At forty, he hadn't done well for himself or the family, always looking for a windfall rather than taking personal responsibility and working for a living. "Maybe this could be the big one," he thought.

The wind-up was working, although the real fun was about

to begin. Alfie, one of the drinking buddies, talked with authority on the matter. He revealed that, to take advantage of the scheme, one had to be married. The lads looked at each other, finding it challenging to keep their faces straight, never thinking for one minute that Gary would fall for it, except he did. Although the conversation moved on to football, the seed had been sown. In his mind, the promise of money in exchange for marriage was a price worth paying. Consequently, it came as quite a surprise, days later, to hear the news that Gary had popped the question to Mary, his long-time partner.

As a couple, they weren't madly in love with each other, more fated to stay together, like so many couples, for all the wrong reasons. Two children were the prime motivation in Mary's eyes for their continued togetherness despite a volatile relationship. They subscribed to the fundamental doctrine that every couple quarrelled, sometimes very loudly. After all, it was what couples did. It was normal; it cleared the air. What else was there?

Their association began in 1963 at the local youth club. Mary's first impression of Gary was that he was an idiot and a loser. He fooled around too much for her liking. His younger brother, whom he cared little for, was the complete opposite of Gary, being puny, gawky and lacking in self-confidence to the point of ultra-shyness. Yet, despite unfortunate negative characteristics, he had a certain likability.

Mary's opinion of Gaz, as he liked to be known, changed one momentous evening, when, as a do-gooder, he came to her rescue. Two youth club members had been taunting Mary relentlessly, leading to the worst embarrassing blush she had ever experienced, upsetting her to the point of tears. Her plight caught the attention of Gary, who knew the two members. He already hated them from earlier encounters and so came to her rescue. Average in stature, Gary could be a veritable terrier, standing up to anybody who dared to confront him. He was fearless and, in defence of Mary, soon saw the antagonists off, one sporting a black eye for his part in the brawl. Dismissing her thanks out of hand, he declared that, coming from Liverpool, 'red,' referring to her blush, was his favourite colour. Touching her hot cheek, he gave her a wink and left. Over the ensuing months, their friendship blossomed, and eventually they became committed to each other. Nevertheless, their relationship was put on hold for eighteen months when Gary, falling foul of the law, served a sentence in youth custody. Following his release from detention, they picked up where they left off, although Mary had seen a change in him, one that would prove disastrous in years to come.

Popping the question was a strange affair. Amidst the loud stage entertainment at the local working men's club, Gary, with a pint in hand, shouted something into Mary's ear. She wasn't sure what he had said, so nodded.

The dawning realisation of her nod came later when the club secretary took to the stage. Music was brought to an abrupt halt, and he announced Gary and Mary's engagement over the microphone. Amid rapturous applause and drunken cheers, the newly engaged couple stood for all to see. And so the engagement became official. Her good friend Betty, the first to congratulate her, leaned into Mary and shouted above the pounding music. "You and Gary engaged, well, what about that–congratulations."

The affectionate kiss on Mary's cheek left her wondering how it had all happened. Holding a glass to her mouth, preparing to take a sip, she wore a puzzled look. All evening, people offered their good wishes, giving permanence to the engagement that she couldn't renege on, even if she wanted to.

The happy day in the registry office was reserved for 4th June, her mother's birthday. The lack of funds, the guiding factor, limited the *soirée* to family members and a few friends.

Dressed in an A-line fitted, peach chiffon dress lent to her, and sporting a pink ceremony posy, Mary stood alongside Gary, minutes away from their vows.

To look smart, Gary wore his only two-piece navy, double-breasted suit. To appear cool, he insisted on turning his sleeves up, an eighties trend, though, in Gary's case, it had the effect of making him look comical. Nevertheless, the nuptial could have been far worse. At one stage in the wedding arrangements, he was serious about wearing his beloved red Liverpool Football cap until Mary threatened to call the whole thing off. He conceded when she gave ground and allowed him to wear a red handkerchief in his breast suit pocket, along with a pair of cool red socks.

The registry ceremony went ahead without a hitch, except for a few latecomers, much to the annoyance of Mary, who gave them a scornful look. She was in no doubt that they had been drinking in the Fox and Hounds close by, losing all track of time.

Facing each other and repeating their vows, Gary slid the ring onto Mary's finger, prompting an emotional moment.

Concluding the matrimonial proceedings, the registrar repeated the phrase she must undoubtedly have thought of every day of her life. "I now pronounce you, man and wife; you may kiss the bride. I hope you will be very happy together." She looked towards the small congregation. "Ladies and Gentlemen, I give you, Gary and Mary Lowe."

As they kissed, nine-year-old Paisley Lowe, seated in the front row alongside his six-year-old sister Kylie, gave way to an innocent outburst. "Good one, Dad!" With exuberance, the two youngsters clapped, joined by the rest of the assembled family and friends. "Now, can we have some cake?" said Paisley, to the delight of the crowd.

Mindful of her schedule and aware that such moments played havoc with her timetable, the registrar cut through the pleasantries to complete the ceremony. "Would the bride, groom and witnesses please come with me to sign the register? You may now take photographs if you wish."

For some inexplicable reason, events such as weddings always seemed to end up with an excess of alcohol. And so it was at the Lowe family reception at the local working men's club. As tradition dictated, the top table was for the bride, groom and their families. Two other tables were for family and friends, or, as Gary put it, 'the hangers-on.'

Mary's mum, Madge, and friends from the knitting club had prepared twenty-five roast chicken dinners to keep costs down. Rose, Mary's best friend, who worked at a local confectioner's, had given the couple a wedding cake as a present, topped with a miniature bride and groom. Unknown to Mary, someone had felt-tipped a moustache on the groom. She was livid. All afternoon, Mary asked her guests if they had a pen or a felt tip she could borrow. Nevertheless, the culprit was wise to her would-be detective work and so avoided being caught, although she had her suspicions that it was one of Gary's feral friends.

With the wedding reception over, amidst a general hubbub, Gary's dad, Ron, a plump, typical Liverpudlian, stood to make a speech.

"Err... well... I'm delighted... "

The alcohol-fuelled din in the room continued, with no consideration for him or his speech. Frustrated by the lack of propriety, he banged the table with his fist and used a turn of phrase guaranteed to gain attention. "Shurrup you lot! I'm trying to make a bloody speech here!"

"Well, get on with it, we're wasting valuable drinking time," complained a guest.

"Err... right, now then." He took a scruffy piece of paper out of his top pocket and attempted to make sense of the scrawl. "First, on a serious note," with a tear in his eye, Ron looked around the room. "I wish your mum could have been here today; she would have been so happy to see our Gary getting married. But I know she is looking down upon us this minute with a smile on her face." He stopped for a moment, wiping his eyes with a serviette. Taking a swig of beer, he composed himself and continued reading from the scrap of paper. "It took time for our Gary to tie the kot."

"Kot? Not another one on the way?" shouted one of the guests. Laughter lightened the proceedings, lifting the mood.

Ron looked closer at his scrap of paper and rubbed it with his sleeve. "Sorry, folks, there's sauce or something on my speech." He started again. "It took time for our Gary to tie the *knot*. So, I'm pleased to say, our Gary's made an honest woman out of Mary."

Mary's colleague, Ruby, known as Ruby Tuesday, referring to *Ruby Tuesday* by The Rolling Stones, couldn't resist a witty remark. "Honest! I don't think so; she's fiddled the social security for years."

Laughter circled the room. Mary jumped to her feet to defend herself. "I do not, Ruby Turpin; it's a lie." Looking around the room, she realised her misunderstanding of the intended joke and sat down, burning crimson.

Ron continued. "Yes, well, I think I can say without fear of contradiction that, since our Gary got to know Mary, he's a changed man."

Witticism at the ready, the best man offered contradiction to

Ron and his speech. "Which one is that, then, Jekyll or Hyde?"

The guests roared with laughter, deeming Gary to be the out-of-control, evil Mr Hyde.

The best man slid under the table to emerge with ruffled hair, shirt collar undone, tie at an angle and a diabolical, contorted grimace, making a superb impersonation of the infamous Mr Hyde.

By this time, Ron was wound up by the interruptions. "For God's sake, you lot, will you bloody well shurrup, I'm trying to finish my speech here." He took a swig from his pint, glared around the room and continued. "Thank you! As I was saying to you, bloody morons, our Gary is a changed man, and we owe it all to our lovely Mary. Now, raise your glasses with me and toast the happy couple."

"The happy couple."

Relieved that the formality was over, Ron had one final thing to say.

"And now, I call upon our Gary to make his speech."

For a while, Gary sat tight, ignoring the request, hoping it would go away – it didn't.

"Speech! Speech! Speech!" The guests chanted.

Pushed to his feet by Mary, he delivered a speech that took just seven seconds.

"Me and the missus just want to say thanks for coming today and being with us when we tied the knot." To everyone's amazement, he sat down, having delivered his very concise speech.

"Was that it?" enquired Ron.

"Yeah, nothing more to say."

"Well, that must have been difficult to write," said Ron, with sarcasm.

"Nah, wrote it on the back of a betting slip in a few minutes;

oh, and Jabba, my mate, helped as well."

"What, you got help to write it?" said Ron, shaking his head in disbelief.

"Well, I can't take all the credit."

The afternoon wore on to a fun-filled celebration. Tables and chairs were pushed back to the sides of the hall, making way for dancing. Gary's best mate, Dave the Disco, set up his equipment for the reception. On cue, he played a romantic favourite – *Greatest Love Of All* by George Benson. Everyone insisted, much to Gary's objection, that he and Mary should take to the floor for the first dance. Considering the amount of alcohol consumed, he made an outstanding effort at a slow, romantic dance. Photographs of the auspicious occasion taken by Madge on her box camera would raise many a happy smile over the coming days. However, by far the best pictures were taken at the registry office. One in particular, of Gary and Mary standing together by a floral display, was destined to take pride of place on the front room sideboard.

The reception and entertainment were in their final throes. It would finish as late as possible if the guests had anything to do with it, or until the club manager decided enough was enough and threw the drunken partygoers out.

FOUR

Quentin boarded a late-afternoon train bound for home; his day had been fraught and intense, unlike any he had ever experienced. No amount of management courses or seminars could have prepared him for such an emotional rollercoaster ride, the likes of which he had never endured before. On reflection, he felt dispirited that his hard-working, dedicated staff were being treated as mere numbers by management. Some were doomed to be cast aside by a decree from senior management that he, as the manager, had to implement. His staff were people with lives and loves, and, as such, deserved better.

In the past, he had always enjoyed the journey home; it was the end of his working day, a time to unwind, relax and look forward to seeing his beloved wife. He placed his briefcase on the seat beside him to peruse documents. Yet his mind drifted; he stared through the carriage window at people as they scurried to board the train before the barrier came down. On time, the guard blew his whistle, and the train pulled out of Southport railway station. It gained momentum as it took up the mainline to Mystic Sands. Wheel traction over the points produced a syncopated rhythm, narcoleptic in its sound, lulling Quentin's tired mind. Unable to keep his eyes open, he drifted off into a restless, dream-like state. People hurled abuse at him.

"He doesn't care. He's got a job."

"He's a manager; see how they all stick together."

"How am I going to pay my mortgage?"

"Tickets, please?"

Quentin was roused from his troubled slumber as the ticket collector walked through the carriage. Relieved to be woken from the disturbing images and sounds still fresh in his mind, he fumbled for his prepaid railcard. The fine tremor in his hand went unnoticed as he held out the card.

"Thank you, sir. There's a signalling fault up ahead on the line, but it shouldn't be more than a few minutes late into Mystic Sands."

"Very good," said Quentin, outwardly appearing normal, yet, in reality, he was in a troubled place. Thoughts permeated his mind. Breaking the depressing news to his loyal staff was upsetting. For a few, their jobs would end. In particular, he felt a great sense of concern and remorse for Angela, the secretary at the meeting, who became so distraught that she needed comforting by a colleague. For twenty-three years, she had worked for the bank, always on time and always trustworthy. If she were one of the staff forced to take retirement, it seemed inconceivable at her age that she would ever get another job. "How can that be?" thought Quentin.

As an investment bank manager, Quentin realised he was in a privileged position and privy to future decisions for the group of investment banks where he worked. He had put forward his branch's case to stay open, as other managers had. Despite that, in the dog-eat-dog world, honour, trust and integrity had given way to fighting your corner. How depressing and troubling it all had seemed to Quentin, how far removed it was from his previous banking years when he was young and carefree. Once again, he gazed through the railway carriage window. Houses flashed past. Curtains drawn tight held the cold night at bay. Streetlights glimmered in the distance like beacons of hope. Life still goes on, he thought. He tried to strengthen his resolve. In reality, dismissing the day's events proved to be a big ask.

Quentin looked down at the seat beside him; the financial paper sat unopened. As a rule, he would have studied it from front to back, giving him an impression of market trends. Over the years, he had cleverly built quite a sizeable portfolio on his vast knowledge of the stock market. Except, of late, the value of Quentin's shares had plummeted with the downturn in the market. He scanned the paper, even though his heart wasn't in it. Taking out a pen, he tried to get into the crossword; however, his troubled mind wandered. He found himself doodling on his financial paper, lost in a daydream.

'Mystic Sands, next stop.' The train's recorded message interrupted Quentin's mental drift, bringing him back to reality.

'Mystic Sands, next stop. Passengers are reminded to take their belongings with them. Please check the overhead luggage rack,' advised the recorded message.

At 6:10 pm, the train came to a halt. Along with other commuters, Quentin alighted at the railway station. He checked his watch to find they had arrived just four minutes later than expected. Commuters farewelled each other as they walked past the ticket collector and down the platform ramp to the roadside and beyond.

Toting his briefcase and umbrella, Quentin headed for the car park. Stopping to catch his breath, he looked at the sky like a wise old sage. The atmosphere was damp and cold, as often occurs on an October evening. Earlier, in Southport, low-level stratus clouds had headed in from the west, signifying rain, so it didn't come as a surprise when he felt droplets on his face. Pulling his collar up, he walked with haste to the car. A welcoming beep and a flash of lights guided him as he pressed the remote on his keychain. Sitting behind the wheel, he caught his breath as the rain began in earnest. Quentin had just made it to his car just in time. Taking a good few minutes to recover from his walk, he started the car engine, hoping his frame of mind would change for the better once he arrived home.

In their up-market, Tudor home in the suburbs of Mystic Sands, Quentin and Eleanor enjoyed a ritual of gin and tonic before their evening meal, a snifter according to Quentin. Usually, a bottle of wine accompanied their main course. Nevertheless, under recent pressure at the investment bank, the ritual had become more of a necessity for him. Alcohol soothed his troubled mind; it brought about a state of calm better than any medication ever could.

Seated at the dining room table, eating their evening meal, Quentin was generally regaled by Eleanor's nondescript day. However, he did not mind; it was so good to be in the presence of his loving wife. Thereafter, if Quentin felt inclined and could slow Eleanor down, he talked about his day at the bank. Most evenings, with a glass of brandy by his side, he fell asleep, having missed most of the evening news.

In no mood to talk and having no appetite, Quentin pushed the food around his plate, as if creating an elaborate, crazed artwork by Salvador Dali. Even the fine Bordeaux wine failed to excite him. Eleanor always knew when Quentin was troubled; it was a consequence of wearing his heart on his sleeve. She broached the awkward silence. "Is the fillet mignon to your liking, darling?"

"Umm?" said Quentin; his mind far away.

"The meal, is it all right?"

"Yes, very good."

"I can get you something else if it's not to your liking."

"No, it's... I'm just not hungry tonight, dear." He sipped on his wine; in reality, he felt bothered – ill at ease.

She tried to draw him out of his melancholy and engage him in upbeat conversation. "Did you have a good day, darling?"

His answer was doleful. "Reasonable."

"Are you sure you are all right, darling? You seem very quiet this evening."

"Just a headache," he said, rubbing his eyes and forehead to relieve the tension.

"Oh, poor you," said Eleanor; her response, although appearing sensitive, lacked emotion. "You haven't forgotten that it's the bridge club tonight, have you?"

"Oh God, not the bridge club." He dropped his napkin on the table and shook his head in disbelief.

"Of course it's tonight, dear. I've been telling you about it all week. Now, go and have a shower, and I'll put your clothes out on the bed. You'll feel so much better at the club with company. Oh, I nearly forgot there is a special presentation tonight from Montgomery Lovett; the theme is 'bridge from around the world.' It sounds terribly exciting."

"I don't think I can make it tonight, Eleanor. You go and give my apologies," said Quentin, as he held his head in pain.

Eleanor's voice became strident, a sure sign she was losing it. "I don't like going by myself. You know that, Quentin. It is very bad form."

He tried to steer her to avoid any acrimony.

"You'll be fine. Ring Joyce and ask if she can pick you up. She won't mind."

Despite careful handling, Eleanor continued with her childlike outburst. "And what do I say when they ask where you are? It puts me in a very awkward position, Quentin," said Eleanor petulantly. "You know I don't like it when you change your mind like this. It is just too much. Do you hear me – too much?"

Quentin felt exasperated by her mini tantrum; he railed against her with uncharacteristic anger. "Tell them anything, for God's sake! Tell them I've left home! Tell them, I'm dead! Can't you understand, I'm not going tonight? What part of no, don't you understand, Eleanor?"

Whether by design or just uncontrolled force exerted when he pushed his chair back wasn't clear. Nevertheless, a loud noise resounded as his chair hit the sideboard. He stormed out of the room and headed to his study, although not before pausing by the staircase, where he took a draught of his inhaler and waited. Once breathing more efficiently, he carried on to his inner sanctum.

The wood-panelled study, with a full-sized oak desk and floor-to-ceiling shelves, contained more than books; they housed an extensive collection of classical vinyl records. The study had become Quentin's domain, his private place, where he spent a lot of time, much to the displeasure of Eleanor.

Ignatius St John, Quentin's father, was an ambitious barrister who practised in the High Courts of London. He always believed his son would follow in his footsteps and carry on the family tradition of legal work. Although he was intelligent and capable of pursuing such a profession, it wasn't for Quentin. He chose a different path in life, disappointing his father so much that Quentin didn't speak to him for years. Undaunted, Quentin attended university after a gap year and completed a degree in mathematics and economics, earning a BSc. Subsequently, he entered the banking world at the age of twenty-three. His early years defined him as a hard worker with an ability to make perceptive decisions. He set himself apart from his contemporaries as a no-nonsense, career-minded, feet-on-the-ground sort of person. Quentin was adept at steering his career in the right direction and making savvy decisions to advance his career. Fairness combined with decisiveness gave him a unique kudos in the City. With financial expertise, he built an impressive CV and was sought after by major banks looking for dependable, smart-minded people at the cutting edge. With age and having achieved so much, he eased back, mellowed and became the Quentin that everybody knew and loved.

Switching the record player on, he placed a disc on the turntable, positioned the needle on the track and settled into his Chesterfield armchair. Reaching for a cigar, he cut it, rolled it about his lips, lit it and sat back, blowing a plume of smoke into the air. His doctor and Eleanor alike frowned upon the bad habit. Even so, nothing would induce Quentin to give up the practice of his adult life – not even the risk of severe and chronic illness.

Mendelssohn's *Violin Concerto in E minor, Op 64,* filled the room with an enduring and passionate orchestral magic, guaranteed to ease him into a better frame of mind. With his eyes closed, the meditative sound soothed him into an Alpha rhythm, something he instinctively learnt when he listened to his beloved classical music. He continued to follow the concerto note-for-note as he read the vinyl sleeve. *The best of the Romantic era composers.* A sentiment he wholeheartedly agreed with as he poured himself a large brandy.

From his desk drawer, he located the chequebook, wrote and endorsed a cheque for £2,000 to himself and placed it in his wallet for safekeeping. Next, he opened an anniversary card he had purchased during his lunch break. Quentin read the verse about twenty-five years of romance, joy, togetherness, and enduring love. He dwelt on the thought for a moment, feeling emotional. However, his impassioned moment was due in part to the words on the card and in part to the unfortunate disagreement he had with Eleanor. A sip of brandy steadied him as he cogitated some more. Upset by the way he had reacted, something he had never done before, his overwhelming urge was to find her and apologise. Yes, that's it; I will apologise and ask for her forgiveness, thought Quentin. Card signed, he put it in his briefcase, ready to surprise Eleanor at the optimum moment.

The final arrangement for the anniversary surprise would be to contact the hotel in Cornwall and book a room. He would do that in the coming week, once he was sure that James had shown confidence in managing the investment bank. Positivity permeated his mind; he felt sure the week's holiday in Cornwall would be a perfect surprise for Eleanor. He also knew that Mr Quentin St John, investment bank manager, would return to work feeling recharged and invigorated, ready for anything.

Leaving the study to look for Eleanor, it became apparent she had already left for the bridge club, presumably with Joyce. Although his work-related tension had abated, the headache persisted, troubling him. He remembered the discussion with James following the staff meeting. "One of Eleanor's sleeping pills, a large brandy and an early night might help," he concluded.

Sitting on his favourite chintz-covered sofa in the lounge, savouring his brandy, he considered innovative ideas to bypass the proposed staff redundancies. Job sharing, working reduced hours, or even taking a pay cut were all possibilities and worthy of further dialogue. Discussing his thoughts with James tomorrow, he hoped they could find a way forward to ease the immediate impact of redundancies on the staff at his branch. That said, it would depend on the staff and upper management's cooperation. To make it work, he would have to sell the proposal and sell it well.

FIVE

In its heyday, the local working men's club served the farming and business community of Mystic Sands seven days a week. Being on the northern clubs circuit, it hosted many famous acts and generated significant income. Over time, and amid a changing socio-economic environment, the club's success declined. People preferred to travel to nearby Stanton Enterprise Park for cinema, bowling alleys, eateries and pubs. Yet residents of the nearby council estate kept the club's continued existence afloat. The club revised its business plan and introduced innovations, such as cheap meals, with the first drink half price, a children's playground, a large-screen television in the bar, and a snooker table in the sports room.

Club snooker took off in a big way, attracting a strong following. Games were always serious, always fully attended, and always enthusiastically supported.

The snooker tournament final went as anticipated. Amidst rapturous applause, Gary and his partner Megha concluded the snooker doubles, with Gary potting the black to win the coveted title. His reward was a free day of beer, courtesy of the club, plus many pints bought for him by delighted members. Even Gary couldn't drink all the pints bought for him in one day, so the barman, Ted, kept a tally of how many pints were still in the pump for him.

Gary lived for snooker; he was a natural, yet like so many of his ilk, he wasted his talent.

Snooker professionals such as Jimmy White and Hurricane Higgins had made a very comfortable living out of their chosen career, making it an attractive profession to pursue. With thoughts of becoming a professional player, Gary emulated his idols, emphasising speed and aggressive play. He searched for a similar sporting nickname like Jimmy – Whirlwind or Hurricane, and settled for Snazzy Gary. It didn't quite have the same ring. Nevertheless, it became his name of choice.

Trophy cup in hand, an over-exuberant Gary punched the air. "Yeah! We've beaten the crap out of them, Megsy."

"Steady on, Gary, it's only a game, you know," said Megha, feeling embarrassed at the outburst. Disregarding his comment, Gary joined his mates at the bar, poured a pint into the cup to celebrate his success and drank. This was very much to the annoyance of the club captain, who hastily ate his words when told to look for another player if he wasn't happy.

Derek, one of the drinking circle, stood at the bar with an empty glass. "So whose round is it, then?"

At the optimum moment (Gary's round), despite having money in the till for free ale, he headed for the toilet, dodging his round.

"Is it me or is Gary over the top today?" enquired Megha, his snooker partner.

"He's been like that since his wedding yesterday," intoned Derek.

"So what's he on, then?"

"Don't ask; you don't want to know. What I can tell you is it's bloody expensive, and he's always on the cadge," Derek held his empty pint glass up. "And he never buys a round – ever."

"What about the family? How does Mary cope with it all?" said Megha.

"With difficulty, I should imagine. If it were me, my wife

would beat the crap out of me. And from what I've heard, things don't look too good at the newlyweds' home, if you get my meaning." Derek's remark raised an eyebrow or two.

The heavy beat of the music in the club was only slightly lessened in the toilet by the closed door. Gary was standing at the urinal, trying to work out if he should have a whisky chaser to celebrate his win, when Craig, a local bruiser, walked into the toilet. Instantly, he saw Gary. This was by far the worst scenario Gary could have ever imagined. Although his feet remained rooted to the spot by the urinal, his head rocked forward, hitting the wall. His face took the brunt of Craig's punch to his back, revealing an immediate swelling to his forehead. Undaunted, he steadied himself by putting his hand up to the wall. "All right there, Craig."

"Never mind, all right there. Where's my fuckin' money?" boomed Craig, in no mood for pleasantries.

Gary zipped his fly and turned to face his nemesis. "I've been looking all over for you, Craig," said Gary, obviously lying.

"Oh, yeah?" Craig grabbed him by the shirt and pulled him in close, communicating his displeasure with a menacing snarl. "Get me the fuckin' money – now! You fuckin' cretin, or else!"

Gary felt his shirt rip. Shaken, he croaked. "Okay, Craig, no need to rough me up, I've got the money."

"What, with you?"

Gary was unconcerned by Craig's expletives; he could give as good as he got in any conversation; however, what concerned him was Craig's menacing fury. He felt his collar tighten all the more. Mindful that the situation was worsening, Gary would say anything to distance himself from Craig, a dangerous criminal and well-known local supplier. Nobody messed with Craig.

"No, not here, back home, two hundred notes," spluttered

Gary, seeing stars.

He had found himself in a similar situation a year ago when he sustained broken ribs, a fracture to his eye socket and a fractured nose. Gary spent five days recovering in the hospital from his injuries and many days in the follow-up clinic. To add insult to injury, he still had to pay the money back to the supplier. Fortunately, Madge, his mother-in-law, came to the rescue. Gary borrowed the money from her on the understanding that he would repay the loan at £10 a week. The arrangement worked well at first, although after a while, the weekly payments dried up.

"Well, you and me are going there right now, and, if you're fuckin' lying, I'll take your fuckin' head off. Do you hear me?"

Gary felt giddy owing to Craig's choking grip, but, in the nick of time, the toilet door swung open, revealing two club members. Ultra-aware of the situation, Craig eased back from his death-rant, changing his demeanour. He put an arm around Gary and, with feigned friendliness, squeezed him. "Okay, Gaz, see what you can do, pal." With his back to the others and to emphasise his threat, Craig put two fingers together and held his hand like a gun. The danger was duly noted.

Keen to talk business with Craig, the men interrupted. "Can we talk, Craig?"

Being a master of opportunity, Gary broke away from the clinch and moved towards the exit. He reached for the door handle. "Yeah, okay, not a prob, Craig, I'll... I'll go and get it right now; back in ten." He raced out of the toilet into the bar area. Adrenalin kicked in like never before. All he could think about was saving his neck. Like a greyhound out of the trap, he headed for the main door in an undignified manner.

Standing at the bar, a bemused Derek held a pint up in the air. "Here, Gaz, I've got you a pint."

"Not now, thanks, Degsy. I've got to go," said Gary, focused on continuing his existence for the foreseeable future.

The lads looked at each other in utter amazement. "Well, bloody hell, that's a first; Gary refusing a pint."

As if pursued by the devil, Gary paced down the main street, intent on avoiding the removal of his head by Craig. He ducked into his 'second home,' as Mary called it.

From the age of seventeen, Gary frequented the bookies. He was desperate to grow up quickly and become one of the clan. For him, this was a place to be with like-minded adrenaline junkies. He experienced first-hand how punters placed their bets. With optimism, they always focused on the 'big win.' It seemed elusive, tantalisingly close and yet so far away. From time to time, Gary won, and when he did, it convinced him that the big one was just around the corner. Living for the *camaraderie* with like-minded people, winning and losing, happy and elated, penniless or despairing, was his want in life. Being hooked, he lived for the enormous buzz.

The bookies heaved with men bellowing at a televised race commentary from Ascot. The atmosphere was electric, comparable to the stock exchange in London; rowdy, with lots of testosterone flying around – men ready to do or die.

The three o'clock race entered the final furlong.

A general hullabaloo grew to a deafening crescendo. Maybe for luck or perhaps just in sheer desperation for a big win, he took a betting slip out of his pocket, kissed it and held it in front of him for all to see.

"Come on, Mr Muster! Yes... Come on! You can do it! Yesss! You can do it! Yesss! Yesss! Ooooooooh, fuck! So bloody close." Gary looked around at his betting mates. He held his hands up in a 'would you believe it?' gesture.

"It was that close. Bollocks, that close." He screwed up the betting slip and threw it to the floor.

"Lost your shirt again?"

He looked around to see who had the temerity to question his betting skills. A poorly dressed stranger, intent on conversation, stood nearby. "Why is it that, with only five runners in the race, we can't even pick a winner?"

"Hey, I do all right, you know, pal," said Gary, feeling quite insulted at the stranger's remark. "Won eighty notes last week."

"Well done! Do you want to earn some serious money?"

It wasn't often that people propositioned Gary about earning 'serious money.' He gave the stranger his undivided attention.

"Mal tells me you can fix me up with new papers."

Gary eyed him with suspicion.

"What do you mean, papers? The Echo, The Mirror, the local freebie, what?"

"Well, I hear you can," he said, looking around, making sure nobody could listen in on their conversation. "I hear you can fix me up with papers, documents. You know, all I need to get me out of this bloody big hole I'm in right now. Is that right?"

"It depends," said Gary, with caution.

"Depends on what?"

"On who you are," Gary scrutinised him cautiously.

Leaving the stranger, Gary strolled over to one of his mates, 'Dixie the Database,' so-called because his local knowledge was second to none. For reliable information, Gary plied him with the occasional pint at his local.

They both looked at the stranger and discussed him at length. Gary rejoined his newfound friend.

"You're all right," confirmed Gary.

"Yes, I know I'm all right."

"Michael Crane – Cranes the butchers. Divorced – no kids –

done two years inside for swindling. Although no one could prove it, they said you sold horsemeat as beef. I think you were tipped the wink before it got too hot, and you bailed out. Your ex is doing a line with Joe from the Rose and Crown, and you've got a bad credit rating."

"My God, it's like the bloody Mafia. Did he tell you what I had for breakfast?"

"Got to know who you're dealing with, Mick. So, what d'you want?" said Gary, enthusiastic about the pending financial outcome.

Looking around, Mick lowered his voice. "I need a completely new identity."

A master of negotiation, Gary reacted with a sharp intake of breath. "Well, you've come to the right man, Mick, but if you want the full works, passport, driver's licence, social security number, that'll cost £850 at least." In keeping with Gary's humour, he couldn't resist a joke at Mick's expense. "That includes VAT."

"What?" said Mick, reacting to such a large sum of money. "£850?"

"Mick, it doesn't come cheap, mate. I put days of work into coming up with the goods; and the risks; my God, I'm shaking in my boots just thinking about it." To add impetus to his negotiation, he imparted apparent information. "It's fraud, you know, Mick. I could go down for ten years at least," Gary picked up a betting slip, straightened it out and passed it to Mick. "Here, write your details down."

"Why do you need them? I need a new identity."

"You want me to get rid of every detail about Michael Crane, don't you?"

"You can do that?"

"Mick, does Dolly Parton sleep on her back?"

Stuart Roberts

Impressed, Mick scribbled his details and passed them back for approval. "Is that okay?"

"Yep, and now the dosh."

Negotiating with someone like Gary wasn't easy; nevertheless, Mick tried to reduce the amount. "You said at least £850. Can you do it for £800?"

With the fish on the hook, Gary gave it a few seconds to contemplate, as if he had to calculate his costs. "Well… okay, but keep it to yourself; I don't want people thinking I'm a soft touch. It's not good for business."

"No, of course not," said Mick, pleased to have negotiated the price in his favour.

Gary held his hand out. "Half the money now, the rest when I come up with the goods."

"I don't carry that kind of money, Gary; there's too many crims around ready to rip you off, you know."

"Tell me about it, Mick. What a crap world we live in, eh? I tell you, when I win on the football coupon, I'm off." He looked around the bookies with a gesture of his head meant to indicate the whole of humanity. "Leave all this shit behind."

"I know what you're saying… are you in tomorrow?" enquired Mick.

"Sure am. I've got a cert for the one-thirty at Redcar – Russian Blue. I know the trainer; he drinks in the White Horse. Put your shirt on it, Mick, it's a dead cert."

"Well, thanks very much, I will. Okay… see you here tomorrow."

"Right, Mick. Four hundred notes in tens and fives and a couple of passport photos." They shook hands like long-lost friends. "See you tomorrow."

Before Gary left, he turned and gave Dixie the thumbs up, licked his finger and struck one in the air. To earn £800 with

Dixie's help meant a pint for him, maybe even a whisky chaser.

Exiting the bookies and crossing the road, Gary kept his eyes peeled as he walked down the street, trying to blend in with other shoppers. He saw Craig and one of his thugs on the other side, entering the bookies; it was time for evasive action. Ahead and to his left, an old lady with a shopping trolley was negotiating the step into the greengrocers. With haste, he darted into the doorway with her. "Here, love, let me help you with that." He glanced over his shoulder. Craig and his accomplice emerged from the bookies and walked on up the street. The threat had passed.

"Thank you, young man. That's very kind of you. I wish more people were like you, helping us poor pensioners."

"That's okay, love; just doing my bit, makes me feel good, you know – helping oldies." As Gary guided the old lady into the shop, he pilfered a carrier bag containing shopping from her trolley. He moved with speed down the street before the lady realised some of her shopping had been stolen. At the newsagents, he filched a newspaper from the rack outside the shop and moved on. Head down, he diverted away from his usual path home to take a more circuitous route. Relieved that the imminent threat of Craig and his accomplice was over, he trudged through the housing estate where he had spent most of his formative years. Children playing in a burnt-out car reminded him of his childhood.

He recalled with fondness playing football with his mates on the grassy area 'the green' in the middle of the housing estate. The 'No Ball Games' sign was uprooted and discarded – another casualty of vandalism. On a typical summer's day, football began in the morning and continued all day or until neighbours, fed up with the noise, chased the young footballers away. Often, hunger was the reason the game had to be temporarily paused. After a break for food, they kicked off again. However, there were always arguments about the correct score; that was the fun of it all, being young, carefree and living for the moment.

Weeks before 5th November each year, branches, mattresses, tyres, sometimes even whole wardrobes or sofas appeared in the centre of the green for the Guy Fawkes celebration. Gary and his friends made their bonfire substantial by clearing the entire local community of unwanted, combustible items. Every year, the Council bans the practice of a bonfire on the green. Every year, a bonfire was built to an enormous size and lit.

Gary passed streets of run-down houses, overgrown hedges, rubbish lying around and gates off their hinges. His gaze was momentarily fixed on a tidy, well-kept home that stood out like a symbol of hope. Purpose-built shops in the crescent serving the neighbourhood stood derelict and boarded. Time and time again, they were the subject of vandalism. Security boarding was ripped down, defying the local council's commitment to safety. The one remaining functional shop, rented by Mr Sing, known to the locals as Sing Song, tried to eke out a living from the estate. However, he was failing. Many thought his days were numbered, and soon, like all the others, he would give up and move on. The estate was all Gary knew; to him, it was his stomping ground, home, and normal; he belonged there.

Making his way down the street of post-war terraced houses, he spotted his personal landmark. In the front garden, a red armchair sat resplendent for all to see; a battered coffee table and a wooden box for a footstool completed the array. Giving directions to people trying to find his house always raised an eyebrow.

"Drive down the street, mate," he would say, "ours is the house with the red armchair in the front garden." In reality, the armchair, coffee table and box, weather-damaged and in an appalling state, were an eyesore, lowering the tone of an already rundown neighbourhood. The local council had written to him on several occasions, pointing out his obligations as a council house tenant. The letter stated it was 'incumbent upon him as the tenant to keep the house and garden clean, tidy and in good order.' His only remark as he discarded the council letter, usually out of the front door, was, "Bollocks, who do they think they are? Cheeky bastards."

As he walked down his street, one of the local busybodies pulled a curtain back to spy on him. With two fingers held high, Gary summoned up his best scary face and yelled. "You'll know me next time, you nosey bitch." The curtains closed immediately.

Making a final sweep of the area to ensure Craig and his thugs weren't around, he headed for his home. His recent brush with Craig still lingered in his mind; he put a hand to his throat, remembering it all too well. So far, his evasive action – being one step ahead had served him well. Satisfied that there was nobody on the radar, he let himself in by putting his hand through the letterbox. There, he retrieved the key, attached to a piece of string.

Gary entered the front door of a three-up, two-down terraced house in need of decoration and general maintenance. A narrow hallway led to a living/dining room on the right. A separate kitchen at the back of the house led to a backyard. To the left were stairs to three bedrooms and a bathroom. Furnishings around the home were sparse and mismatched, indicating they were second-hand or from charity shops. The only exceptions to the tired, bedraggled-looking interior were a toaster, kettle, washing machine and vacuum cleaner, acquired by Gary instead of payment for one of his dubious jobs – no questions asked. The occasional cheap flourishes of curtains or cushions were Mary's attempt to smarten the interior. Except that they had little effect when nearby wallpaper hung off the wall, and a threadbare carpet showed the passage of feet over the years.

Upstairs, Mary prepared for evening work at the casino. "Is that you, Gaz?" she called.

"No, it's the rent, man. Who do you think it is?" replied Gary – always the joker.

Mary hastened downstairs, almost tripping over the children's school bags and coats strewn across the stairs.

"How many times have I told you to hang your things up when you come in from school?" yelled Mary. "Get here right now and do it, or else no tea and straight to bed."

Gary felt nervous at the mention of tea; any minute, Mary would ask for the shopping. The moment of truth was always a long way away for Gary. Old habits died hard; the temptation for a pint and a bet was too strong to resist when he had money in his pocket.

Preparing herself for work, it was clear from her appearance that Mary hadn't spent money on herself in a long time. Her clothes looked tired and dated. Her dyed blonde hair needed the roots touched up, and her shoes, apart from the scuffs, could be trendy for a second time around if kept much longer.

"Did you get the shopping, Gary?" said Mary in anticipation as she prepared to cook tea.

He handed her the carrier bag and walked into the living room with his paper, bracing himself for the imminent diatribe. Nervously, he prattled on about their neighbour. "That nosey cow Martha was at it again." He settled into his favourite chair and opened the paper. An ominous silence hung in the air; he couldn't avoid it any longer. Looking up, he saw Mary in the living room doorway, gaping into the carrier bag.

"What th...? Two tins and a jar of," she held the jar up and examined the label. "A jar of bloater paste for £10." As if that wasn't clear enough, and in total disbelief, she felt compelled to repeat it, this time much louder. "Three damn items for £10. Is this a joke?"

"Oh, hey, love, things cost a lot, you know, the prices at that supermarket they're... "

Mary stuttered with rage. "A tin of... of corned beef, a tin of rice pudding and a jar of... I don't even know what the hell it is... a jar of soddin' bloater paste." She held the bag open as if expecting the contents to change miraculously. "Three items for £10. Tell me I'm not seeing this."

Gary hid behind his newspaper.

Then it all became clear. "You've been out drinking again, haven't you?"

"Don't start!" said Gary.

Mary was incensed. "Gary, we're skint, do you understand? We've got nothing, and you spent the only money we had on beer. How am I supposed to run a home? How am I supposed to feed the kids?"

He chose to ignore the point of the argument. "You've got spuds, haven't you?"

"What...! Of course, I've got spuds! It's one of the few things I do have in this bloody house and only because mum bought them for us yesterday."

"Well then, chips, corned beef and then rice pudding; very tasty. There you are, that's easy, tea sorted. And you've got the jar of... of the other thing for again when you want it." He raised his paper, blocking out Mary from his sight, hoping for an end to the conflict; however, she wasn't giving up so easily.

"Gary, that's not the point!"

He had a clever knack of sidestepping the main issue by engaging in minor, superfluous points, frustrating her all the more. If she were more like her friends, Mary would have thrown a plate or ornament at Gary.

Following a heated dispute, her friend Eunice threw a plate at her husband. He needed to attend A&E to have five stitches in his forehead. From then on, her husband was careful not to annoy Eunice, notably when she laid the table or cooked a meal.

Even so, in the Lowe household, circumstances were different. If Mary threw something at Gary and it smashed, she would have to clean it up herself. Left to Gary, the broken pieces would stay on the floor forever.

However, the best story in Mary's eyes came from her friend Sandra. It seems that her husband complained that the stew was cold; he had been out drinking and was back home late for his tea. Sandra picked up the remaining pan of stew and poured it over his head. What great fun that was when they met and talked about it over coffee.

"Look, I wasn't going to have a beer," said Gary, lying, "I was on my way to the supermarket and saw Megsy. He'd been to the docs – problem with the kid's guts or something. Anyway, he couldn't buy the prescription, so I bought it for him out of the £10. I only had enough left for the corned jock, pudding and the thing, the other... thing. He said he'd give it back to me tomorrow." Gary hoped his explanation, although a complete fabrication, would be enough to pacify Mary. But she wasn't falling for such a tall story.

"What a bloody liar you are, Gary. It just rolls off your tongue, doesn't it?"

"What do you mean?" said Gary, feigning offence.

"Well, I happen to know that Aisha, his wife, and the kids travelled to Birmingham yesterday to stay with her mum for a few days. And anyway, you don't pay for a kid's prescription. Therefore, you, Gary Lowe, are lying through your teeth. The truth is, you went straight to the club and spent the money on booze, didn't you? Didn't you?" Her body language was in an aggressive forward stance – fists clenched, eyes glaring. Her face displayed murderous intent. "You went and did what you wanted, didn't you? It doesn't matter about us. It's all about you, Gary soddin' bloody Lowe. Well, that's it, you bastard."

"That's what?" said Gary, out-gunned and out-manoeuvred.

"That's it, you lying, cheating, low-life scum bag." Mary headed for the kitchen. She slammed pots and pans about, but couldn't let it go. She walked back into the living room. "What a useless load of... of rubbish you are, Gary Lowe. I hate you, you good-for-nothing, scrounging, useless bum."

Gary threw the paper to the floor. The children stared at the television, oblivious to the quarrel; they'd heard it all many times before.

"Shut up, for Christ's sake, you silly bitch; you're doing my head in. I've just about had enough of your stupid crap!" He stormed out of the living room, kicked the door and stomped upstairs to the bedroom for peace and quiet. He slammed the door behind him in a display of anger.

Nevertheless, Mary had to have the last word. She bellowed upstairs. "Yes, that's it, pretend it isn't happening! Play games on your bloody, stupid toys!"

This was the final straw; he threw a box across the room in anger. "Bitch! What does she know about anything? She'll eat her words when I wave eight hundred notes in front of her, the stupid little cow. She'll be all over me when she sees the dosh, but then I'll tell her to piss off."

The Lowes' bedroom showed little resemblance to a place of rest and more closely resembled a storeroom, with boxes, some bursting at the seams. Against one wall, IBM computers, cables, floppy discs and a variety of computer parts littered the area. The only concession to a bedroom was a double bed pushed into a corner, with a dressing table and a wardrobe vying for space. A small table full of Gary's latest projects held pride of place by the bedside. He showed a great deal of flair with computers, considering the industry was still in its infancy in Great Britain. Computers would not develop user-friendly software for some time to come. Despite that, Gary was at the cutting edge. His ability in computer technology, learnt in a young offender's prison, combined with art, writing skills and photocopying, helped him to emerge as a local forger. Within the criminal fraternity, he felt proud of his talent, as it set him apart from the ordinary criminal. He possessed a unique aptitude and was capable of greater things. Alas, he chose the wrong path in life, missing a tremendous untapped potential.

Such was the anti-establishment camaraderie in detention centres. They were intended to rehabilitate young offenders and show them the error of their ways. In reality, the centre was a breeding ground for an apprenticeship in illegal practices.

Gary locked the bedroom door, pulled back the rug, and took up a small floorboard where he kept a stash of blank passports, bankbooks, and other illegal papers and documents. "Now let's see what I can find for my mate, Mick."

Suspecting that the air had cleared an hour later and expecting a meal, Gary walked into the dining room. The children tucked into corned beef and chips. Even so, Mary hadn't forgotten or forgiven. As he sat at the table, she slammed a plate of chips topped with bloater paste down in front of him, scattering chips across the table.

Gary looked at the plate with incredulity.

"What's this?"

"Your tea, idiot," snarled Mary.

"This isn't a proper tea."

"I know. Who's a clever boy, then?" As she turned to walk out of the dining room, the children looked at each other with raised eyebrows.

"Your mum's in a bit of a strop today, isn't she, kids?"

"I heard that, Gary Lowe," said Mary, standing in front of the hallway mirror as she primped and preened herself, ready for work.

Maybe it was working at the casino, where she met interesting people and saw a different side of life that preserved her sanity or perhaps just a break away from the crazy home environment. Whatever it was, Mary always came home from work the following morning feeling tired, yet optimistic about her lot in life, more so than she had felt the previous day. She felt sure that, although not a perfect marriage, it would continue. With hope, it would get better as Gary mellowed and matured, leaving behind his foolish ways.

"I don't suppose you asked your dad about working for him?" enquired Mary, already knowing the answer.

In no mood to talk after her harsh criticism, Gary offered his feeble stock-in-trade answer. "How can I work with my back? I have pain all day."

"You don't seem to have a problem with your back when you go to the club," said Mary, backcombing her hair and spraying it with lacquer. "I mean, it must take effort to stand there, pint in hand, with a bad back. Or do you ask one of your mates to hold the glass to your lips so you can take a sip? No, I know, maybe you have a straw. Yes, that must be it; in agony, you lower your head to the straw and take a much-needed sip to relieve the pain in your back. Diddums."

Gary cocked a snoop at Mary's sarcasm, making the children

laugh.

"Don't let the kids stay up late tonight, and make sure they do their homework."

The chips and bloater paste weren't going down too well; in fact, they tasted awful. It took a few seconds for Mary's last remark to dawn on him. "What d'you mean, homework?"

"The kids, you're looking after them tonight. I'm working. You know that thing you have to do to bring money home to survive."

Looking down at her tights, Mary realised she'd snagged them. "Oh, balls. I'll have to change." As she ran upstairs, she barked an order. "Gary, get the kids their rice pudding."

Unhappy with the prospect of babysitting, he sauntered towards the kitchen to collect two bowls of rice. On the hallstand, he saw Mary's bag hanging, waiting to be plundered. In double-quick time, he gave the children their puddings and headed back into the hallway. Sneakily, he looked upstairs to make sure all was clear, then opened Mary's bag. There he found her purse and took £5, quickly replacing the purse in the bag, he hung it back on the stand.

SIX

At seven o'clock, Madge prepared herself for a quiet evening, safe in the knowledge that no one ever called at that time of night. She changed into her nightdress and dressing gown and relaxed in an armchair, ready to watch her favourite soap. At about ten o'clock, she tended to retire for the night, depending on television programmes.

Since the sudden death of her husband, Harold, from a heart attack, Madge had floundered. After the funeral, she retreated to her home and hid from life. Then, four days later, the isolation ceased, and Madge, to the astonishment of everyone, was back to her usual self. Despite repeated requests to divulge what had happened in the intervening four days, Madge kept her counsel and never spoke about grief or bereavement again. In reality, scrying (contact with the spirit world) had saved the day – maybe even saved her life. She would never have considered committing suicide; it was against her religion. Even so, in the wee small hours, when desperation reigned, who knew what might have transpired.

Following a bad night, she woke tired, depressed, and uncertain about life. She wondered if what people said was true: 'You cry so much that you can't cry anymore.' If that was the case, she thought, then why do I continue to cry?

A low-level amber glow illuminated the bathroom from a single streetlight outside the window. She ran water into the bathroom sink to see if maybe a wash could freshen her up – make her feel a bit better. Turning the tap off, she gazed wearily into the mirror.

"Oh, Harold, where are you?" she said aloud, feeling desperate and forlorn. About to immerse her hands in the water to splash over her face, she stared aimlessly into the sink. Then it happened. As if by magic, she saw the image of her beloved Harold in the water as it floated in and out of focus. It wasn't clear, but she knew the face of her husband; there was no mistaking, this was Harold. Madge wasn't scared; if anything, quite the opposite. She felt re-energised, her sadness lifted. From that day on, she knew that Harold was still part of her life; he had made contact. He had given her a purpose and energy to continue living. Harold's countenance had brought her back from the brink.

She didn't tell Mary how or why her life had changed for the better. She merely said that the brief withdrawal allowed her to put things into perspective. Which was quite correct, but it didn't tell the whole story of how she achieved the transformation.

The following day of rest, Sunday, Madge encountered the most amazing endorsement of Harold's presence in her life. It was on a cold, miserable morning, and she decided to have breakfast in bed. In the kitchen, she prepared tea and toast, then placed them on a tray. The familiar sound of the letterbox rattle in the hallway confirmed that the Sunday paper had been delivered. As planned, she could have breakfast and a leisurely read in bed. But when Madge returned to the kitchen with the paper, to her surprise, she saw a single dandelion on the tray. Her shocked expression turned into a smile as she remembered how Harold always brought her tea in bed before he set off for work. Depending on the season, if flowers were available in the garden, he placed a bloom, usually a carnation, on the tray of tea to see her reaction and beautiful smile. She recalled on more than one occasion in autumn, with no flowers in the garden, that he picked a dandelion to put on the tray. Madge knew this was validation of his presence.

The little things he had done for her in his life meant so much. To many, it might have seemed silly, although to Madge and Harold, they were precious moments. He was one in a million, which made his passing even more difficult to accept. Of course, given a choice, she would have given anything to have Harold back. Although that wasn't possible, she had him with her in spirit every day, and that was miraculous; it filled her with happiness and gave her the will to carry on. Madge kept going for the love of her daughter and grandchildren more than anything else, yet she longed for the day when God would take her. Then, reunited with her beloved Harold, she could be at peace once more.

Later that evening, sitting comfortably with her feet on a stool, cup in hand, poised to dunk a biscuit in her tea, she heard the front doorbell. Madge eyed the clock. "Who could that be this time of night?"

Making her way to the front door, she peered through the spy hole to see Gary and the children. Removing the security chain, Madge opened the door. "Hello, Gary, what are you doing here?" Surprised and confused for a moment, thoughts of whether she had forgotten a prior arrangement ran through her mind.

"Hi, Madge, sorry to trouble you. Mary said, 'Could you look after the kids for her tonight?' She's working, and I'm seeing a man about some business. We wouldn't ask as a rule, but... well, you know. What are Nans for? Everything all right? Good." He pushed the children forward through the door, without waiting for her to agree or disagree. Gary walked away. "Ta, Madge, you're a goodun. Don't let them stay up too late;

they need their sleep, you know. Oh, and make sure they do their homework." He looked over his shoulder and waved. "Bye."

Having learnt little from the spat with Mary earlier, Gary headed for the local club, keen to see his mates. Along the way, he kept a wary eye open for Craig, just in case. That said, he knew full well that nighttime for Craig was better spent at a more lucrative haunt in town, so he felt reasonably safe. Tonight, he could enjoy a drink with the lads without concern for Craig, the bruiser.

Pint in hand, Gary circulated the bar area, talking to strangers, a sure sign he was tipsy. As he looked around, two girls having a quiet drink caught his eye. "Hello, girls, been stood up, then?" slurred Gary.

One of the girls, sporting pink hair and a penchant for tattoos, demonstrated her annoyance at the intrusion. "What's it got to do with you, creep? Now piss off."

"Okay, no need to go ape shit, love. I was going to fix you up, but now..."

Before he had time to finish his silly remark, the second girl, with blue eyeliner and matching hair, waded in with a final onslaught. "Get stuffed, old man. Piss off before I call the bouncer."

He took the hint and staggered off, bumping into one of his buddies, Kelvin, a thin, unkempt Rasta, with body metal and tattoos. He was a rare breed of hippyfied dude and a known supplier.

"Hey, Gaz, my man, how the hell you doin'?"

"Yeah, cool, Kel, still trying to make it and buy that Porsche, you know," said Gary, with a silly throwaway remark.

"You don't want a Porsche, Gaz. Too much on the eye, my man," Kelvin gave an all-knowing tap on the side of his nose.

"Take it from me; you need a crappy little Mini to fly under the radar, man."

"Yeah, right." Gary took a swig from his pint and overbalanced. As he did so, he slopped beer on the floor. "Quiet here tonight, Kel."

Kelvin held his hands out to steady Gary, manoeuvring him to the corner of the room. Covertly, he looked around to make sure they weren't being observed and slipped Gary a pill. "Here, try one of these; made 'em today. This'll put hair on your chest."

Gary downed the pill with a swig of his beer, paying no heed to the safety of such a trusting gesture. In reality, it could have been arsenic; such was his faith in Kelvin. "Ta, Kel, you're a goodun; is it the real deal?"

Already high, Kelvin nodded. "Couldn't get any better, Gaz. Made 'em for Gypo; he's got the outlet if you know what I mean, and I'm not talking about a stall on the market."

As a couple approached the fruit machine, Kelvin directed Gary a few paces away and continued the clandestine conversation. He lowered his voice. "If you want to earn some hard cash, Gaz, find me some punters, and I'll see you right."

"Okay, Kel, you can count on me, mate." Gary tried a wink, but it was more of a squint. "I'm off to the footie on Saturday; big one for Liverpool, so I'll get rid of a shed load there."

"Good man, Gaz. Come round to ours in the morning, about eleven."

From the other side of the club, one of Gary's mates shouted for his attention. "Hey, Gary, come on, we're up next for the snooker doubles."

Hearing this and aware of Gary's inebriated state, Kelvin was intrigued.

"Snooker doubles... Gaz, you can't even stand. Do you know which end of the cue to hold?"

"Yeah, not a prob, mate." In a drunken brain, disconnect from his legs, Gary staggered back two steps, trying to steady himself and save his beer. He over-compensated and lurched forward. Kelvin caught him in the nick of time.

"Now, where was I?" said Gary. "Oh yeah, I know. The thick end's for holding. I know that because..." He stopped for a moment and searched his mind for a ditty. "That's it, thick stick near my dick." As he verbalised the ditty, his voice elevated on the words, 'near my dick,' turning heads in the bar. The club owner, serving a customer, looked over at Gary and gave him a disapproving shake of the head. Unperturbed, Gary continued. "The pointy ends for whacking the balls into the holes. If I get stuck, someone'll put me right."

"Gary, we're ready to go. Get your arse over here, now before it's too late!"

SEVEN

Since she could remember, Eleanor had always been an early riser, a routine instilled in her from prep school.

Her morning routine comprised a shower, drying and styling her hair, and selecting an outfit from the more than adequate walk-in wardrobe. After that, she applied makeup and headed downstairs to read the morning paper in the kitchen-diner. There, she savoured a cup of coffee in her favourite china cup. It was an essential start to the day; anything less was inconceivable to her.

Quentin stirred before the alarm. He'd had a miserable night, despite the brandy and sleeping pill. Getting out of bed, he pulled on a dressing gown and headed to the bedroom window; he threw it open, gripped the windowsill with both hands, and leaned forward, taking in the cold morning air. From habit, he found that the stance tended to help his oxygen-starved lungs. Mornings were always a bad time for him. Be that as it may, Quentin saw the morning's usual slow start even more difficult thanks to a hangover. He checked his emergency oxygen supply and decided against using it, since his breathing seemed to be improving, albeit slowly. Had the sleeping pill he took last night had an adverse effect? It wasn't clear; nevertheless, the outcome was that he felt jaded before the day had begun. A lack of adequate sleep left Quentin unable to perform his role as manager effectively. Tiredness slowed his thought processes, increasing the risk of errors and misjudgments. If he made a mistake due to fatigue, he had a bad day and had to play catch-up to correct matters. In due course, this compounded his inner vexation, knowing he was capable of better. Speaking to his contemporaries at managerial meetings, he found that tiredness and work pressure were commonplace. All feared burnout, a condition rarely recognised and rarely discussed.

Like most housewives, Eleanor understood Quentin very well. She played her part in his daily organisation and chivvied him along. Her organisational skills were exemplary; however, for some, she was annoyingly super-efficient.

Eleanor was already on her second cup of coffee and halfway through the paper, at the fashion page, when Quentin entered the kitchen. Tie askew, hair awry, looking unprepared for the day, he headed to the Aga to pour a cup of coffee and pop bread into the toaster.

"Are you all right, dear?" intoned Eleanor.

"Not really, I had a bad night."

She eyed him fleetingly and continued to read her paper. Christian Lacroix, an up-and-coming French fashion designer, had opened a haute couture house. His latest exquisite creations impressed her. In particular, she admired a floral, fitted, skirt suit and thought it absolutely divine, one she would dearly love to wear. She made a mental note to talk to the girls about Christian Lacroix next time they met.

Checking his diary, Quentin made amendments and reviewed the rest of his appointments for the day whilst drinking coffee.

"Aren't you going to ask about the bridge club last night?" said Eleanor.

"Umm?" Quentin's mind meandered as he reviewed the events of his busy schedule at the bank. He wondered why his diary was always so full these days.

"Oh, never mind." Some mornings, she found Quentin irritating when he didn't pay her the attention she wanted. Reaching for her coffee, she immersed herself in the health page.

A loud knock on the back kitchen door startled Eleanor.

"What now?" Unsettled by the interruption, she opened the door to reveal the gardener, ready for a morning's work.

"Good morning, Mrs St John. Would you like... ?"

Rudely, she gave him short shrift. "Start with the lawn." She slammed the door in his face.

Quentin was aghast. "Eleanor, I know he's only the gardener, but there's no need to be rude."

Characteristically, Eleanor disregarded his comment and continued with other matters. "I need your car this morning."

Both had their own cars. Eleanor used hers as a run-around, attending meetings, organising and meeting friends at the local Soroptimists – an international volunteer group. Quentin used his car to drive to and from the railway station. There he parked up, caught the train to Southport, and then back again at night.

"You can't. I need it for the station run."

Eleanor was insistent. "Well, my car is going in for a service today. Therefore, I need your car this morning. I have such a busy day."

"But..."

"Now, don't be silly, darling. I need your car, and that's all there is to it. I'll drive you to the station and pick you up tonight."

He was unhappy with the arrangements; however, it seemed that he had little choice in the matter. Eleanor, as usual, was in an unequivocal mood. Equally, he didn't want a meaningless conversation at that time of the morning; he needed to focus on his demanding day ahead.

"What about your toast, darling?"

Quentin looked at his watch. "Goodness, I've got no time for it now. I'll get something later."

Early morning sun filtered through the living room's net curtains. Gary stared at the ceiling as he lay reclined on the sofa, still wearing his beer-stained clothes from the night before. Nearby, on the coffee table, sat a crowbar.

The front door slammed. Mary walked past the open living room door to shout upstairs. "Come on, kids, time to get up." She hadn't noticed Gary sprawled on the sofa. More often than not, she wouldn't expect to see him up and about till late morning.

As part of her routine on arriving home from work, Mary put dishes and cutlery on the table and filled the kettle, preparing breakfast. She took a carton of milk out of her bag and placed a box of cereal on the table. She was surprised not to hear Kylie, always the early riser. Mary called again. "Kylie! Paisley! Come on; you're going to be late for school." Her concern kicked in when, after a few minutes, there was still no movement from upstairs. "I bet Gary let them stay up late last night. Typical." She skipped up the stairs to rouse the children. Doors opened and closed with a heavy thud; Mary let out a sickening cry. "GARY!"

Frantically, she ran downstairs, stopping at the living room door to see Gary lying on the sofa. In an instant, she was at his side.

Mary didn't see the dark, diaphanous figure standing behind the living room door.

"Gary, the kids, they're not here. What's happened? Where are they?"

He didn't answer her desperate plea; instead, he continued to stare at the ceiling.

"Gary, for Christ's sake, the kids, they're not here, where are they – speak to me?"

"I know they're not here," said Gary in a cold, weird, detached manner.

Mary was frantic. "What do you mean, Gary, for Christ's sake, talk to me, where are they?"

He sat up facing her. "They're in Hell, the little bastards, and you're going to join them, right now."

Mary looked at him, dumbfounded. "What?"

She had never seen him like this before and was frightened by his freaky behaviour, but she was ultimately more concerned about the children.

"Two little bastards burning in Hell, where you'll be in a few minutes." He stood up.

"Gary, you're frightening me." She backed off as he became more agitated. He kicked out at the coffee table. The crowbar fell to the floor. "The little shits are dead. But don't worry; you'll be seeing them very soon. Now come here, you fuckin' little slut I'm gonna smash your crap face in!"

Gary's invective pierced her to the core. She squealed, turned and ran for the stairs. The split second it took Gary to pick the bar up gave Mary a head start. Halfway up the stairs, she tripped. He grabbed her ankle, releasing it as Mary kicked back; her heel caught him in the face, stunning Gary. She regained her footing and made it to the bedroom. As she slammed the door, Gary was on the other side. Mary wrestled with the door handle as he tried to turn it. Frantic, with the strength of panic, she succeeded in locking the door, breathing a sigh of relief. All the same, the danger wasn't over; he beat the door relentlessly with the metal bar. In fear for her life, Mary dragged boxes in front of the locked door. In reality, the boxes would do little to stop a madman; still, the psychological reassurance they gave her helped.

"Open the door, you bitch, I'm gonna beat the crap out a yer!" he ranted like the devil possessed.

Mary couldn't believe this had happened to her and the poor children. "Where are they?" she cried in floods of tears. Last night she had set off for work, leaving Gary with the children. Then, through no fault of her own, she had been immersed in a crazy, life-threatening situation.

He continued smashing the door with the metal bar. It was beginning to have the desired effect. The plaster from around the door casing fell away. "Get away, leave me alone," she cried. Tears streaked her mascara.

The door rattled as Gary tried to kick it in, sending more plaster crashing to the floor. Looking around in desperation, Mary ran to the window, opened it and leaned out, screaming for help. Nobody was about. It was too high to jump. What could she do? All seemed lost when, with luck, a passer-by appeared, walking his dog. "Help! Get the police; he's killed the kids!"

From inside the double garage, Eleanor opened the car door and sat in the driver's seat.

"Oh," said Quentin, "I was going to drive."

"Quentin, you are going to be late if you don't move yourself. Now get in, and then we can go."

The course of true love never ran smoothly. Quentin knew when not to question Eleanor. "Yes, dear," he said as he placed his briefcase on the back seat.

Rush-hour traffic to the station that morning was heavy. It always seemed to be the case when running late; fate took a hand and conspired to cause more delay. *En route*, they encountered road works and waited in line for traffic lights that seemed to take forever to change. The red of the light ahead matched his mood. Quentin rolled the window down, craning his neck to see ahead. "What are they doing up there, for God's sake?"

"Well, we are evidently waiting for the lights to change, and then we can go." Her annoying retort didn't help Quentin's frame of mind; in fact, it unsettled him. Eleanor turned the radio on for a traffic update. They sat and waited a few more minutes, listening to the eye in the sky's update on the morning's traffic.

"We've been waiting here far too long. Sound the horn," Quentin demanded.

"I will not, don't be silly; it will change in a moment." The traffic in front moved slowly. "There, what did I tell you?"

He took a handkerchief out of his pocket to mop his brow and looked at his watch again. Further on, cars slowed to negotiate a minor accident. Traffic flowed sluggishly. Quentin rechecked his watch.

"Oh, my God, this is appalling. Can't you go any faster, Eleanor? I'm going to be late," said Quentin, exasperated with, in his eyes, her foolish behaviour.

"I'm not driving any faster, Quentin. This is a thirty-mile-per-hour zone."

He glanced at the car's Speedometer. "Yes, but you are only travelling at twenty-six or is that twenty-five miles?"

In no mood to listen to criticism, she chastised Quentin as a mother would her disobedient child. "Quentin! Calm yourself. I will get you to the station on time. If you distract me, it only slows me down. Just another five minutes and we will be there."

He rechecked his watch. "I'll have to leave the petrol and fill the car up tonight."

"Fine," said Eleanor as she changed gear. Her inclination was to scream; nevertheless, she held it together for the sake of peace.

As they pulled into the station car park and came to a halt, Eleanor passed her cheek. "Goodbye, darling, do try to have a good day."

He kissed her goodbye, exited the car and paced out towards the station. The slight incline up the ramp to the station platform caused him problems; he experienced the precursor of an asthma attack. Putting his briefcase down, aware his wheezing chest was worsening, he took a deep draught of his inhaler, which steadied him. Holding on to the rail, he waited. With the passage of a few minutes and a burgeoning control over his breathing, he continued to the platform.

The street where the Lowes lived hadn't seen so much drama since the fire at number twenty-six, two years ago. On that occasion, the police sealed off the street for the day. The fire brigade and ambulance were also in attendance. Mary, like most people, thought it was an unfortunate accident. Yet, Gary believed differently. He was convinced it was deliberate and an insurance job. Stan, the owner of the house and a DIY fanatic, was good at electrics. According to Gary, he rigged the television so it would overheat and catch fire.

The street was sealed off. With growing expectation, police in riot gear amassed outside the Lowes' family home, ready for action.

Distressed and in floods of tears, Mary hung out of the window and yelled. "Break in, he's off his head; he's killed the kids. Please hurry."

The police sergeant, an old hand at domestic violence, tried to find out what had happened to assess a deteriorating situation. He shouted to Mary. "Are you safe?"

"Only just," came her reply, "but he's trying to get to me. He's smashing the door in." She looked back at the door as if to confirm what she had said.

"Is he armed?" yelled the police sergeant.

"Yeah, he's got a bloody big metal bar, and he's smashing the door right now. Quick, he's nearly through!" squealed Mary, in fear for her life, "He'll kill me if you don't hurry. Quick, stop him now!"

With no other choice, the sergeant gave the order. "Okay, lads, break it down!" The door took several mighty thuds from a metal ram; in the end, it succumbed to brute force. Police in protective gear stormed the house. Outside, the crowd grew. Local television crews and reporters raced to the scene. Overhead, a police helicopter flew low, adding a sense of drama to the street where the Lowes lived.

EIGHT

As he made his way to the platform, Quentin was shaken to see the train already waiting at the station; he had made it with seconds to spare. Under normal circumstances, he would have allowed himself five or ten minutes before the train arrived. These extra few minutes were his safeguard in case of unforeseen problems. It gave him time to chat with fellow passengers waiting for the train or to buy mints from the railway kiosk. Except today was different; he didn't feel his usual self.

Sitting back in the first-class carriage, Quentin emitted a pent-up sigh, closed his eyes and tried to compose his whirring mind. He needed all the strength of body and mind to deal with the day's schedule and its myriad of decisions. During the day, he would see staff, individually if necessary, to discuss their worries and concerns. As a manager, he knew there would be awkward questions to answer. Nevertheless, that wasn't enough. Quentin was sure he had to do more for his staff. He needed to speak with head office about the proposed redundancies. In his mind, he had hatched a plan which needed head office approval before he could discuss it with his staff.

In recent months, Quentin had found it difficult to relax and achieve inner calm. Being a lifelong asthma sufferer, he had noticed his condition worsening, more so of late. A specialist had talked long and hard about the virtues of calming his troubled mind and taking control to reduce his stress levels. He had suggested relaxation techniques. Yet, it all seemed alien to

Quentin's understanding of relaxation. No, for him, relaxation was a glass of brandy and a cigar as he listened to his favourite classical music. New Age relaxation mumbo jumbo, as he referred to it, sat cross-legged on the floor, thumbs and first fingers together, chanting 'Ommm,' wasn't for him.

The journey time from Mystic Sands to Southport was thirty-three minutes. *En route*, Quentin usually read his financial paper, checked the day's markets and made a start on the crossword. However, this was unlike any other day he had experienced before. Staring out of the window, he was lost in a dream, oblivious to the train as it stopped at stations. He knew the route well and, as a rule, checked his watch at stations along the way to confirm that the train was on time. Even so, things didn't matter anymore. Nothing seemed to matter. He was lost in ephemeral thoughts – his own inner dimension.

At peak times, Southport train station was a bustle of commuters exiting the station, headed to their respective jobs. In the main, Quentin would take a taxi for the short drive from the station to the bank. To the minute, the train stopped on time at the terminus, emptied in its usual frenetic way and sat, waiting to be cleaned, checked and readied for its return journey. Despite that, Quentin didn't alight; he sat motionless, staring out of the carriage window.

The routine maintenance for the train as it arrived at the terminus went ahead as usual. A team of domestics set about cleaning the first train of the day. As they entered the first-class carriage, they saw Quentin sitting in his seat – motionless. They became concerned, thinking something serious could have happened to him, particularly as he didn't respond to any contact. The station guard, alerted by a domestic, walked into the first-class carriage to sort out the problem. Only once before in his career had he attended a similar situation; then, the passenger had experienced a fatal heart attack, making life all the more difficult, as the police classified the carriage as a crime scene. The train didn't move all day, disrupting the railway's schedule.

"Excuse me, sir, this is the end of the line, we're at Southport." Quentin didn't respond or acknowledge the guard. "Sir, are you all right?" Quentin remained inert. No amount of questioning elicited a response; his only option was to alert the railway police.

"He's in here," indicated the guard as he led the police through the carriage. As before, Quentin remained in his seat, immobile.

"Excuse me, sir. Are you all right?" enquired the police officer. "Sir, can we help you?" With no movement or response, the policeman adopted a different approach. Putting a hand on Quentin's shoulder, he gave a gentle shake. "Excuse me, sir; we're police officers. Can we help you?"

'We're police officers,' was said as if confirmation of being an officer in some way would bring Quentin out of his trance. It didn't.

The guard looked at the policemen and shook his head, as if to say, "I've tried that."

Next, he raised his voice. "Are you all right, sir? Can we help you?" Like a mannequin, Quentin continued to sit rooted to the spot; he didn't move, nor react to stimuli, but stared out of the carriage window.

"How long has he been here?" enquired the officer. The guard looked at his watch. "Well, the train got in at eight-thirty, and it's now eight fifty, so twenty minutes without a peep."

With a concerned look, the guard confided. "It doesn't look good, you know, maybe he's had a stroke or a brain haemorrhage? I did first aid twenty years ago, so I know all about these things."

Trying to appear in control of an unusual situation, the policeman donned his medical cap and looked at Quentin's face. "I don't think so, but his colour is poor. I think we'll get an ambulance, to be on the safe side."

Upon her return home, the gardener confirmed that her car had been collected by the garage for servicing. By this time, her frame of mind was a bit more forgiving towards him, yet he knew she could be tetchy, something he ignored, putting it down to her being a posh so-and-so who probably spoke to other menials in very much the same way.

Busying herself around the house, she changed into a silk robe, put the washing in the machine and filled the kettle, placing it on the Aga. Making tea in a plain white cup and saucer, she placed it on the kitchen table, opened the door, and caught her gardener's attention.

"Gardener, cooee, I have tea for you; come right now, or it will be cold."

She left the door ajar and stood by the window, watching as he approached. He knocked at the door and waited.

"Come in, gardener," said Eleanor. He entered, standing submissively by the door. As she pointed to the table, her loose robe gaped.

"There's your tea; be quick about it and don't spill it on my clean floor... well, go on."

He touched his forelock. "Yes, ma'am." However, instead of heading to the table, he walked over to Eleanor. They looked at each other impassively. Moving closer, he enveloped her in his strong, muscular arms, kissing her fervently, wantonly. With eagerness, they kissed, with passion, they groaned. Eleanor wrapped a leg around his strong, muscular legs as if dancing the

Argentine Tango. With deepening fervour, she broke away from the passionate kiss.

"That's very familiar of you, you naughty gardener, taking advantage of a defenceless lady, maybe I'll have to tell my husband."

He ignored her remark, running his hands over the robe and pulling the tied belt clear of her waist.

Their passion became urgent. Crashing about the kitchen, they slammed into the table. Eleanor rolled back across its surface. As she graciously fell into a seductive heap, her silk robe fell open, exposing her sensual, seductive nakedness. Luckily, the morning breakfast dishes had already been cleared away; however, the cup and saucer fell to the floor, smashing into pieces. Tea splashed everywhere, making a dreadful mess. But neither were concerned; they had only one thing on their minds. Breathing intensely, the gardener broke away from the intense passion and uttered, "I'll give you 'get on with the lawn,' Mrs Eleanor Smarty-Pants St John."

He took a firm hold of her hand and pulled her without grace to the doorway leading to the hall and beyond. For some time, the broken cup and saucer and spilt tea would remain on the kitchen floor while the amorous couple dealt with their passion.

NINE

Set in a semi-rural location, the new £3.4 million department of psychiatry, built to serve the Metropolitan Borough, was a veritable jewel in the crown. In keeping with modern trends, the unit boasted male and female admission wards, a well-equipped outpatient's day hospital, and an Occupational therapy unit (OT), completing the first phase of the building project. Set in the extensive grounds of the old general hospital, the new department of psychiatry, deemed revolutionary, was built amid some opposition from residents. The first of a two-part phase was due to government investment. Planning was underway for a new state-of-the-art maternity unit, scheduled for opening in 1993.

In full regalia, the mayor opened the Mystic Sands Department of Psychiatry, amidst a fanfare of trumpets and celebration. At the inaugural opening, members of the public were invited to tour the new unit, thereby promoting goodwill and education and dispelling the myths of a 'Mad House.' The open day was fun-filled and saw families with children, members of the local council, hospital representatives and the press. Drinks and nibbles, along with music, balloons, and staff on hand to answer questions, made it an enjoyable, informative, and fun day. From the public relations point of view, it was a great success. A local newspaper report likened the new department to a 'First-Class Hotel,' which gave the media's seal of approval for its future success.

Despite its good intentions, the new department of psychiatry faced opposition from within at the planning stage. Staff unacquainted with mental illness predicted untold emergencies and problems brought about by a psychiatric unit in the grounds of a general hospital. Despite that, the planning team, in association with members of the psychiatric team and local community representatives, were confident it would work seamlessly with the rest of the hospital services.

Mid-morning – light traffic traversed the 'A' road into town and beyond to the hospital. Blue lights flashed as an ambulance sped across town, its destination the new Department of Psychiatry. Admission to psychiatry in an ambulance with blue lights flashing wasn't a usual occurrence, and so Gary had secured the notoriety of being the first such admission. Reversing towards the single-storey male admission ward, the ambulance came to a stop. Ambulance doors swung open to reveal an outraged Gary, sitting handcuffed between two brawny police officers. The transition from the ambulance to the admission ward was difficult. Like a mighty atom, with the power of ten men, Gary made it clear that admission would not happen. With the collective determination and professionalism of the nursing staff, they moved him through the reception area and into the admission ward without a problem. Police followed the entourage in case of further trouble.

Consultant psychiatrist for the Psychiatric Unit, Dr Sharif, tall and, to many of the ladies, debonair, tried to speak to Gary, who only responded by trying to head-butt him. "Don't come near me; you fuckin' witch doctor!" Nursing staff held him in check as Dr Sharif leapt back.

"Let go, you fuckin' bastards," screamed Gary, with fury. The kerfuffle, without a doubt, turned heads.

To try and defuse the situation, Dr Sharif instructed the sergeant to remove the handcuffs. With incredulity, officers looked at each other as if to say, 'big mistake.' Unknown to the police, the experienced psychiatric staff were more than capable of dealing with an awkward admission. With training and know-how, the aggressive admission – Gary, progressed without a problem.

"Okay, take him straight to the side room," said Dr Sharif, as he followed. If the admission hadn't been so serious, it might have been funny. From a distance, the nurses appeared as a mass of white coats surrounding one person. In essence, it was like a manic rugby scrum moving left to right towards the emergency side room. Midst a venomous tirade, Gary saw his destination. "Get your hands off me; you fuckin' bastards; I'm not going in there." With perseverance, the staff steered him into the room. He continued to scream and yell.

Making a quick appraisal of the situation, Dr Sharif realised that a regular admission wouldn't be possible and so discussed the options with the charge nurse, Mr Elwood.

"We can't evaluate him right now; he's too disturbed. However, his GP has just contacted the department, and it seems that, apart from a lower back problem, there are no physical problems, so I'll write him up for a tranquilliser and we'll see how he is in a couple of hours."

Gary's overt psychotic episode tested the staff and doctors. They wouldn't forget the Gary Lowe admission in a hurry.

A nurse entered the side room with a syringe to administer a tranquilising injection. Gary continued his verbal tirade, though, given time, he reluctantly accepted the inevitability of his confinement to the side room.

TEN

Curtains pulled tight to block out the day created a cosy, intimate atmosphere in the luxurious bedroom. The Egyptian cotton sheets, plush duvet and feather pillows exuded quality. The large bedroom chandelier boasted opulence; the ivory-coloured, deep-pile carpet, so dense it massaged bare feet, oozed decadence. Clothes strewn on the bedroom floor showed the urgency of their immoral passion.

Eleanor lay cocooned in the gardener's strong arms; her head on his chest, she listened to the soothing cadence of his heartbeat. She kissed his tanned, muscular chest, gazing up into his deep, lustful eyes. "You most surely know how to please a lady," she purred.

"Lady, what lady would that be, then?" he said tantalizingly.

"You impudent little pup." Sitting up, she mischievously clipped him across the head. Ready to play her at her own game, he rolled Eleanor over onto her back, pinning her wrists to the bed. She tried to retaliate by arching her body upwards, but her paramour was too strong. He pressed the length of his body against hers and kissed her with passion. Naked contact ignited her sexual yearning. She left behind the facade of being a lady and wanted basic, primitive, sexual fulfilment. Nothing else could sate her craving.

The bedroom telephone rang, interrupting their moment of passion. She shook her head as if to say, 'Can you believe the timing?' Pulling back the sheet, Eleanor swung her legs over the side of the bed. She looked at the hunk of a man in her bed.

"Don't go away." She padded like a cougar over the deep pile carpet to the French dressing table. Her sense of deportment showed, even after many years. The finishing school had taught her well. Unlike other women of her age, Eleanor continued to look after her body, working out at the local country club, spa and gymnasium. As well as having a gifted mind, Eleanor was enthusiastic about maintaining a fitness regimen. To this end, she looked svelte for her age of forty-nine and could have passed for forty. Except, already, life had programmed fine wrinkles on her face, something she felt determined to eradicate with the help of cosmetic surgery in the coming months.

"Hello," said Eleanor into the mouthpiece of the landline.

"Is that Mrs St John?"

"Yes, it is. To whom am I speaking?"

As the gardener listened to Eleanor's voice, he found it hard to believe that it belonged to the same woman he had just bedded. His overriding boyish urge was to creep up to her and tweak her firm, pretty bum, yet he knew that would be the wrong thing to do. Her affected speech intimated superiority as she spoke on the phone, a voice she played on to her advantage, time and time again.

"This is Southport General Hospital, and I am Sister Jean McDonald. Is Mr Quentin St John your husband?"

"Yes, he is." Eleanor's demeanour changed to one of guarded concern when she heard 'hospital.' "Is everything all right, sister?"

The sister continued. "We just wanted to inform you that your husband, Mr Quentin St John, has been brought into casualty."

"Oh my God, what happened?" The gardener was more than curious as he pieced together Eleanor's words. He left the King-sized bed to join her and pressed his ear to the receiver, listening in on the conversation. Eleanor detested such common behaviour; in her world, it was the height of bad manners and took liberties far beyond the accepted norm. She pushed him away in annoyance.

Reeling from the odd behaviour, he couldn't help thinking what a strange person she was. She represented another world, one he could never understand if he lived with her for the rest of his life. It seemed it was all right to violate her body in sexual intimacy, not forgetting it was adulterous, but he was forbidden to press his ear to the phone when she was taking a call. He concluded, "Women, I'll never understand them." There again, did he want to understand her? Their closeness was wanton sex. No, he decided, this was the easiest money he had ever made, and he would do well to keep his thoughts to himself and play along with the shenanigans.

"There's nothing to be alarmed about. It's merely a precaution," said the sister.

Eleanor was distracted for a moment as she looked at the gardener standing alongside her with his sexy, beguiling body. She realised that pushing him away in a dominant act had excited her. For a moment, the phone call lost all precedence; she stared at his manhood and his, oh, so perfect body. "Sorry, did you say precaution?"

"Mr St John was apparently found unwell in a railway carriage at Southport station and brought by ambulance to us here in the accident and emergency. We weren't able to contact you initially as your phone was out of order."

"Really?"

"Yes, when I couldn't get through, I reported it to the telephone company."

"How extremely kind of you," said Eleanor.

"Not a problem... Of course, you will appreciate that I can't discuss personal details about your husband over the phone..."

"Quite."

"Nevertheless, I can tell you he will be transferred to another hospital."

Eleanor found it difficult to concentrate; sexual feelings played havoc with her mind. She turned to face the dressing table, but that only made matters worse. The dressing table's oval mirror framed his very adequate appendage like a cameo. She lost her train of thought; her mind went blank.

"I do beg your pardon, nurse, can you repeat that?"

The nurse felt it was pretty understandable that Eleanor would be unsettled by the news of her husband's unexpected admission to the hospital. "Your husband will be transferred to Mystic Sands, department of psychiatry, admission ward, when we can arrange transport."

"Psychiatry?" said Eleanor, in a questioning tone.

"The doctor thought it appropriate for admission to a psychiatric hospital for further investigations."

"This is very disconcerting. Are you sure it is completely necessary?" said Eleanor, resolute in wanting to bring the conversation to a close and fulfil her deepening impulse.

"You will be able to talk at length with the psychiatrist, at Mystic Sands, Mrs St John. I'm sure he will allay any concerns you may have."

"Oh, I see. Would you know how long it could be before he's transferred?"

"Difficult to say with certainty, but I would think about two hours. I'll get them to ring you when he arrives. Oh, one final thing. Apparently, the bank where your husband works tried to phone you much earlier when Mr St John didn't turn up for work. Because they couldn't speak to you, they reported the matter to the police, who confirmed he had been taken to the hospital feeling unwell."

"I see. Well, thank you, nurse, that was awfully thoughtful of you to let me know–good morning."

Stood behind Eleanor, the gardener kissed her shoulder as he held onto her hips, which had a devastating effect on her uncontrollable desire. Containment wasn't a choice. Eleanor was ready to pop like a cork from a Champagne bottle.

"Well?" said the gardener, curious to know the outcome of the phone call. "What gives?"

Nevertheless, Eleanor's unstoppable urge was paramount. She took him in her arms, pressing into his remarkable athletic body. Sexually aroused, they kissed with passion. His tongue probed her moist, sensual mouth. The intimate contact fired her lust.

"Well, what?" she said tantalizingly as she caressed his firm buttocks.

"There's obviously something wrong. Spill the beans."

Like a spoilt child playing a silly game, she refused to divulge any more information. This was her prerogative. She would only talk when she was good and ready. But, right now, she didn't want to talk; all she wanted was action. Taking both his hands in hers, she led him to the bed. With surging desire, they stopped and kissed. Running her hands over his chest and back, she drew him into her soft, luscious curves. The sumptuous bed made a gentle whoosh as Eleanor pulled her personal sex machine sprawling across the bed—a moment of curiosity from the gardener persisted.

"Is he all right?"

"Oh, yes," said Eleanor, breaking away from the passion. Her hands roamed his body, fulfilling her lustful, tactile desire. "Quentin was always a bit of an actor. He takes after his mother, you know. He'll be right as rain by tonight."

"You'll have to contact the bank, won't you?"

Like putty in her hands, Eleanor rolled the gardener onto his back and straddled his strong hips. Her beautiful, manicured nails lightly scratched his hairy chest, exciting him all the more. She kissed all six abdominal muscles of his stomach, firing his desire.

"Let me worry about that. Right now, I have something else on my mind and you, my naughty, alluring gardener, haven't earned your wages yet, so I will have to take payment in kind."

Like a well-rehearsed scene from a love film, she pulled the sheet over both of them and slid seductively down his muscular body.

ELEVEN

What should have been another typical day in the life for Mary turned out to be a rollercoaster ride full of aggression, fear, uncertainty and trauma. She arrived home from work, tired and ready for bed. However, for some inexplicable reason, Mary was beset by a violent onslaught from Gary. He had become a crazed, psychotic individual, prepared to kill. Undeniably, if she hadn't moved so quickly and found sanctuary in the bedroom, Mary could have been another casualty of domestic violence. Finding Paisley and Kylie missing, presumed dead, was the biggest shock she had ever encountered in her whole life.

Hours after the attack, she still relived the horrific, violent moment. The trauma consumed her to the point where she vowed never to see Gary ever again. Because of her upbringing, violence had no place in Mary's life. She was committed to peace, love, and respect. Violence was alien to her and was never to be tolerated. Yet she was human; when provoked and tested by Gary's crazy, selfish ways, she sometimes lost her self-control.

Her loving parents weren't very religious; even so, they trod the path of gentle people with Christian values. They attended church at Easter and Christmas, and for weddings and funerals, or on the odd occasion when they felt inclined. Nevertheless, they were kind, caring, God-fearing people who were the salt of the earth.

Since meeting Gary, Madge had seen the adverse effect on her daughter. On many an occasion, she was of a mind to point out her concern, yet held her tongue for fear of causing problems or alienation.

Contacted by the police on the morning of the attack, Madge left her household chores to rush to Mary's side. Typical of most mums in an emergency, she was a tower of strength and committed to giving practical support for as long as was necessary. As she arrived at Mary's home, the family doctor was leaving.

"Are you Mary's mother?" he said.

"Yes, I am. I've just heard the news from the police. Is she all right?"

"Yes, she'll be fine. More shock than anything else."

"Oh, thank God for that." Madge was so relieved; she almost hugged the doctor.

"She's taken a sedative, and I've left her with two more days' supply," continued the doctor, "just enough to calm her and help her through the worst of the trauma. Let me know if there are further problems, but I don't expect any. Try to get her to talk about the experience; it will help."

"Thank you, doctor."

Mary ran to the door as soon as she heard Mum's voice. It took a long time to calm her; however, in due course, she settled and talked about the unforgettable events of the morning. Upon being informed that the children were safe and unharmed, Mary let out tears of joy and relief. With patience and understanding from a caring mother, Mary's emotions began to level out; the tears and shakes gradually gave way. With encouragement, she talked more coherently about the attack.

The phone rang. "Don't answer it, mum. It'll be the press again," said Mary, irritated with the constant intrusions.

"I do wish they'd leave you alone, Mary. It's not as if it's news, is it?"

On the contrary, the attack and later removal of Gary from the house by the police was very newsworthy. In the hands of an experienced reporter, the news could have sounded astonishing.

"I know. They're so nosy." Mary peeped through the curtains, making sure she couldn't be seen, "Just look at them, they're like vultures."

"I'm just so glad the police are outside, Mary, aren't you?" said Madge.

Mary didn't answer; she had a lot on her mind. The attack was so unreal and still fresh in her mind, although the sedative and lack of sleep had begun to blur her memory of the raw emotion.

In continual need of reassurance, Mary repeated the same question she had asked at least twice before. "Are you sure the kids are okay, mum? Gary really took the kids to you last night?"

Madge moved close and put an arm around her shoulders. "Mary, they're fine. Yes, they were with me last night, and yes, I took them to school myself this morning and saw them in the school gates." She looked at the clock. "Anyway, they'll be home soon; you'll be able to see them for yourself."

Curling a soggy handkerchief around her finger, Mary gave a half-smile. "Why do you think he said such terrible things and attacked me, Mum?"

"Seeing as you ask, I think he's off his head." Madge was happy to give her opinion, a secret she had kept for a long time. "Well, I did warn you, Mary, and now it's happened; booze, drugs, not eating and look, his head's gone."

"Okay, mum, you don't need to drag it *all* up." Mary regretted opening the can of worms. "It's just... I'm trying to make sense of it all, but can't."

"Well, you need to face reality, Mary; he needs professional help." Not content to divulge her innermost thoughts about Gary, Madge indulged in an 'I told you so' moment. "There was only one in that family that turned out to be half-decent, and you gave him his marching orders."

"Mum, please."

"I'm right, aren't I? Two brothers, and you had to choose the reject." She stopped at the word 'reject,' realising how ill-chosen it was under the circumstances. She regretted her loose tongue and moderated her tone. "As nice as he can be, he doesn't take life seriously. You and the kids aren't his priority, Mary; you have to understand that."

Just then, there was a knock at the door. Mary jumped to her feet and ran into the hallway. Wrenching the front door open, she found her two children standing on the doorstep, looking around, bemused and uncertain, wondering why so many people and police had congregated outside their house. With unbelievable relief, Mary fell to her knees; her arms embraced the children with intensity.

"You're here. Oh, thank God, you really are here." A battery of press cameras came to life, lighting the area as if a film star had just stepped into the frame. A cacophony of questions were hurled towards the joyous scene. A few enthusiastic reporters pushed forward. Police stepped up as the scrum showed signs of breaking past the cordon.

Unaware of the morning's events, the children looked on with uncertainty. "Of course, we're here. We've just got home from school, haven't we?" Paisley looked at the crowd. "Mum, what's going on? Why are all these people here? And why are you on your knees, squeezing us?"

Mary looked heavenwards. "Thank you, God, for looking after them. I'll always believe in you now." With unimaginable happiness, Mary felt compelled to hold on to the children, afraid to let go. "This is the best present I've ever, ever had." She looked heavenwards again, "Oh, thank you, God." Cameras continued to flash, lighting up a scene destined for the front page of the local newspaper, possibly even the national press if the news of the day were unremarkable.

Madge knew that her daughter was overplaying the situation and tried to normalise the homecoming. "Mary, love, let the children in and close the door."

"Mum, what are you doing?" said Paisley, as he tried to push his mum away. "Stop it, mum, me mates are watching. Anyway, why are you crying?" Mary released her hold on the children, stood up and tried to compose herself. As she looked out onto the street, a huddle of busybodies gawked and exchanged comments.

The press fired questions at her, hoping for the lowdown on the morning's events.

"Mrs Lowe, how do you feel?"

"Over here, Mrs Lowe – Liverpool Echo – how's the family holding up? Is your husband in the hospital?"

"Mrs Lowe – Evening Post. Can you give us the exclusive?"

"Piss off, you nosey bastards," screamed Mary with venom as she slammed the door.

Untidy as ever, the children threw their coats and bags on the floor and then ran to the upstairs window for a bird's-eye view of the gathering crowd and reporters.

"Hey, Kylie, did anybody say anything to you?"

"No."

"I thought me mate Jono was talking rubbish. He said our street had blown up."

Madge and Mary picked up the coats and bags. However, this time, Mary didn't complain about their untidiness. She was so thrilled to see the children safe and sound at home, and their untidiness was a welcome sight; it was positive reinforcement of the actual reality that helped chase away the nightmare and dispel Gary's cruel assertion that the children were dead.

Five minutes later, Kylie had seen enough. She came downstairs to join Mum and Nan, more to find out about the strange events that had taken place in their street and see if she had missed anything.

"Mum, has Dad seen all this?" She pointed towards the window, then realised something wasn't as it should be. "Mum, where is Dad?"

TWELVE

Following Eleanor's busy morning in the bedroom, she elected to have a day of pampering. As well as beauty treatments, she tried on a few clothes and decided to clear her wardrobe of items she no longer favoured. Donating her unwanted clothes to charity satisfied her altruistic self, making her feel good. This gave her a good reason to travel to London with her friends on a shopping spree, where she bought haute couture to replenish her dwindling wardrobe and, of course, dined at the best restaurants. Money was no object.

As she tried on a full-length, beige diamante evening dress, the bedroom telephone rang. Undaunted, she continued with her clothes moment, allowing the answering machine to pick up.

"Hello, Mrs St John, my name is George Macey, and I'm a staff nurse from the Department of Psychiatry admission ward, Mystic Sands Hospital. Your husband, Mr St John, has been transferred to us here at the hospital, and Dr Sharif, the Consultant Psychiatrist, will be on the ward from five o'clock onwards this afternoon. Should you wish to see him, he will be happy to answer any questions you may have. Thank you."

The approach to the Department of Psychiatry snaked its way from the main road along a tree-lined avenue. The modern unit, encircled by lawns, garden borders, shrubs, and seating areas, although public, communicated a feeling of peace and serenity. It had the feel of a small park, hidden away from the noise and humdrum of modern life. Parking for visitors and staff, with a drop-off point for taxis and ambulances, afforded ample space.

"So this is how they spend our taxes." Eleanor intoned as she parked up, making her way to the main entrance. Surprised by the interior decoration, she eyed the stylish reception area, noticing the colourful prints of one of the masters – Vincent Van Gogh: Sunflowers, Irises, A Vase of Roses, Olive Trees, and Wheatfield under a Cloudy Sky. The person who chose the prints had, in her estimation, superb taste.

"Can I help you?" said the receptionist.

"Thank you, yes. I'm here to see Dr Sharif."

"And you are?" said the receptionist, a little too brusquely for Eleanor's liking. She had become accustomed to fawning receptionists and the like, filling her full of self-importance.

"Mrs Eleanor St John."

"Take a seat. I'll let the doctor know you are here." She gestured to the seating area opposite, dismissing Eleanor. Gentle, agreeable music played in the background, another surprise for Eleanor. She had never heard background music in private hospitals, let alone in NHS hospitals. The *ambience* was surprisingly agreeable to her senses.

The consultant, Dr Sharif, was instantly pleasing to Eleanor, with his good looks and *savoir-faire*. He walked to the reception area with a young couple and said goodbye. Turning to Eleanor, he shook her hand and invited her into his office. From the rug on the floor to the aged mosaic artwork that hung in pride of place on the wall behind his desk, she speculated that the well-furnished office suggested Moroccan or North African influence.

Eleanor recalled her private school days. As a young lady learning about the Berber race, she and other young ladies in her year travelled on an organised trip to the Bardo National Museum in Tunisia. There, she saw first-hand the selfsame mosaics and statues that adorned his office. Her first trip abroad without her parents seemed so much fun, so grown-up. It felt wonderful with her life ahead of her. Eleanor questioned incredulously where time had gone.

"Please take a seat, Mrs St John. Would you like tea, coffee or a cold drink?"

"No, thank you, Dr Sharif, I am fine. But, please do call me Eleanor."

"If you prefer," said Dr Sharif, with his well-educated English accent.

Eleanor smiled sweetly. She looked at his nameplate on the desk and thought of his surname, Sharif, just like the film legend Omar Sharif, a charismatic star that she couldn't forget in a hurry.

Her impression of the doctor was that he came from a wealthy family and had lived in the United Kingdom from a young age, or maybe lived here all his life. He was obviously a gentleman of breeding.

"So, how is my husband, Dr Sharif?"

"Apart from his asthma, physically, he appears quite well for his age. Nevertheless, it isn't easy to obtain a full history from him. You see, he has a memory problem. He only speaks when prompted."

"Oh. That's unusual for Quentin; by and large, he normally has a lot to say for himself."

Dr Sharif smiled. "And has he ever had any problems with his memory before?"

"No, nothing at all. In fact, I would go as far as to say he has an outstanding mind." She tried to imagine Dr Sharif's family status. He wore a ring, so he was married. Yet she saw no personal photographs of his family around the office. His clothing looked immaculate and expensive. Eleanor always accompanied Quentin when he bought his clothing. In reality, she felt he wasn't to be trusted to make the right decisions on dress and style. Her father always bought clothing in Savile Row, London. For Eleanor, it was essential to maintain social standards and dress well.

Dr Sharif continued, "I see. Has he had any illnesses of late, Eleanor?"

"No, although he has been sleeping poorly."

"And his asthma, how has that been?"

"Absolutely fine."

He wrote in his notes. "And what is your husband's profession, Eleanor?"

"He's a manager in investment banking."

"So quite a stressful job; deadlines to meet, targets to achieve, etc."

Eleanor was dismissive of the doctor's suggestion that the work of an investment manager was stressful. She gave him the impression that the team at the bank, with his accomplished assistant manager and handpicked staff who bore the brunt of responsibility, enabled Quentin to have precious time for managerial matters.

Dr Sharif continued writing in his notes. "Do you think Quentin is a happy person?"

"What do you mean?" said Eleanor, unsure if he was implying something aberrant.

"I'm trying to understand Quentin's mood and what led up to his admission here today, Eleanor. For example, has he talked about being depressed or has he sounded strange at any time?"

In her mind, Eleanor had dismissed the unfortunate words they had had the previous night as inconsequential, putting it down to tiredness and a headache on Quentin's part.

"Oh no, nothing like that," said Eleanor, wanting to distance herself from any suggestion of abnormality. She smiled as if recalling his image. "Darling Quentin."

"And is he under any personal financial strain?"

"Oh no," declined Eleanor, "we have no financial problems at all."

"Well, thank you, Eleanor. I think that's enough information for now. I'm sorry about the questions. Some of them must have seemed personal, I'm sure. However, it's all very relevant. We need to have a full picture if we are to do our best for your husband."

"Of course; please don't apologise. It's extremely kind of you to have my husband's well-being at heart."

Dr Sharif smiled. "So, now it's a case of observing your husband here in the unit, completing a full range of blood tests, X-rays, scans and assessment by my team. Then we should have a better picture of his problem."

Eleanor took a moment searching for words. "I hope this isn't going to sound pompous or anything, Dr Sharif, and it doesn't reflect on you or your hospital here." At that point, she looked around the office with an approving smile. "We have health insurance, and I would like to have Quentin cared for in a private ward if that can be arranged."

"I'm sorry, Eleanor; there aren't any private facilities in this area. Besides, he couldn't get better treatment anywhere else. In this hospital, we pride ourselves on patient care. You will have noticed we are a new unit here and are at the cutting edge of modern psychiatry. In short, I'm saying we are very professional and have very high standards."

"Well, if you think. It's just... we have always had private medicine, and I feel comfortable with that."

"I understand, Eleanor. Let me assure you, I will oversee your husband's case personally and will make sure he is well cared for."

"Thank you; that is very reassuring. So do you have any idea what might be wrong with him, Dr Sharif?"

"It's difficult to say at this juncture without all the test results. Still, presuming that they all check out normal, I think we could be dealing with dissociative amnesia."

"Goodness."

"Nothing to worry about."

"Oh, I'm not worried; it just sounds so terribly medical."

"Yes, I'm sure it takes a lot of understanding and getting used to, especially as it all came out of the blue."

Dr Sharif stood up and offered his hand. "Let's see how we go, Eleanor; it's early days yet. Now then, the nurse will take you to see your husband. He's in the quiet room so that you won't be disturbed. Just the same, I must warn you, don't expect too much from him. It will take some time, and you will have to be very patient with him."

"Thank you for your help, Dr Sharif, terribly kind of you. Goodbye."

The nurse led Eleanor down a corridor to a door labelled 'Quiet Room' and opened the door for her. As she entered, Quentin was sitting in a corner. He didn't react, nor turn his head; he stared out of the window, lost in another world, appearing afflicted by an eerie, disconcerting torpor. Eleanor felt upset to see him looking so meek, unlike his former self. She pulled a chair up and sat beside him.

"Hello, Quentin, darling," she said, expecting him to acknowledge her despite the doctor's attempt to prepare her for the worst. But he didn't react to her greeting. She tried again. "Hello, Quentin, it's me, Eleanor." Because of her proximity to him, Quentin turned his head to look at the stranger speaking – unconvinced, he turned away. She tried a more direct approach. Her hand covered his. "Darling, it's me, Eleanor."

He pulled away. "What? Who are you? What are you doing?"

"It's me, darling, your wife, Eleanor." Her contact with him wasn't working; she was out of her depth. His rejection of her was distressing and upsetting.

"No, you're not, now leave me alone."

Irritated by the stranger, Quentin moved to another chair and turned his back on her. Akin to a rabbit caught in car headlights, Quentin continued to stare out of the window.

The Following Day.

With trembling hands and a vacant look on his face, Gary sat facing Dr Sharif in the consulting room. Gary's disturbing behaviour had abated. No longer did he ply the staff with a venomous tirade of obscenity. Quite the opposite; he appeared quiet and sullen. Given the short time since admission, this showed that the treatment was working. The interview was conducted to assess his present mental state.

"The staff tell me you're settling in well, Gary." No response was forthcoming. Gary stared at Mr Elwood, who stood nearby.

"Can you remember being brought into the hospital?" Gary shook his head.

"Can you remember anything at all?"

"Wife... kids."

"Okay, that's a good start. Do you recall saying anything bad about your children before you came into the hospital?" Gary's demeanour and fixed stare had a menacing edge to it – he glared at the doctor with enmity.

"How about your wife; did you say anything nasty to her?" said Dr Sharif, looking for a response. No answer was forthcoming.

"Do you remember attacking your wife?"

Without speaking, Gary glowered with menace. For an inexperienced doctor, this situation could have been unnerving. Nevertheless, with many years of experience, the consultant had seen it all.

When he was still a junior trainee, many years ago, he recalled a patient who took exception to a question put to him. The patient launched himself over the desk to grab Dr Sharif. Luckily, staff were on hand in the interview room. The patient acquiesced when two large psychiatric nurses bore down on him. The whole experience was one that Dr Sharif had never forgotten. After that, he always ensured a member of staff was present when he interviewed a potentially problematic patient. It seemed self-evident to him that when, for example, he interviewed a frail old lady, there would be no need for a minder. Then again, maybe his logic would let him down one day. Who knew what was in the mind of a disturbed patient? Anything could happen in psychiatry, and on occasions, it did.

"Attacking?" intoned Gary.

"Yes, your wife."

"No, you're lying, I wouldn't." Gary's nostrils flared with rage; his hands reached for the armrests as he prepared to stand in confrontation. It could have deteriorated into something nasty except for Mr Elwood stepping forward, ready to restrain if necessary. Nevertheless, Dr Sharif's finger was already making for the emergency button under his desk in case the interview went belly up, requiring reinforcements.

"Okay, Gary, keep it calm," said Mr Elwood, in a low, calming, resolute voice.

Like many other men at the end of the Second World War, Mr Elwood looked around for a job. With work thin on the ground, he entered mental nursing as a means of paying the bills. At the outset, the job was just a stopgap. When things levelled out, he would look for something better. That said, surprisingly, he enjoyed the work and continued to qualify as a Mental Nurse. Throughout the years, working with aggressive and disturbed patients, he had accumulated a vast knowledge of nursing skills. Besides his natural ability to care for patients, he had a compassionate side and spent many hours tending to patients when and where needed. In his early days of nursing, he had experienced patients with psychotic disturbance and aggression. In extreme measures, if the patient required restraining, he was placed in a straitjacket, administered a calming injection and put into a padded side room. He had witnessed every conceivable condition and treatment imaginable in the world of psychiatry. Well-liked by his staff, Mr Elwood assumed a place of respect and admiration.

Dr Sharif followed up with calm reassurance. "Okay, Gary, not a problem, let's leave it there. I'll give you something for your tremor; it should work pretty quickly and make you feel more comfortable."

The Following Day.

After lunch, patients relaxed in the day room, chatting, reading or watching television. A group played dominoes in the corner of the day room. Gary was undoubtedly feeling more together and sat a few chairs away from Quentin.

"Gary," he said out loud.

In a world of his own, Quentin continued reading his newspaper.

"Gary Lowe!"

Quentin lowered his paper and looked at the individual sitting near him. He stared in bewilderment. "What?"

"My name... Gary Lowe."

"Oh, yes, very good." He turned his attention back to the newspaper and continued reading.

"And yours?" said Gary.

Quentin felt irritated at the interruption; he lowered his paper again. "Quentin, they tell me."

Although Gary's thought processes were still impeded, he was together enough to find the remark unusual. "What d'you mean, they tell you. Can't you remember your own name?"

"I can't remember. That's why I'm here." Quentin's mind functioned well enough with day-to-day events, but, despite that, his memory refused to respond. No amount of forced or deep concentration on his part would free his amnesic mind. Locked in the depths of time, it refused to budge. He accepted reassurance about his amnesia and, with encouragement, he was able to control his troubled mind. All the same, the frustration of not knowing who he was or where he came from far outweighed any positivity.

"No shit," said Gary.

"Excuse me?" said Quentin, with indignation at the crude vulgarity.

"Err... sorry. I mean, no way. And your other name?"

Quentin looked at the front of his newspaper where his name was written. "Quentin St John."

Gary's face lit up. "St John! Not *the* St John?"

Poor Quentin couldn't believe his misfortune. He had been dragged into a pointless conversation with a crude individual who wanted to talk when all he wanted to do was sit and read his paper in peace. He shook his head in disbelief as Gary continued the *tête-à-tête*.

"Ian St John, the best Liverpool player of all time. In four hundred and twenty-four games, he scored one hundred and eighteen goals for Liverpool. I can still see him scoring and the Kop going wild." At the mention of the Kop, he automatically stood, raised his arms, and began chanting, but soon realised he was drawing unwanted attention to himself. Hospital admission to the psychiatric unit was still very fresh in his mind, and he did not want to be seen as being out of control and receive another injection, so he sat down. "Err, *that* Ian St John. You must have heard of him."

"No, I haven't, and no, no relation."

Quentin's answer had a finality to it. He buried his head in the newspaper to discourage any further intrusion.

THIRTEEN

In between doing good work for the Soroptimists and being on the board of trustees for the Women's Institute, Eleanor was also an active member of the committee for the local orchid society. She led a busy social life, often meeting up with close friends. To this end, Eleanor arranged to meet with two of her dearest friends at an Italian bistro.

Arriving at the *soirée*, she located her friends on the far side of the room and made her way over, negotiating tables as she meandered toward them, smiling at acquaintances. At one point, she stopped to say hello to a member of a committee she chaired. Such was her popularity. Finally, she reached her table.

"Frances, darling, how are you?" said Eleanor as she leaned in and air-kissed her friend.

"More to the point, how are you? Are you managing by yourself in that big house?" said Frances.

"Darling, I've always been by myself."

Eleanor embraced Cynthia. "Cynthia darling, how's Gerald?"

"Oh, don't ask, he's frightful."

As they sat, the waiter approached. "Mrs St John, so lovely to see you again." He took her hand, bowed reverently and kissed her hand.

"The pleasure is all mine, Giovanni." Eleanor ogled him in a display of unfettered lust. She adored his charm, his swagger and his beautiful Michelangeloesque face. The waiter, in his thirties, tall and trim, with dark, passionate eyes, was a hit with all the ladies. He played upon his looks for the good of the bistro and, of course, his own ego. Because of his notoriety at the bistro, the owner, Mario, allowed him certain privileges and more leeway than other members of staff. Even so, there were occasional heated spats between him and the manager when he took too many liberties. Impassioned moments were ordinary in the fiery Italian world of interpersonal relationships, where egos vied for dominance as would-be alpha males. The exception was that the boss, as the owner, always had the last word.

"Giovanni, we'll have three very dry, very large martinis," she held her finger up for his attention. "Remember olives." She waved him away as the girls caught up on gossip.

"So tell us all about Quentin, how is he?" enquired Cynthia.

"Well, the consultant, who I might add is rather handsome and very sophisticated, thinks he has amnesia."

"Oh, how awful," replied Frances. "Is that a similar thing to Agent Kay in the film Men in Black, where he erases people's memories with a neuralyzer?"

Eleanor and Cynthia looked at each other quizzically and burst into laughter.

"What are you talking about, Frances?" They giggled so much; it brought tears to their eyes. Frances's continued protestations made their hysteria even worse.

"Well, he did." She held a rolled-up napkin to her right eye and uttered "poof," simulating the neuralyzer.

"Oh, Frances, stop it, I can't take any more," said Cynthia, as she dabbed her eyes with a tissue and tried not to ruin her makeup.

"Oh my God," said Eleanor, trying to calm her fit of the giggles. "How enormously funny; that is the best tonic I have had in a long time." The laughter subsided as Eleanor perused the menu. "Do you want to choose your own, or shall I order?"

One of the reasons for their enduring friendship was in part due to mutual respect. Eleanor, an authoritarian, ready to direct at a minute's notice, preferred to be in control. Her friend Cynthia, although equally accomplished at organising, was more than happy to leave it to Eleanor. Frances – well, Frances was the person who didn't have to try hard to be loved. She was pleasant and engaging, a butterfly flitting from one situation to another, at times getting it completely wrong. She was a beautiful, fun person who didn't have a nasty bone in her body, which made her all the more adorable.

"We will have asparagus wraps for starters," said Eleanor, ordering from the menu, "*Pasta Alle Vongole* and for the sweet *Zabaglione*." She took a moment to look at the wine menu; Giovanni stood, pen poised.

"And a bottle of *Pinot Grigio* will suffice. Make sure it is served chilled, Giovanni."

"Certainly, and if I may say so, Mrs St John, you have

chosen a perfect meal for you and the ladies." Giovanni fawned as only he could.

"You may say so." A wave of her hand, and he was gone.

"I believe it's your silver wedding anniversary next week, Eleanor?" said Cynthia.

"Yes, the third of November."

"Twenty-five years married – how wonderful. Do you have anything planned?"

"No, nothing at all. With this hospital fiasco, nothing at all will happen, I fear."

"Awwh," said Cynthia, with a look of sadness.

The starter, main meal, and sweet, served with panache, were among the reasons for the bistro's popularity amongst the elite.

Later, Mario, the manager, came over to add his personal acknowledgement to the lady clients. He clicked his fingers in the air for attention. Giovanni scuttled on over. Mario pointed to the half-empty wine glasses. This wasn't a great crime, merely a display of authority for all to see over the young pretender. His action of pointing to the glasses annoyed Giovanni. Later, there would be a gnashing of teeth between the two, and Giovanni would threaten to leave. Sleeping on it, he would turn up for work the following day as if nothing had happened – a non-event.

"So, Cynthia, how is Gerald? You said he was frightful."

"Oh, my dear, you won't believe it. Yesterday, he told me we had to be more prudent with our finances. More prudent," Cynthia rolled her eyes. "Now, remember," she held up her finger for emphasis," this is the same man who bought himself a Lamborghini recently... I ask you."

"Midlife crisis," exclaimed Eleanor, quite matter-of-fact. "Just ignore him," she said with disdain. "Quentin's always saying ridiculous things like that."

"Well, so does Gerald, but this time he means it. He's asked me to review my allowance to see if I can make any economies. I ask you, economies."

"I know," Frances interjected, "Julian had a fit the other night when he saw the account from Harrods. Well, I mean, if he wants me to look after the home, he has to jolly well pay for it. Don't you agree?"

"Hear, hear. That is more than enough of this vulgar talk about economising. Shall we have three Sambucas?" dared Eleanor.

"Yes, let's," agreed Cynthia.

"I don't think I should," said Frances with concern, "I'm already a bit squiffy."

"Oh, go on, it will do you good."

"Talking about doing good, how's the gardener?" said Cynthia, probing for all the lurid details. Eleanor smiled. Although she hadn't talked about the gardener to her friends, they had seen him working at Eleanor's house and had arrived at their own conclusions.

"Come on, spill the beans," said Frances, "and I want to know everything, darling."

"Yes, I am sure you do." Eleanor, more outspoken than usual because of the drink, leaned in close and imparted the licentious details to a host of unbelievable gasps.

"Oh, my God, really?"

"He did what?"

"Well, I've been married for forty-three years, and I have never even heard of that." Frances pulled a face. "I mean, how on earth can one do that?" Puzzled, she tried to work out the gymnastics.

"Darling, he sounds absolutely divine," confirmed Cynthia.

"He sure has lots of va va voom," said Eleanor.

"I'm sure he does."

Cynthia took a moment to phrase the words of her next question with care. "I think he's... he's, shall we say, a little bit younger than you, isn't he?"

"Not just a bit younger, a lot younger. Darling, that is why I employ him."

"So how do you keep up with him, I mean... ?"

"Zumba," intoned Eleanor.

"What on earth is Zumba?" said Frances. "It sounds like a place in Africa."

Cynthia looked at Eleanor with a smile on her face.

"Don't start, Frances, or I will have an accident."

They could see Frances turning something over in her mind

as they waited for the pearl of wisdom. She lowered her voice to proffer some well-meaning advice. "If you have a problem, Cynthia, I believe you can now buy something to wear inside your briefs."

Eleanor looked at Cynthia and shook her head, as if to say, 'Here we go again.'

"You put a pad in the waterproof pants and..."

Cynthia raised her hand to end the conversation.

"No, enough, I'm fine, thank you." She smiled at Eleanor, enjoying the fun.

"Cynthia, darling, would you like me to mention you to the gardener. Maybe he can fit you in," said Eleanor.

"Don't be silly, darling; we live in a penthouse. How could I justify employing a gardener chappie?" All three laughed hysterically, turning heads.

The waiter, Giovanni, was happy that the threesome were in good spirits. He knew that a sizeable tip would be left for him, rewarding his time at the Bistro, grovelling and smiling like a jackass at their silly, self-important behaviour, very worthwhile. In truth, he hated their superiority and pretentiousness.

The *soirée* had gone well and was destined to continue for some time longer. Coffee liqueurs were next along, with more gossip and more hoots of laughter.

FOURTEEN

Since Gary's admission to the hospital, Mary had involved the children more in the running of the home. Both had taken on the responsibility of cleaning and tidying their bedrooms. Be that as it may, it wasn't up to Mary's standard, but it was reasonable enough to make her proud of them for trying. Mary questioned why she hadn't involved them before now; however, times had changed, and so had family dynamics. Paisley appeared to have taken on the male role, feeling protective towards his mum. She felt proud of him and saw him in a completely different light. In many ways, he had shown more common sense and aptitude than his father ever did. Good, it would seem, had emerged from adversity.

As a treat and to save cooking, Madge bought fish and chips for tea. Choosing her moment, she broached a sensitive subject.

"Mary, love, when are you going to visit Gary?"

"I'm not," said Mary, with vehemence.

"I'll look after the kids if you want to go," said Madge, pressing the point.

"Mum, I can't."

"But I'm sure he didn't mean to... " Madge stopped mid-sentence, just in time. The children were paying close attention to every word of the conversation.

Mary cared deeply for the children; her mission was to protect them from the cruel realities of life. With this in mind, she had been careful not to mention the attack at the hands of Gary. It was nigh on impossible to explain to young children how or why their dad had lost it and attacked their mum. She didn't know herself. All she knew was that for the time being, it was far better to keep it to herself. Of course, the near blunder by Madge made them more curious.

Madge continued. "He only did *that* because he wasn't well, Mary."

"I know, but I can't take that chance again, Mum." Emotions ran high: "You didn't see him, and you didn't have to run for your life to get away, did you?" Her impassioned recall surprised her. She had just said too much in front of the children and felt annoyed with herself; the big dark secret had just slipped out.

Kylie wanted to know more. "Mum, what do you mean? You had to run for your life, why?"

For once, in a rare moment in Mary's life, she was speechless. She had divulged an account of Gary's attack, and the carefully guarded secret was out in the open. Her strategy had been to rehearse what had to be said to the children and tell them when the time was right. Instead, the plan had been scuppered by her stupid tirade.

Madge came to the rescue. "Your dad wasn't very well, he got confused and took some tablets that made him ill."

"Now that's enough, our Kylie." Mary wanted to draw a line under the whole sorry saga. "You're always asking questions. Now, eat your fish and chips before they go cold."

They continued their supper in stony silence. Mary gave mum one of her well-rehearsed, withering looks as if to say, 'It's your fault, look what you've done.'

All the same, Madge had seen this look many times before. Mary had a lot on her mind and needed support and guidance to navigate the morass of confusing emotions that had surfaced and overwhelmed her. Only since Madge had slept over had she realised the depth of despair and unhappiness that consumed Mary. In reality, she had a husband who didn't take married life seriously, who lacked commitment, and who played his own silly, immature, and selfish game of life. She understood the pretence that had taken place. Her daughter had gone without, made do with second best, and all to put the children first. Although Mary could not see it at that moment, Madge truly understood her plight. Madge vowed with every breath left in her body to put things right for her beloved daughter and grandchildren. It was her mission in life, and she wouldn't rest; she couldn't. It was her *raison d'être*. Madge was sure that, before she died, Mary's life would improve. It was a big ask. Even so, she was very resourceful. She vowed with every bone in her body to make it happen, come what may, or die trying.

FIFTEEN

Every Tuesday and Friday, Dr Sharif held a patient review meeting in the conference room, along with his junior doctor, the charge nurse, the staff nurse, the social worker, and the occupational therapist. The meeting was conceived to maintain a formal oversight of patients' progress; the review afforded the opportunity to assess individual patient treatment and care. It brought together all disciplines and allowed staff the opportunity to comment on medical care and development.

Eager to start, Dr Sharif called the meeting to order. "Unfortunately, we have a time constraint on our meeting this morning. I have to attend the coroner's court at eleven thirty, so we'll push on and see if we can be finished on time. So, let's take a look at our two most recent admissions, Gary Lowe and Quentin St John." He looked at Mr Elwood.

"Okay – Gary Lowe. Forty-year-old male, married with two children. He was admitted on Wednesday morning in an aggressive, disturbed state, following an attack on his wife at home, according to the police report."

Dr Sharif intervened, requesting a social report on Gary, with the usual background checks, family, work, etc.

This was duly noted, and Mr Elwood continued.

"We got him settled in, and he has responded well to a major tranquilliser. There was a slight reaction to this, so he was prescribed something to help with the tremor. He slept well for the first two nights and is a little groggy and slow in the mornings. There are no signs of aggression, disruptive behaviour or psychotic features. In fact, he has settled in well, and staff report that he is pleasant and cooperative. There is, however, one significant health problem we need to be aware of, but I will let Dr Reece tell us all about that."

Staff nurse Gwyneth Jones provided more information. "Gary's urine sample on admission was interesting. It tested positive for amphetamines. Although he didn't admit to taking drugs, he displayed the classic signs. He had dilated pupils, elevated blood pressure, an abnormal heart rate, rapid breathing and restlessness. Two days later, his signs are more within normal limits. We took a blood sample for complete analysis and are awaiting the results."

Dr Reece, the junior, nodded in agreement. "Just to add an important point on Gary's condition," said Dr Reece. "At the first opportunity, I did a full medical examination on him and found he had a heart murmur."

The news surprised Dr Sharif. The general practitioner had reassured him over the phone that Gary was fit and well.

"I've made arrangements for him to be seen by a cardiologist at the first opportunity," said Dr Reece.

"Fine; keep an eye on him and let me know if there's a change in his condition," said the consultant.

The consensus for Gary's treatment plan was to carry on with the present drug therapy and get him to the Occupational Therapy Department (OT) on Monday. The consultant stressed that it was essential to keep a close eye on him. He believed that drug abusers could be difficult to nurse because of their dependency and could, at any opportunity, take more illegal drugs, even while being nursed on the ward.

"Just to give you an idea," said Dr Sharif, "how challenging it can be to nurse a drug-dependent patient. When I was a junior doctor, I worked on a drug dependency unit. I remember we were having problems with one particular patient, Jonathan, who regularly, before his admission, took a variety of banned substances. He admitted to having tried smoking, snorting, injecting and taking by mouth every banned substance you could think about. That said, even though he was a patient on the ward and unable to take any substances, the team couldn't understand why he seemed high at times if he wasn't able to get hold of drugs. It wasn't until we isolated these moments of elation that we realised they coincided with his wife's visits. Then we began to get a handle on the mystery. We found out his wife was feeding him illegal substances passed on to him in a kiss."

The attending staff looked at him in surprise, thinking he had misremembered the incident.

"Before his wife left at the end of visiting time, she always used the toilet, which seemed odd, maybe even obsessional. However, it was a casual remark from one of the staff that helped to make the connection. When she emerged from the toilet, she would say goodbye, kiss him and then leave. It was soon after that we had problems with his behaviour. Later, when questioned, she admitted to passing him pills via her mouth in a kiss. She had previously popped the pill into her mouth during the toilet visit. It all looked very innocent and, as far as the staff were concerned, nothing had been passed to him by hand. The reason I'm telling you this is so you know the potential problems of a person with an addiction. Moreover, I wanted you to understand the lengths to which some people can go to feed their habit. Now, I may be doing him an injustice," cautioned Dr Sharif, "he may just abuse drugs from time to time, so I will reserve judgment until we find out more about Gary."

A knock on the door revealed catering staff, with mid-morning coffee and biscuits for the meeting. This was a welcome diversion for Dr Reece, who had been on-call for 24 hours and had already experienced a busy night. As an American working and training in the UK, he had commuted over the big pond to celebrate his parents' Golden Wedding anniversary. On his return, he had stepped off the Red Eye from the States, showered, changed and reported for duty. The consultant understood the life of a junior, having been one himself, and so ignored it when Dr Reece closed his eyes in the meeting. Junior doctors were expected to work long hours, with little sleep, throughout their medical training. In the elite club of trainee doctors, there was an unwritten requirement for psychological and physical endurance.

"Right, Quentin St John; how is he, Mr Elwood?"

"No trouble at all. Quentin St John. Fifty-three-year-old male, married, no children, admitted on Wednesday, found sitting in a railway carriage, stock-still, staring out of the window. His unresponsive nature caught the attention of the railway staff. I might add that the train was at the terminus, and he had been sitting in the carriage for some time. His reason for being in a railway carriage was that, during the week, he travelled from Mystic Sands to Southport, where he worked as an investment bank manager. Paramedics conveyed him from the station by ambulance to Southport General. After an initial assessment, he was sent to us here. On admission, he was cooperative and, I would have to say, an absolute gentleman. I wish we had a few more like him." He looked around the room for nods of agreement. "Staff have talked to him regularly to reassure and help with his memory loss. He has no recollection of his past, even when prompted. But he does accept his name is Quentin. Just as an aside, it seems curious that, when his wife visits, he becomes quite agitated."

"Yes, I've seen this reaction before in anxiety-depressive cases," said Dr Sharif.

"He has been examined," confirmed Gwyneth. "Apart from his asthma, he is a little overweight, with slightly high blood pressure. That said, he is good for his age, considering he works in a sedentary job." Gwyneth paused for a moment. "There was evidence of nicotine on his fingers to suggest he had smoked recently."

Keen to add to the proceedings and stay awake, Dr Reece interjected. "That's right. When I first saw him, he had a bronchodilator inhaler for his asthma. I checked his airways, and there was evidence of a high-pitched whistle on the out-breath. He has used his inhaler on the ward a few times, so I thought we might add steroids to his regimen for a week to reduce any inflammation. Also, I'm sure he smoked before admission. Of course, not good for an asthmatic. However, he has no recollection, so we can't counsel him on the perils of smoking."

"Yes, I concur," said the consultant. "Let's start him on steroids, keep an eye on his physical state and check his bloods carefully when they come back. We should confirm with his wife whether or not he smoked. Regarding his memory, I have already spoken with him, his wife, and his GP. Let's consider trying regression therapy with Sodium Amytal. I'm convinced we are dealing with a Dissociative Amnesia here," he looked around the room at intrigued faces. "Let's explain the treatment to him and get him to sign the consent form. Dr Reece, have you seen regression therapy with Sodium Amytal?"

"No, I haven't."

"Then you shall. Mr Elwood, could you get everything organised for Quentin's regression on Monday morning?

SIXTEEN

Quentin reached for his alarm clock as it danced around his bedside locker. "Good morning, Gary."

"Yeahhhh," said Gary, grumpy and wanting to sleep on. Night staff began their final round to rouse any remaining patients who were still intent on turning over for a few more minutes. On cue, Alf, the night nurse, switched the dormitory night-lights to normal mode. Akin to a nocturnal creature looking for refuge, Gary pulled the covers over his head.

"Hell, it's the middle of the bloody night," said Gary, reacting to the blinding light as if he were a vampire.

"Good morning, gentlemen." Alf opened the blinds and windows. "What a beautiful day, the sun is up, and the birds are singing."

"No, they're bloody not," said Gary.

"I slept like a top last night," said Quentin as he stretched.

"Go away, Alf," was the response from the bundle of bedclothes where Gary lay. Nevertheless, change was afoot. Like a whirlwind on a mission, Alf pulled the covers back from Gary, shocking his fragile system. To add insult to injury, he hummed a strident racket, much to the annoyance of Gary.

"Come on, Gary, move yourself, it's already five past seven," said Alf.

"Bollocks" was the response. Yet he knew the wake-up call was for real and required nothing less than compliance. Alf wasn't the sort of person to shirk his duty.

Standing at the base of the bed, Alf took hold of the frame

and rocked it. "Come on, Gary, come on, Gary," trilled Alf in a singsong voice, refusing to give up, much to the amusement of Quentin. With no alternative, he swung his feet out of bed and sat in a stupor, knowing this was the only action that made Alf go away. So began the fourth day of hospital life for two people brought together in extraordinary circumstances, requiring treatment for their unique mental conditions.

Quentin enjoyed the early morning routine. He shaved, showered, and dressed in slacks, brown shoes, a shirt, and a cardigan. At breakfast, he didn't bother with cereal; instead, he opted for eggs, bacon, and tomato with toast, followed by a cup of tea, which, by hospital standards, was quite good.

Showing signs that his brain was out of sync with his hands, Gary sat opposite Quentin, attempting to butter his toast. As he did so, he created an unholy mess on the table. Watching him drink coffee wasn't for the faint-hearted. Noisy slurps and coffee trickling down his chin indicated he was a moron, lacking in social grace. He wiped his mouth with his sleeve, oblivious to etiquette or decorum. Quentin looked on and said nothing.

Allowing his breakfast to digest, Quentin sat in the dayroom, reading his pre-ordered Saturday newspaper, a substantial read and enough to keep him engaged for many hours.

Unable to settle, Gary chatted to a patient in the dayroom. He always enjoyed a good chinwag, although it did have a purpose. There was a part of his mind that functioned as a computer hard drive. He stored useful information, ready for recall at a later date. One such snippet of information had helped him recently wriggle out of a very awkward situation with some difficult people in town. It worked well time and time again, giving credence to the idea that nosiness was clever.

Having exhausted his inquisitive nature, Gary headed back

to Quentin, who was methodically working his way through the crossword.

"Hey, Quent, you won't believe what I've just heard," said Gary, unable to contain himself.

"No, I'm sure I won't," said Quentin, dryly.

"That man over there," he jerked his head backwards to indicate. "The one with the dark hair – Stan."

Quentin was uninterested; however, not wishing to be impolite, he looked up from his newspaper.

"Yes, him over there. He just said he went into town yesterday; he's a punter, like me. He got to the main junction in town and wanted to cross over the road to the bookies, but the lights were on green, and the traffic was whizzing by, so he had to wait for the lights to change."

"Is there any purpose to this story, Gary?" Quentin was impatient to return to his unfinished crossword.

"Oh, aye, yeah; there's more. So, he gets to the traffic lights and stands waiting for the lights to change. Just then, he looked up to the police station, which was down the road; it had a massive aerial or something big on the roof."

"So?"

"So, he stood there; he wanted to cross the road to the bookies, you know."

"Yes, we have already covered that part of the story."

"Then, he said the aerial beamed a ray down on him, burning the back of his neck."

"Oh, poor man," said Quentin, in a low voice.

"Wot?"

"Poor man, having such disturbing thoughts."

Gary's anecdote was in tatters because of Quentin's interruptions. As far as he was concerned, this wasn't how it worked. It sure as hell wasn't how the lads at the club would have reacted. Gary pushed on. "Well, he just pulled his collar down and showed me the back of his neck. It's as red as…" He searched his mind for a word to complete the simile.

"A cherry."

"Wot?"

"Red as a cherry. It's what could be said in such circumstances."

"Right… Red as a cherry."

"Don't you feel sorry for the poor man?" said Quentin, again showing empathy.

Gary disregarded the comment. "Anyway, when he got to the bookies, he'd won twenty notes on a horse. And, get this. The horse's name was." His voice elevated on the word 'was' to add impetus to the story, "Red Robin. I ask you, Red Robin. So how's that for a humongous coincidence?"

"Fascinating."

Gary leant in to impart his considerable wealth of knowledge on the matter. "He's in the right place, you know, mad as a March hare."

Not at all impressed with his levity, Quentin took him to task. "I say, Gary, that's a little insensitive, isn't it? He is in a psychiatric unit, and so are we, in case you had forgotten."

Standing upright, with a puzzled look on his face, Gary tried to grapple with the logic. "But we're all right, aren't we, Quent? I mean, we're normal, aren't we?"

The life cycle of the psychiatric admission ward was fluid as it functioned on a sequence of admissions and discharges. Therefore, patient numbers increased or decreased regularly. Monday to Friday consisted of admissions, discharges, assessments, treatments, OT, and other supportive treatments. Given good progress in a patient's recovery, weekend leave was encouraged to bridge the transition from hospitalisation to eventual discharge. Weekends on the ward were, by and large, quiet, with few patients remaining.

Lunch over, the rest of the patients sat in the dayroom. "I'm off out to see what the gee-gees have done; see you later," said Stan.

"Yeah, see ya," said Gary, deep in thought.

He drummed his fingers and looked around. Saturdays back home weren't very different from weekdays for Gary. The significant distinction was that at weekends the children were at home. Mary organised her working week as a casino dealer, working Monday to Friday nights. While they were in school during the week, she caught up on her sleep, but at weekends she cared for Paisley and Kylie. Gary never offered to look after the children, and Mary never asked him; she considered him to be too irresponsible as a parent.

Late mornings, Gary got up, usually worse for wear from a night of overindulgence. Later, feeling a bit better, he headed into town to the bookies, where he talked with his mates and studied form. If he was lucky with the horses, he collected his winnings from the previous day. Later, he would have a pint at the working men's club, either bought by him or cadged. In extreme circumstances and when broke, he offered himself to the club owner for work. Moving crates and kegs and stacking shelves for a pint or two all depended on the amount of work. Mid-afternoon, he walked home via the bookies, checking his bets, forever hopeful of a big win. Arriving back, he expected a meal, which wasn't always forthcoming, especially if money was tight or Mary could smell beer on him. On many an occasion, she would say to Gary, "What is more important to you, food or beer?" Of course, he wanted both. Yet, Mary was making an important point. Life was about choices. It would appear he chose beer over food.

The lack of finances continued to be a significant problem for Mary. As the purse holder, if she had any money, it was her wages or tips from work that kept things ticking over. Given a tip of £10 or more, which sometimes happened, depending on the punter's luck, Mary had the money earmarked for buying something for the home or children.

Contrary to this, if money were ever in the hands of Gary, he spent cash without a thought for anybody.

"It's quiet here today," said Gary. His comment barely registered with Quentin as he read the paper. "I was thinking we could go out for a walk."

"A walk?" said Quentin, looking up from his Saturday read. A puzzled look suffused his face.

"Yeah, you know, that thing you do when you put one foot in front of the other."

"I know what walking is, Gary. I just hadn't thought of going out of the ward, I suppose."

Gary acted on impulse and called into Mr Elwood's office. "Err, sorry to trouble you, Charge," said Gary. "It's a nice day, and me and Quent thought we would go for a walk; is that okay?"

Mr Elwood took a moment to reflect. "Okay, Gary, you've settled in well, and we haven't had any problems from you, so I'm willing to give it a go. Is Quentin there?"

Quentin stepped into the office. "Yes, sir, I'm here."

"How are you feeling today, Quentin?" said Mr Elwood, trying to gauge his state of mind.

"I'm feeling okay, thank you. It's quiet, so we thought, seeing as it was such a nice day, we'd go for a walk around the grounds. That's if it's okay with you, sir."

"Sounds reasonable; yes, I think it would do you both good.

Make sure you stay together, don't go too far and stay in the hospital grounds."

"We will," said Quentin. "Thank you."

"Have you got your inhaler?" enquired Mr Elwood.

He patted his pocket. "Yes, I never leave home without it." Quentin smiled at his joke.

Mr Elwood mentioned a few landmarks of interest within the grounds, including office buildings, flowerbeds, and a fishpond. On the western portion of the grounds, staff cottages bordered a canal. To the east was a tract of land, destined for the new Maternity Unit. With a sense of intrigue, he mentioned 'pretty cabbages' and to look out for them. Gary thought he'd lost the plot; however, Quentin believed he knew the answer to the puzzle.

It felt good to be out, stretching their legs and experiencing life outside. The ward was comfortable with the food provided and with the staff caring for them. Nevertheless, it was an unnatural, sheltered existence, and walking the hospital grounds gave them both a sense of normalcy. They meandered and chatted in the extensive grounds, enjoying the morning sun, unusual for late October. Ahead, they approached the red-bricked office block dating back to the 19th century – the earliest part of the hospital's buildings. Opposite the offices, the manicured lawns and borders, planted with an array of bedding plants, shone with colour and form. Quentin pointed to the vibrant purple, green and white ornamental cabbages.

"There they are. Cabbages," said Quentin, having solved Mr Elwood's riddle.

"What's the idea of putting cabbages in with flowers?" said Gary, looking quite perplexed.

"Well, border plants are in short supply in autumn. The weather becomes cold, and summer plants can't survive the fall in temperature. So, they make use of ornamental cabbages, grasses, pansies, polyanthus and sedums for a splash of colour." Without thinking, Quentin had just drawn on his extensive knowledge of gardening.

"How do you know all this, Quent?"

He stopped and thought deeply. "That is an excellent question, Gary." his puzzled look said it all. "I don't know. Hmm, I just don't know."

In the distance, a tree-lined drive meandered to the main gates. They walked on to find the pond and a garden seat nearby, allowing an unrestricted view of Goldfish, Orfe and Shubunkins swimming around, enjoying the sun. Ornamental shrubs and trees bordered the little oasis, creating a sanctuary of peace and serenity.

"Let's take a seat," said Quentin, eager to take in the ambience. They sat in silence for a moment, reflecting.

Gary picked up some gravel and used the nearby waste paper bin as a target. "You had a visitor yesterday; was that your wife?"

"I don't know."

"You don't know who she was?"

"That's what I said."

One of the stones landed in the bin, pleasing his tiny mind. "I saw her at reception and thought I heard her asking for you. Suppose it could have been a relative or a social worker. I just saw her and thought, 'That's Quentin's wife there.'

Quentin snapped with frustration. "Will you stop talking about my wife? She wasn't my wife! I don't know who she was!" He rose from the seat and walked on, closely followed by Gary.

"Sorry, I was only chatting," said Gary as he paced out and caught up with Quentin.

The rudeness displayed was uncalled for, and Quentin

knew it. He didn't know his true self and wasn't sure if he would ever regain his memory. This seemed to be the catalyst for his outburst.

"Gary, I am so sorry, I didn't mean to bite your head off. I just didn't…"

"That's okay." Gary dismissed his apology, focusing on a pinecone that sat in the middle of the path ahead of him, destined for a classic John Barnes chip, floating it into the border.

"I don't know any more. Nothing seems to make sense. Some days, I seem to remember things from my past. Then, just as swiftly, they're gone again. It's so frustrating not knowing who you are or knowing the people around you."

"Yeah, it must be the pits. I'm forgetful when I'm brain dead after too many bevvies," said Gary, as he tried to lighten the mood.

Quentin smiled at the humour. "So, I'm sorry, Gary. Can you forgive me?"

"Not a prob, mate."

"How about you?" said Quentin, "Have you got family?"

"Oh, yeah, big style. My wife, Mary and I've got two kids, Paisley, nine, and Kylie, six," he thought for a moment. "She's a little princess."

"How nice. I always wanted children." Quentin stopped and looked at Gary. "Why did I say that?"

"Say what?"

"Say, 'I always wanted children.' I don't know if I'm married or even if I have any children. How odd."

"Maybe you're married with ten kids…" Gary floated another pinecone in for an incredible header from Peter Beardsley, scoring with only seconds to go before the final whistle. He threw his fist up in the air and waited for the Kop to go wild.

Quentin smiled again.

"Mind you, just think of all that family allowance for ten kids." Gary focused on the money, disregarding the slight inconvenience of ten kids.

Looking heavenwards, Quentin took in a deep, invigorating breath. "Let's take a seat over there by the Acer Palmatum shrubs."

"More gardening info," said Gary, intrigued.

"Yes, it's an interest of mine," he stopped. "There, I go again. I just said, 'It's an interest of mine.' This is incredible; I'm talking as if I know myself, but I don't. Maybe it's your skills in psychotherapy, Gary."

"Oh, aye, yeah," said Gary, not understanding the last part of Quentin's remark.

They took a seat and looked around. Just then, an aged male patient from the hospital ambled up to Quentin. "Have you got a cigarette, boss?"

"No, sorry, I don't smoke."

"Can you lend me a pound? I'm waiting for my Giro," said the patient.

Quentin rummaged in his pocket and produced a little change. "I've got a one-pound coin or this loose change."

"That'll do." Without waiting, the patient reached out, snatched the money and walked away.

"Hey, you come here." Gary was ready to chase after the thief.

"No, it's all right, Gary. Leave it; I'm not bothered."

"You don't wanna do that, you know," said Gary, determined to show Quentin how foolhardy and trusting he had been.

"Do what?"

"Splash your money about like that."

Quentin was a little perplexed at Gary's comment. "He only wanted a pound until his money came through; besides, what's a pound?"

Gary shook his head in frustration. "Let's walk; if we sit here much longer, there'll be a queue of people wanting money from the friendly bank of Quentin."

As they arrived back on the ward, Mr Elwood followed them into the day room. "Did you enjoy your walk?"

"Yes, it was excellent," said Quentin.

"And we found the cabbages," said Gary. "If it's cabbage for tea, I'm not having any. You never know where it's been, dogs and all that, yuck."

Mr Elwood had heard enough of Gary's puerile talk and changed the conversation. "Can I have a word with you in the office, Quentin?"

While they were out for a walk, Eleanor called to see Quentin. Despite the opportunity to wait in the quiet room to see him, she had declined the offer, left a fresh change of clothes, a cassette player and tapes, and departed.

Mr Elwood handed him a small travel bag. "I want to ask you a favour, Quentin, and, in so doing, I'm taking you into my confidence." Quentin looked on, intrigued. "Because of Gary's condition, we have to make sure he doesn't... how can I say... leave your company and go off by himself. So, if you don't mind my asking, when you are out together, can you keep an eye on him?"

"Most certainly, Mr Elwood, you can count on me." Quentin wasn't entirely sure why he had been enlisted as a minder, but felt pleased to be helpful in some small way. He suspected the concern for Gary stemmed from a rare illness, so he readily obliged.

"Thank you, Quentin," he smiled, "this is just between you and me.

To Quentin's surprise, when he laid the contents of the bag out on the bed, the clothes were his size and very much to his liking. However, the attire and, in particular, the cassettes and player were a complete mystery to him. Although the items were in some way familiar, he couldn't quite understand why they had been left for him. Subsequently, he called the charge nurse's office to ask about the items, particularly the person who had brought them in for him. Unfortunately, the charge nurse's explanation hadn't helped much. So, with the mystery still bugging him, he decided to accept the items and sit in the day room, where he played the cassettes, finding them very pleasant and just his sort of music. They gave him a sense of comfort and familiarity, which only added to the ongoing uncertainty in Quentin's mind.

SEVENTEEN

With Sunday lunch over, Quentin relaxed in the dayroom listening to a cassette tape. *Hebrides Overture (Fingal's Cave)* by Mendelssohn sounded fleetingly familiar to him. He read the cassette sleeve to see if it gave any clues to explain its significance, yet nothing gelled in his mind. The swell of the orchestral strings evoked images of waves crashing into the Hebridean cave; the sound reverberated in thunderous magnificence. Then the anticlimax, the diminishing ebb of the waves, left a moment of anticipation until the next sonorous sound. He searched his mind to get a handle on it, but nothing was forthcoming. The frustration of being unable to remember something from his amnesic past unsettled him. For all the world, it was as if he were up against a brick wall, with no obvious way forward. However, advice from the hospital psychologist had helped him back off and let things roll off him a bit more. According to the psychologist, frustration and intensity thwarted any progress and were counterproductive. It was most important for Quentin to remain relaxed if he ever hoped to make inroads into his amnesia. Easy for him to say, thought Quentin, when *he* hadn't lost his memory.

Although he couldn't recall the occasion of the music, it held special meaning because it was the highlight of a holiday spent in Scotland early in their marriage. They had arranged a tour from their hotel on the Isle of Iona in late April to visit the Island of Staffa. Eleanor was eager to see the Puffin population,

"Darling little things," she said. Quentin enthused about the Island's famous watery inlet cave, with its unique, natural basalt lava pillars. Still more was the cave's architecture, which produced distinctive sounds. As waves rushed in and out of the cavern, they created harmonies full of drama and awe that inspired Felix Mendelssohn to write his Hebrides Overture. Quentin, not often affected by displays of emotion, showed a child-like excitement as he took in the grandeur of the grotto. The fact that many years ago, Mendelssohn had stood in the very same spot and listened to the same sounds that Quentin was experiencing rendered him full of wonder. After that, whenever Quentin listened to Fingal's Cave overture, he did so with excitement. He visualised waves crashing in and out of the cave as he gloried in the oceanic symphony.

For the first time since his admission, Madge, along with the children, called into the psychiatric ward to visit Gary.

"Gary, you've got a visitor!" announced one of the nursing staff, having opened the ward door for Sunday afternoon visiting.

"Take a seat in the day room," said the nurse, remembering that the quiet room was off-limits with his visitor. Dr Sharif's story about the patient fed drugs while an inpatient made the staff more aware of people with a substance use disorder and their possible covert behaviour.

Madge, Paisley and Kylie were pleased to see Gary; even so, he wasn't the person they remembered. He was quieter and more introspective than Madge recalled. She felt sorry for him, yet didn't know why she should feel such emotion. Being organised, she had brought in a few personal items: underwear, socks, T-shirts, and clean jeans.

"How are you today, Gary?" said Madge as she sat down and

unbuttoned her jacket. She handed the carrier bag over.

"Okay," he said, looking around. "Mary not here?"

"No, she couldn't make it," said Madge.

"Oh." Gary didn't let the disappointment show on his face. He reached for the children, ruffling their hair. "And how are you two monsters?"

"Okay," said Paisley, as he stared at a football match playing on the television. Regrettably, it wasn't his beloved Liverpool; just the same, it was football, and that held his attention.

"And you, Kylie, how's my best girl?"

Kylie was in a strange mood. "I'm all right." Nevertheless, curiosity overcame her; she had a pressing question that needed an answer.

"Dad?"

"Yeah."

"What's wrong with you? Why are you here?"

Madge scolded her. "Kylie, I told you about that."

"No, it's okay, Madge, the kids need to know."

"Well... your old dad hasn't been very well because he took some pills and then had a bevvy or two, and well... it made me ill."

As far as Kylie was concerned, Dad had bared his soul and paved the way for more questions. "But what did mum mean when she said she had to run for her life... or something like that, I think?"

Gary realised his simple explanation hadn't satisfied her curiosity. "I don't know, Kylie; I can't remember... It's like a blur, like a dream." He looked to Madge for help.

With tact, Madge changed the subject. "Kylie, show Dad what you did in art class on Friday."

"Oh yeah, Mr Perkins wanted us to paint an abstract picture. I didn't know what abstract was, so I watched my mates and painted this." She took a piece of folded paper out of her pocket. It had stuck together, needing careful handling to pull it apart. With pride, she handed it to Dad.

He struggled for words as he examined the painting in detail. "Very good, love."

He turned the painting 180 degrees. "I like it. I like it a lot. You've really got the..."

"Abstract!" said Kylie.

He looked at the painting as if pondering its merits. "Yes, you've got the abstract thing well here."

Kylie pressed him for more superlatives. "Do you know what it is, Dad?"

In reality, his artistic merit was zilch; nevertheless, he wanted to please her. "Well, I think it is a very abstract painting that came from your head, and I think it looks terrific. In fact, it's the best I've ever seen."

Kylie bristled with pride.

"What do you think, Madge?" said Gary, as he tried to steer Kylie away from further questions.

"Yes, she's got talent, just like her grandfather."

"What do you mean, Nan?"

"Well... your grandfather was good at art; he had a natural flair. If he'd continued with it, I think he could have been famous. As it was, all those years ago, there was no money in painting, and he had to get a job in the local factory to bring money in."

Madge cherished fond memories of Harold sitting at his easel, painting. He brought the subjects to life before her eyes. She always found it amazing, given that whenever she tried to draw, it looked childlike. Horses were his favoured theme, captured in oils. He had a liking for the subject, which seemed to derive from his upbringing in rural Yorkshire, where he worked on farms and stables for pocket money. His first serious subject was a sketch of his uncle's shire horse, called Noddy. They called him that because the farm horse made comical nodding movements with his head. When people stood nearby and spoke, he nodded, as if in agreement with them. Harold captured an incredible likeness of him and later sold the drawing to his uncle for two and sixpence (2/6d).

"Sometimes mum helps me with my homework and does drawings," said Kylie.

"Yes, she's good at art," Madge glowered at Gary. "Shame, it was all wasted."

Towards the end of visiting, the shop trolley came around, selling goods. This was a perfect opportunity for the children to crave sweets and try to get as much out of Nan as they could. The sweets kept them quiet for another ten minutes, giving Gary time to talk to Madge in private.

Later, in the background, a bell rang.

"Well, that's the end of visiting; real nice painting, our Kylie. I'll stick it on my bedside locker, so everyone can see how clever my little girl is."

Not content with that, Kylie wanted to see his locker, where he would display her famous painting. Madge had the perfect answer to curb her enthusiasm. "We can't, Kylie; it's the end of visiting. Maybe some other time."

"Yes, your Nan's right, got to go." The children stood up, ready to make for the main door.

"Bye, kids, see you soon," said Gary, as he hugged Kylie. Questions answered, she was ready to go, chewing her gum.

"Look after yourself, Gary; I'll see if I can call again during the week," said Madge.

Gary kissed her on the cheek. "Talk to Mary, Madge; see if you can get her to visit."

"I'll do my best, Gary," she said, lowering her voice. "But she's still shocked and very hurt at what happened."

"Try to explain to her." He looked contrite. "Tell her I'm sorry. I've been a fool; I know I have. Tell her I'll never touch drugs or drink ever again, I promise. I'm serious about that."

"Well, I'll try, Gary, but you know what she's like when she's made her mind up. She can be stubborn; takes after her mum," confessed Madge.

He smiled, picturing her. "I know, you're right. Thanks for the visit, Madge." He held the carrier bag up. "And thank you for these."

As they made their way to the door, he called out to the children. "Look after your mum for us."

"Okay, we will."

Gary felt a great deal of emotion at their departure. They were his children; he had fathered them. Even so, he had never had such strong feelings for them before now. Maybe his absence from the family had caused him to feel this way; he wasn't sure.

With a carrier bag by his side, Gary sat on his bed and stared at the wall. He considered his marriage to Mary, the events that led to his conflict with her, and his subsequent brush with the law. There and then, he made his mind up, vowing to turn his life around, to do the right thing and make Mary and the children proud of him. With all his heart and soul, he firmly believed change was in the air.

Quentin looked out of the window at the cloudy autumnal day and decided that if the rain held off, a repeat of yesterday's walk would be enjoyable. He found Mr Elwood in the treatment room, checking the medicines cupboard. "Is it okay if we go out for a walk again, Mr Elwood?"

"Yes, I reckon that will be fine, Quentin. How did it go yesterday? Did you find the goldfish pond and the gardens?"

"We certainly did, and the bedding plants were absolutely splendid."

"Any after-effects from the exertion?"

"None at all, and everything else was fine," said Quentin in coded language, meaning everything went well with the escort duty.

"Good, well, enjoy your walk... oh, and there'll be no need to ask for permission in the future. Just let a member of staff know when you are going out," he gave Quentin a wink as if to say, 'Well done.'

"Very good, sir."

"And I think we can drop the formality from now on, Quentin."

"Very well, thank you, sir."

Since it had chilled down, Quentin decided to wear a light jacket. He found Gary putting his clothes away in his bedside locker.

"Would you like to go out for a walk, Gary?"

"Aye, that would be good," said Gary, in a subdued manner. "Just got to put these things away, and I'll be with you. Best ask the Charge if it's okay; got to keep him sweet, you know."

"No need, I already have. We must be doing something right," said Quentin. "In future, if we want to go out, all we need to do is tell a member of staff."

They passed the office block and extensive lawns that highlighted the grandeur of the old general hospital; the sun peeped out from behind the clouds. There was no purpose or direction as they strolled, just a joy of being out and about, meandering to their heart's content.

"Let's go up there." Gary pointed towards the main driveway. Quentin instantly demurred. It was the main exit out of the hospital, and he had given his word to stay within the grounds. Undaunted by such trivial matters, Gary pressed on, daring to walk further. At the point of near disregard for the rules, Quentin came to a stop. The ornamental trees and shrubs bordering the driveway continued the theme to the entrance roundabout. A central elevated bed, made up of coloured succulents depicting the word 'Welcome,' took pride of place at the entrance to the hospital. Quentin felt full of foreboding; if he continued further, he would be damned to eternity.

"I think this is as far as we should go, Gary," said Quentin, aware that they were within sight of the main road that passed the hospital.

"It's okay, Quentin. No big sweat; this isn't Colditz, you know. We're only looking, aren't we?"

Quentin didn't respond.

Gary pointed in the distance on the far side of the road. "Look, are those shops I can see?"

"Yes, I do believe you're right," said Quentin, happy just to be observing.

Gary put his hand on Quentin's arm. "What've you missed here more than anything in the whole wide world?"

"Well... I don't know, Gary; I can't give you a definitive answer because I can't remember. Having said that, I do feel something *is* missing in this chaotic world of mine, but I can't put my finger on it."

"So, something missing; like what?" said Gary, pushing for an answer.

Quentin shrugged his shoulders.

"Okay, so, if you're a fella and normal like me, then you must be missing a pint and maybe a ciggie."

Quentin half-agreed. "Maybe."

Gary continued. "Now take me. I like a pint to relax when I'm out with my mates. So, unless you're teetotal or something abnormal like that, then you'll be ready for a pint. I know I am."

"I suppose that makes sense," agreed Quentin. "But I really have no idea." Then he began to get a handle on Gary's logic. "You aren't suggesting for one minute that we leave the hospital grounds and go for a drink, are you?"

"Well, yeah, just a quick one. Nobody will know."

"No, Gary, definitely not. Besides, Mr Elwood said we must not..."

Gary completed the mantra. "I know, leave the grounds. Do you always do as you're told?" Quentin's face confirmed his suspicion. "Just as I thought. Look, Quentin, nobody does as they're told. Besides, if we only have one who on earth would know?"

Gary's persuasive argument challenged Quentin's moral principles. Nevertheless, he felt sure that, if Gary were to go to the pub alone, he would have let Mr Elwood down. "Sounds tempting, but I'm not sure it's such a good idea. Besides, the staff on the ward would smell alcohol on our breaths. So I'm sorry, I would have to say no."

"Aha, not if we drank vodka," said Gary, obviously having thought it through and aware he was about to win the argument. Quentin wavered. The persuasive tongue on a susceptible Quentin made him easy prey.

"Well," he urged, with an encouraging pat on the shoulder. "Go on... just one... it won't hurt, Quent."

Looking around, Quentin searched for a reason why he should refuse. He faltered. "Go on, then, just one and then straight back to the ward."

"Good one, Quent... mind you, you'll have to buy them. I'm

still waiting for my money to come through."

"It would be a pleasure, Gary."

"Oh, and if you don't like the booze, as a good friend, I'll finish it off for you; that's what friends are for, right?"

The deed was done; they had enjoyed vodka in the Pie and Eel. However, while drinking, Quentin experienced an oddity, a link to his past, but not one he could share with the nursing staff. He made an instant neural connection when he smelled the glorious aroma of a cigar being smoked. At that moment, impressions came rushing back to him in the form of taste, smell, enjoyment and fulfilment. It all seemed so strange, yet it confirmed part of his past life. The compulsion to smoke a cigar was overwhelming. Like a person with an addiction, and without any further ado, he bought himself the most enormous cigar in the pub, lit it up and savoured the reward that came from abstinence.

Even though Quentin's memory was still blank, he felt encouraged. The cigar had given him a link to his forgotten past, prompting him to guess and speculate.

Gary talked about himself and his life, carefully avoiding mention of his chequered past. Time flew by, and, at the insistence of Quentin, they headed back through the hospital grounds in a jovial mood towards the psychiatric unit. In the distance, the office block loomed, indicating that they were just a few minutes away from the ward.

As they neared the fishpond, Quentin pointed to the garden seat. "Should we sit for a few minutes, catch our breaths?" On the walk back from the pub, he had stopped to use his inhaler. In truth, the cigar, although enjoyable, had triggered a reaction within his lungs; despite that, he didn't want to acknowledge the fact.

The late afternoon sun cast long shadows across the lawn. Dappled light glinted across the surface of the pond. The occasional splash of water broke the surface, as fish leapt in a feeding frenzy to devour unsuspecting midges. Quentin smiled, finding the diversion from his asthma helpful. Feeling better, he made an observation. "You seem to be a happier person than when we met a few days ago."

"Yeah, I know. I've got my mojo back."

"Why had you misplaced it?" said Quentin.

"No, you don't get it. It's not something you lose, Quent. Well... it is, and it isn't."

This confused Quentin.

"You see, yer mojo is something inside. You know when you haven't got it and know when you have."

"Oh, I think I see what you mean," said Quentin. "What you are referring to is your inner spirit, your *joie de vivre.*"

"Is it? Not sure about that Froggy stuff you just said, but yeah, I've got my mojo back, and it feels good, really good."

Whether it was the drink talking or a genuine feeling wasn't clear. Even so, he felt happy and looked forward with optimism to his discharge date, when he would see the lads in the club and the bookies once again. He yearned to play his beloved snooker and help the team to another victory. Earlier thoughts about Mary and the children seemed to have faded into self-indulgent hedonism.

Putting his head back, closing his eyes, Quentin relaxed, breathing out a contented sigh. "I could stay here forever. How about you?"

"Oh, aye, yeah," uttered Gary in one of his stock-in-trade retorts, meant to sound positive even if, in reality, he didn't agree or understand.

"Well, we should be getting back; it will be tea time soon,

and we don't want to miss that, do we?" said Quentin.

"Aye, you're right... D'you think I came up with a good idea, popping out of Colditz for a tipple?"

"Excellent idea, Gary. I didn't know vodka tasted so good. It makes it a little bit more bearable somehow, doesn't it?"

"Dunno about that. Makes me think what a nice holiday camp this is."

"What, Billy Butlins?"

"Who?" said Gary as he scratched his head.

They ventured back to the ward, laughing and joking.

"Now don't forget, Quent, not a word when we get back, or else they might put two and two together."

"Quiet as a church mouse, Garry."

Quentin felt satisfied that he had performed his escort duty well in a difficult situation. Gary hadn't suffered any problems or setbacks, although God alone knew what would have happened if *he* had taken a turn for the worse in the pub. Just as dangerous was the possibility that Quentin himself could have suffered a severe asthma attack in the pub or outside in the grounds of the hospital, raising all kinds of searching questions. Working on the premise that everything would be all right could have been a risky strategy.

Gary patted Quentin on the back.

"My mates call me Gaz."

"Right, *Gaz,* it is then."

They strolled along like two long-lost friends, talking about nothing and yet everything. Within minutes, they had returned to the ward. All in all, it had turned out to be a pretty remarkable weekend for both of them.

EIGHTEEN

Gary and Quentin, brought together on a psychiatric admission ward, formed a tenuous relationship through the commonality of mental illness. Sleeping in the same dormitory, they revolved in and out of each other's worlds to forge a burgeoning friendship. It would be correct to say that, had they met in civilian life, neither would have looked at each other for a second time. Like chalk and cheese, they came from different social and economic worlds, which made their growing friendship all the more remarkable. Hospital routine solidified their companionship; they spent time together over breakfast, lunch and tea. They made their beds, showered, shaved and kept their lockers tidy. Collective responsibility fostered a sense of purpose and camaraderie, engendering mutual respect and appreciation for each other's worlds.

The social difference between Gary and Quentin was immense. In the Lowe family home, Gary didn't always find bread in the morning for a piece of toast. Meals such as pizza, burgers, and fish and chips were regular fare in their household.

On the other hand, Quentin and his wife ate well. Expensive wine from their cellar accompanied evening meals. On occasions, they ate out at the golf club and in fancy restaurants. Clothing, holidays, and costly possessions were commonplace and were bought and paid for without concern for money.

As Gary and Quentin finished their breakfast, Mr Elwood approached. "You're both down for OT today."

"I don't think I can do it," said Quentin, concerned at the prospect of something new taking him out of his comfort zone. He was feeling flat, which didn't help his confidence.

"That's okay, Quentin; you can take it slowly and, if you have any problems, we can sort it out. I think you will like Sara, the Head Occupational Therapist." Mr Elwood tried to paint a glowing picture of the department for Quentin. "So, Gary, you can attend this morning, and Quentin, you will be able to attend this afternoon."

Having cleaned his teeth and brushed his hair, Quentin sat in the dayroom. A male nurse found Gary in the dormitory, sitting on his bed as he changed into his trainers.

"Ready to go, Gary."

"Yep, all ready."

Without further ado, they headed off to the OT department situated next door.

Historically, Occupational Therapy, conceived after the Great War, was vital for the health and recovery of soldiers returning home suffering from the horrific effects of conflict. Many needed both physical and mental help to recover. Sadly, there was an even greater need to restore confidence in the broken and shattered minds of injured soldiers experiencing dreadful injuries and trauma. Workshops conceived within military hospitals encouraged disabled men and women to work with tools and machinery, exercising their damaged bodies, gaining confidence in a broken world. Taking months and sometimes years of treatment in the hospital, they found some sense of normality.

Based on workshops, Occupational Therapy Departments became a popular concept in hospitals, where psychological and physical injuries benefited from OTs' on-site availability. The war to end all wars didn't stop a Second World War as it ran its evil course in Europe and beyond. Many more injured soldiers returned home from the conflict in need of help, treatment and understanding. Once again, OT played an essential part in rehabilitating, except that the support had become more professional, more refined and tailored to individual needs.

The nurse introduced Gary. "Sara, this is Gary, admitted last Wednesday; he's feeling a lot better now and looking forward to OT."

"Hello, Gary," said Sara, shaking his hand. "Come and sit down over here, and we'll get you started." She pointed to a large craft table where various craft projects were underway. There was basket-weaving, knitting, art of differing types and printing. A therapist introduced him to fellow patients as they worked. To assess his dexterity, she started him on basket weaving to test his hand-eye coordination. Within minutes, Gary wove as if he had done it for years.

"Hey, it's all right, this." Typical of his outgoing nature, he chatted with others as he worked, familiarising himself with their worlds.

In the office, Sara, Head Occupational Therapist, looked through Gary's notes.

"Dr Sharif wants us to keep a close eye on Gary," said the nurse. "He was admitted in an agitated and aggressive, paranoid state. Having said that, he has responded well to medication. His blood tests on admission tested positive for methamphetamines. So, maybe a regular substance abuser."

"Okay, we'll watch him," said Sara, a regular face at ward meetings. "I'll make sure all the staff are briefed."

"Good morning, Quentin," said Dr Sharif, finding Quentin

in the day room. "How are you today?"

"Not too bad this morning, thank you."

"We are just about ready for you, so if you would like to follow me, I'll show you the procedure."

They made their way to a room set aside for therapies. It was furnished in neutral colours, giving a feeling of tranquillity and warmth. From the date of his admission, Quentin felt a great deal of confidence and respect for the staff and, in particular, Dr Sharif, whom he saw as a gentleman and true professional.

"Take a seat, Quentin." The consultant pulled a chair up. "Over there is the medical couch. In a few minutes, I will ask you to lie down on the couch and make yourself comfortable. Then, if you feel relaxed and wish to continue, we will administer an injection. You will feel a bit drowsy but not sleepy. When we are certain all is well, we will dim the lights, and then I'll talk to you and ask you some questions. How does that sound?"

"Yes, that sounds fine by me. Will it be just you?"

"That was my next question. My junior, Dr Reece, hasn't seen this procedure before and, if you are agreeable, he would like to sit in and observe."

"I have no problems with that at all. I have met Dr Reece and find him very agreeable," Quentin chanced a bold remark. "But I would have to say, Dr Sharif, I do think you are working him a little too hard. There are days he seems to be overly busy and positively tired out."

Before he could comment, there was a knock at the door. A somewhat flustered junior doctor entered, carrying a small tray with the injection. He was running late.

"Good morning, Quentin. How are you this morning?" said Dr Reece.

"I'm fine. Thank you."

"Now, shall we make a start? I'll help you to get settled on the couch and then Dr Reece will administer the injection."

With blinds drawn, a 'Do not disturb' sign displayed, and chairs placed close to the couch, they were ready to begin. The injection, administered with ease, began to take effect.

Dr Sharif began the session *sotto voce*.

"Now then, how do you feel, Quentin?"

"A little strange but okay."

Gesturing to the light switch, it was dimmed, a recorder set in motion, and the session began in earnest.

"You said you felt strange; can you describe the feeling for me, Quentin?"

"I feel as if I'm not here, floating, so to speak." His speech was slower than usual, yet easy to comprehend.

"I see. Can you hear my voice well enough?"

"Yes, I can."

Dr Sharif looked over to his junior, hoping the semi-darkness and soothing sounds didn't lull him to sleep. On the contrary, Dr Reece hung on every word.

He continued. "Good... What is your name?"

"Quentin St John."

"And do you live in a nice home?"

"Umm..."

"You're not certain, or you can't remember?"

"I don't know."

"Do you think you live here in Mystic Sands?"

"That name is familiar... maybe... I just don't know."

Controlled reassurance and guided questioning led Quentin on an investigative journey to recover his lost memory.

"It's not important, Quentin. Can you remember anything? Can you see anything in your mind's eye?"

"I can see... a beautiful garden."

"And is this your garden?"

"I don't know... it seems enchanting."

"Do you like gardens?"

"I like colourful gardens with flower beds and shrubs."

"Can you see anything else?"

"I see a lawn... it has just been cut."

The next question reinforced and immersed the patient in visualisation, an experience that few patients had.

"Excellent, Quentin. Can you smell the freshly cut grass or the scented flowers in this garden?"

Quentin moved his head and inhaled. "Yes, I can."

"Excellent. When you talk about gardens, you sound happy – relaxed."

"Yes, I've always liked..." He stopped mid-sentence, as if unsure or uncertain why he should be answering the question positively.

"You were saying, 'I've always liked;' were you going to say, always liked gardens or gardening?"

"Maybe... I'm not sure."

Dr Sharif looked to his junior. This was a significant learning experience for Dr Reece, one that would encourage him into psychiatry as a lifelong career.

"I would like you to imagine you are walking in this beautiful garden," said the consultant.

"Okay."

"As you look around the garden, you see many flowers. There is a beautiful fragrance in the air. You walk across the lawn, taking in the sights; you hear birds singing. It seems familiar, you feel happy, no worries, no pressure – all is well with the world."

"Yes, I feel good."

"You feel the sun on your face, and it feels so good to be alive.

Can you see and feel it all?"

"Yes, I can."

"Good. A lady calls to you from the house."

"I don't know her," said Quentin, mildly agitated and submitting a denial of her existence. He appeared ill at ease.

"That's okay, Quentin... she's a very nice lady."

"No, she isn't!" Quentin raised his voice.

Dr Sharif looked to his junior as if to say, 'A breakthrough.' He gave Quentin a moment to compose himself.

"Okay, Quentin. Nice and calm... breathe slowly...   you're in control... You are safe... nothing will happen to you. Imagine your body feeling floppy—floating. Breathe slowly... good... do you feel relaxed?"

"Yes."

"So you are in this beautiful garden. You walk across the lawn. Do you see anything?"

"I can see a fence, trees..."

"What else?"

"A footpath and a potting shed."

"Good. You're happy because it's a beautiful day. You feel good; you look around, what else do you see?"

"A potting shed."

"Another potting shed or the same one?"

"The same one, I don't like it... I don't want to go in there. Please don't make me?"

"Why don't you want to go in, Quentin?"

"I hate it."

"You hate the shed?"

"Yes, I hate it... I... I... she shouldn't!"

His breathing increased rapidly. Panic was taking over. Dr Sharif had to take control fast.

"Okay, Quentin. Listen to my voice, breathe slowly... nice

and slow... that's right... nice and slow... Listen to my voice. You are safe here... nice and slow. We are here with you; nothing will happen to you... relax... relax... Very good. All is well."

Dr Reece's pager flashed; he felt mildly annoyed that his first abreaction was curtailed by what might be an unnecessary or time-wasting call. Being on-call, as he found, was like being a general dogsbody. If wards weren't sure how to handle a situation, they usually beeped the on-call doctor.

Using a phone in the charge nurse's office, he hoped for a quick resolution and then speedily back to the abreaction.

"Dr Reece," he said into the mouthpiece.

"Emergency in OT, Dr Reece."

"On my way."

As he entered the Occupational Therapy Department, Gary sat slumped in a chair. He held his chest – lips were blue – he grimaced with pain.

"Hello, Gary, what's the problem?" No answer. The doctor took a stethoscope out of his pocket and listened to Gary's chest, detecting an irregularity in his heartbeat. He called for a blood-pressure meter.

"When did this happen?" said Dr Reece, looking to Sara for information to assess the problem.

"Just a few minutes ago. One of the staff called me over; Gary looked ashen, holding his chest in pain. I got them to call you straight away and took his pulse, which was very erratic."

"So how do you feel now, Gary?"

Maybe because of professional attention or perhaps because the discomfort had eased, Gary spoke with guarded optimism. "A bit better now, doc... must've eaten something that upset my guts."

"Okay... let me know what you ate, Gary, and I'll make sure I don't eat it," said Dr Reece. It was the doctor's sense of humour that patients and staff liked so much; he showed his human side and was a natural with people. He intended to pursue a career in psychiatry, hoping to become a consultant psychiatrist himself one day.

Many junior doctors working their training rotation in a psychiatric hospital considered mental illness too imprecise and challenging to handle. Appendicitis or a fracture was predictable and straightforward to treat. However, psychiatry was a whole new ball game; it required understanding and imagination. Only the chosen few felt a leaning towards the challenging career.

"Let's get you back to the ward, and then we can get you checked over."

Gary attempted to stand.

"No, don't move, we'll get you your personal chariot."

Leaving Gary, he headed to the storeroom, emerging with a battered but usable wheelchair. Meanwhile, a staff nurse arrived from the ward to assist the doctor.

"Here we go, Gary, now stand up slowly; the staff nurse will help by moving the wheelchair behind you."

Before long, they were headed back to the ward at a quick but dignified speed.

"Get him onto the bed in the side room; start him off on oxygen. Wire him up to a monitor and get a line in. Full observations and a member of staff with him at all times. I'll contact the cardiologist."

Given time, Gary's elevated blood pressure reduced, and ectopic heartbeats and chest pain decreased.

The 'Do not disturb' sign on the door had been removed. Dr Reece entered and found Quentin sitting in a comfortable chair, recovering from his therapy.

"Come in, Dr Reece."

The session was over, and Quentin looked none the worse for his part in the discovery of the truth.

"Quentin's regression is over, and it proved to be very successful."

"Good, I'm glad to hear that," said Dr Reece, "I'm just so sorry to have missed most of it."

Dr Sharif looked at his patient and continued with more questions. "Now then, Quentin, are you recovered enough to talk about the regression?"

"Yes, I feel good and somewhat relieved."

"Can you explain, relieved?"

"Well, even though you assured me all would be well. I didn't know what to expect, so I was a little apprehensive about today."

"I see. So, do you remember what you talked about in the regression?"

A sense of solemnity descended upon Quentin. "Yes, I remember it well. I talked about a garden, realising it was my garden I was describing. I talked about my hatred of all things, the garden shed. And I remember feeling a deep sense of sorrow as well as anger."

"You mentioned finding a pocket knife."

"Yes, I did. I remembered finding a pocket knife in the bedroom. It was just behind the bedside cabinet."

"*Your* bedroom?"

"That is correct. I found the knife and knew it wasn't mine, and it wouldn't have belonged to Eleanor, that was for certain."

"So you now know your wife is Eleanor?"

"Yes, my mind has cleared. I remember my wife, myself and where I work."

"That is impressive, Quentin. So, can you remind us about

the connection between the knife and the ensuing events, if it doesn't trouble you too much?"

His face changed, reflecting a saddened individual who felt the enormity of the events that had brought him into the hospital.

"At first, I didn't know what to do with the knife; it played on my mind. The only thing I could conclude was that it belonged to the gardener, except then I thought, why would it be in the bedroom? All the same, I had an idea: I put the knife in the shed and waited till the gardener had been working for a day. It was a Sunday; I remember it well. Later, I checked the shed; the knife had gone."

"So, in your conclusion, did you think there was something suspicious in finding the gardener's knife in your bedroom?"

"Well... yes."

"And were you making a connection between the knife, the gardener and your wife, Eleanor?"

"Precisely; if the knife was claimed then..."

Clearly upset, he took a handkerchief out of his pocket and wiped his eyes. Dr Sharif leaned forward, putting a hand on his arm.

"We can stop if it's becoming too much, Quentin." Dr Sharif looked to his junior, who echoed the sadness.

"Thank you, but I would prefer to carry on." He rubbed his face, trying to wipe away the sadness and to compose himself, "I said nothing to Eleanor... well, I didn't know what to do. It played on my mind. I couldn't stop thinking about Eleanor and the... well, you know. I thought she loved me, and we were still together." He took a moment; a dawning awareness washed over him. "It's our twenty-fifth wedding anniversary tomorrow," said Quentin, as he wrestled with the humiliation.

About to compliment Quentin on his anniversary, Dr Sharif

stopped himself in time. Although congratulations would have been a normal response, under the circumstances, it seemed inappropriate – a crass thing to say.

"Twenty-five years. That has got to count for something, hasn't it?" The question was rhetorical. "Surely she wouldn't," said Quentin, unsure of their future togetherness.

"And what was the last thing you remember before coming into the hospital?"

"I recalled Eleanor driving me to the railway station for work, although I don't remember why she was there." His train of thought broke for a second. "The next thing I recall was being here in the hospital, yet not knowing how or why I was here. It was total insanity – excuse the expression. By far the worst, though, was not having a memory to work things out; it was like a vicious circle, with no end in sight."

"Should we leave it there, Quentin?"

"Yes, I think so. I have a lot to think about and a lot of catching up to do."

"Very well."

"Just one last thing, Dr Sharif. This is such an unusual feeling, having regained my memory, and although I can remember, there are things I still can't – it's a bit hazy."

"That's a normal response under the circumstances, Quentin. All the same, I need you to be patient; give it time, and your memory will return. I want you to continue seeing the psychologist. Talking things over with him will help greatly. Now, Dr Reece will see you out, and I'm sure a member of staff will get you a cup of tea."

Later, Dr Sharif discussed Quentin's case with his junior. In summation, he believed Quentin was a sensitive person under enormous pressure at work. Coupled with his wife's possible indiscretion, it all became too much. In his opinion, the mind had 'switched off.'

Following lunch, Quentin had recovered from his regression and felt well enough to potter. He knew his name and the circumstances surrounding his admission, yet a question mark hung over him. Why hadn't he had any personal possessions about him or in his locker? With his newfound memory, it was clear that his wife had brought in fresh clothes, music on cassette and tapes, and a small amount of money. Except that he didn't possess a watch or a wallet.

All became clear when he talked to Mr Elwood. "That's easy to answer, Quentin. Upon your admission, we conducted an inventory of your possessions, and the items were stored for safekeeping in the patient's property. In fact." Mr Elwood opened the desk drawer to retrieve a receipted copy of Quentin's possessions. "Here you are." He handed him a pink slip of paper.

Quentin scanned the list. "I see. So, can I access these items right now?"

"I'll send a nurse with you to the patient's properties, and you can sign out what you want. I must point out, though, if you have possessions here on the ward, they are your responsibility. Once you have signed for them, the hospital can't be held accountable for their loss."

"No, that is perfectly clear, Mr Elwood," he looked at the slip and saw 'briefcase and papers, wallet and watch.'

"Good, I'm more than curious now to see the contents of the briefcase."

"When you get back, please use the quiet room. You won't be disturbed."

Quentin turned to leave, then remembered having seen Gary back on the ward earlier. "I hope you won't mind me asking, Mr Elwood. Is Gary all right? I saw him in the side room, lying on the bed, receiving treatment."

"Nothing to worry about, Quentin. We are trying to help Gary with a recurring physical problem. The only difficulty is that Gary won't help himself."

The rest of Monday was given over to rest and relaxation. Quentin had asked to be excused from OT so he could have time to digest the morning's session. Working through the contents of his briefcase, he hoped it would help answer some of the many questions that floated around his mind.

Gary, the impossible patient, continued to recover, with hourly observations showing near-normal vital signs. An ECG for confirmation established that he had a heart murmur, which wasn't about to go away anytime soon. He needed to understand his illness so that he could take responsibility for it. To help Gary appreciate his condition, the consultant took time to explain the nature of the problem. More than likely, he was born with the condition, and he should know the dangers of over-indulgence in alcohol. An even more significant concern was the danger involved in taking illicit drugs. Surprisingly, Gary agreed with the consultant and approved reducing his intake and considered moderate exercise upon discharge. That said, Dr Sharif thought his agreement to do the right thing sounded too good to be true. His willingness to comply was a tad insincere and superficial to a trained professional.

Nevertheless, Dr Sharif was still more than surprised to find out that Gary had a heart murmur. His GP had reassured him that all was well apart from a lower back problem. All that he could presume was that his heart murmur was overlooked and only became apparent when he began to take illicit drugs. At any rate, he needed to abstain from taking illegal drugs and listen to medical advice if he hoped to live a long and healthy life. However, Gary was his own man who rarely took advice, except when it suited him.

Quentin kept very much to himself for most of the day. He chatted with Gary for a few minutes in the side room, establishing that he was on the mend, and promised to get him a sports paper to occupy his boredom. As soon as Dr Reece considered him well enough, and for the sake of peace, he was moved back into the four-bedded dormitory, so long as he agreed to bed rest.

There was no immediate rush to discharge Quentin from the hospital. Nevertheless, the consultant thought it prudent that he should have one or two days' leave of absence from the ward to see how he coped with home life and ultimately his relationship with Eleanour.

As evening approached, Quentin felt jaded. Although not sleepy, he decided to retire early and relax. Showered and changed into his pyjamas, he switched the four-bedded dormitory lighting to nightlight and turned in for a restful night. He was surprised to see Gary asleep at such an early hour, but believed it was possibly due to new medication causing sleepiness. Aware he wouldn't be able to sleep so early, Quentin was pleased with the opportunity to relax and reflect on the day's events. No matter how many times he ran the scenario through his mind, the outcome would not change. It seemed patently clear that Eleanor had been unfaithful to him; even so, he considered his culpability in the whole sordid mess. Maybe he could have been a better husband, he thought. Should he have engaged in a more meaningful conversation with Eleanor? Perhaps he should have considered socialising more or taking weekend breaks in London to see a show and dine out. Could he have worked harder to cement their relationship? Although in reality, he hadn't known anything was wrong. Thoughts whirled around his mind, but no answers or different insights came to the fore. After an hour of soul-searching and examining life in general, his mind became weary.

The distant hum of people talking on the ward, the drone of traffic far away, and the sound of a dog barking in the distance all acted like a narcotic. He drifted off to sleep, secure in the knowledge that he could now remember.

NINETEEN

Quentin woke early Tuesday morning. As he lay awake in the dormitory, his mind drifted as he contemplated yesterday's bittersweet return of memory. Unable to go back to sleep, he accepted the inevitable and sat on the side of the bed. Sliding his feet into suede mule slippers, he pulled on a dressing gown. Strolling to the dormitory window, he gazed out upon a typical misty, autumnal morning. The day should have been a happy, momentous occasion for both Quentin and Eleanor, a milestone in their lives that would never come again. However, as with so many personal plans in life, nothing was ever certain. He cursed the lousy timing that had cheated them of their anniversary celebration. Be that as it may, although disappointed, he was determined not to dwell on the misfortune.

Twenty-five years ago, at the age of twenty-eight, he married Eleanor in the historic town of Chester. Luck was on their side. On the day of their marriage, they were blessed with fine, albeit chilly weather. Quentin smiled at the thought of his best man, who appeared even more nervous than he did. They both drank a sizeable brandy before the ceremony, to calm their nerves and stave off the cold.

As Eleanor stood at the altar alongside Quentin, she showed surprise at the smell of alcohol on his breath at eleven o'clock in the morning. With a smile, she mouthed, "Where is mine?"

His love for her began at a charity ball in Chester Castle.

Dressed in a tuxedo and looking dapper, Quentin stood with his friends on the edge of the dance floor. In the distance, the most exquisite lady Quentin had ever seen came into view. She was dancing to a Waltz – *Roses from the South* by Johann Strauss Jr. Not for one minute had he considered asking her for a dance, particularly when he saw all the would-be suitors waiting for an opportunity to dance with her. Contenting himself, he watched from a distance, imagining what it would be like to be in the company of such a beautiful, elegant lady. She possessed the potential to illuminate and fulfil his incomplete life; however, it wasn't to be. As he stood alone on a balcony, taking in the cool air, music drifted through the open doors, bathing him in a musical experience. Drink in hand, he smoked a cigarette and looked up at the night sky. Although he had enjoyed the ball, he wondered how much longer he should stay, when out of nowhere a very polite voice enquired. "Do you think I could trouble you for a cigarette?" He turned to see the radiant belle of the ball in front of him. With speed, in case she changed her mind, he offered her a cigarette.

Things like this don't happen to me, he thought. They talked, laughed, and exchanged pleasantries until Quentin, encouraged by their comfortable togetherness, asked for a dance. From that day on, a beautiful romance developed.

They saw more of each other over the coming days and weeks, finding togetherness a joy, the parting till next time unbearable.

One of his great loves was listening to classical music, in particular the music of one of his favourite composers, Johann Strauss Jr. Quentin always felt his first meeting with Eleanor was pre-ordained, particularly because she came from Richmond, London. She was to him his very own Rose from the South, as in the musical work of Johann Strauss Jr.

Gary came to yawning loudly, interrupting Quentin's nostalgic reverie.

"It's no good jumping out the window, Quent; we're on the ground floor, you know."

"Yes, thank you, Gary, for that pearl of wisdom."

"Good morning, gentlemen," said a bright and breezy staff nurse, Tony Holmes, as he entered the dormitory. "Lie on the bed, Gary, so that I can take your blood pressure."

"There's no need, mate; I'm okay now."

"Let me be the judge of that." Nurse Tony wrapped the blood pressure cuff around his arm.

"How are you feeling this morning, Quentin?" said the nurse as he tried to assess his mood.

"Good. I slept like a top until about twenty minutes ago."

"That's progress. And how do you feel about going to the OT this morning?"

"Is Gary going?"

"Well, unless his blood pressure is doing crazy things or his heart's doing the rumba, I reckon he will. Maybe the two of you could look after each other?" said the nurse. "Just like Darby and Joan."

Keen to have an input, Gary confirmed. "Well, I'm going, whatever my ticker's doing."

"In that case, I will give it a try," confirmed Quentin. He picked up his towel and toilet bag and headed for the *en suite* to shave and wash.

Tony checked Gary's blood pressure and, in a humorous moment, confirmed, "Yes, you'll live, for a little while longer, so long as you do as you are told." He smiled.

Each four-bedded dormitory had a well-appointed *en suite* that comprised two washbasins, unbreakable safety mirrors over the sinks, two shower cubicles and toilets. It allowed patients the luxury of shaving and chatting together at the same time.

"Load of rubbish, that, taking my blood pressure," said Gary, minutes later, as he ran water into the sink, preparing to shave.

"So what happened yesterday, Gary? I came out of therapy with Dr Sharif and saw you in the side room, doctors and nurses all around you, with machines flashing and beeping."

He shook his head. "I think they're just looking for work, Quent. Got nothing better to do, you know." Scrutinising his face in the mirror, Gary held his chin out and applied shaving foam. "I just felt a bit queasy in the OT. Before you could say Liverpool is the greatest, there was the doc. They brought me back to the ward, made me lie on the bed in the side room and did loads of tests. Said I should take it easy, but, as I told them, there's no need. I've had this loads of times before, and I ignore it. Or, if it happens in the club, one of my mates buys me a brandy, so I down the freebie and think, what's the prob?"

"Well, you should listen to them, Gary, and take it easy; it is for your own good, you know."

Quentin finished his shave, dried off and applied Cologne.

"I'm going to the library this afternoon after dinner; are you coming?" said Gary.

"Dinner? Do you mean lunch at one o'clock?"

"Yeah, whatever. Sara from OT told me there was a hospital library by the... now, what did she say? Oh, aye, yeah, by the administration block. What do you reckon? Give it a go?"

"Okay, I'll come for the walk, but better clear it with Mr Elwood first."

OT for Quentin didn't come easy. He wasn't adept at basket

weaving and proved to be all fingers and thumbs. Nevertheless, with help from the staff, he slowly made inroads into dexterity. Later, as planned, they walked the short distance to the library after lunch. Gary was under strict instructions to contact the ward immediately if he felt unwell or experienced anything unusual. Be that as it may, and because he was with Quentin – the sensible one – the risk was substantially minimised.

Mr Hall, the librarian, a polite and helpful man in his mid-fifties, chatted with Quentin as Gary mooched about the library. For most of his working life, the librarian had worked in the North-West of England. He became a University archivist and spent much of his time working behind the scenes. In his early days, he enjoyed the job and found it challenging and engaging. Just the same, he kept a big secret; all of his working life, he suffered from depression, took medication, told nobody and continued to work. In the end, maybe because he was determined to soldier on, paying little attention to his body and mind, he suffered a major depressive bout. Unable to continue working in his capacity as an archivist, he accepted early retirement on health grounds from the University and was released from his position. After eleven months of treatment, he recovered, feeling well enough to take a low-paid librarian's post at the hospital. His limited capacity for work fitted in well with the easy 30 hours per week job. The hospital library was very popular with patients and offered a comprehensive selection of books, magazines, cassette tapes, and newspapers. Although its star attraction was a small glazed atrium, people took advantage of it for its pleasant ambience. It was perfect for reading or just sitting and contemplating.

Gary came across a computer, tucked away in a corner on a small table. Much to the annoyance of people in the library, he shouted. "Hey, Quent! There's a computer over here; ask if we can use it?"

With the librarian's definite yes and undaunted by the slow computer speed, Gary set about showing his prowess. Fingers flew over the keys with dexterity; screen images flashed by at speed. By the time he had finished working on the computer, it ran much faster. He didn't shed light on his misspent youth; when asked about his processor skills, he merely replied. "Oh, just one of my many talents."

"Can you find the London Stock Exchange on the computer?" said Quentin; he wanted to see how the financial world was performing.

"No, not on this piece of junk. But, if you want to see stocks and shares, I could bring it up on the ward's television, that's if it's got Ceefax." For the time being, Quentin contented himself with the library's daily edition of the financial paper.

Collecting his briefcase the day before from the patient's properties was a revelation for Quentin. He checked papers and reacquainted himself with the investment-banking sector. Although his amnesia had lasted a week, the return of his memory was a bit of an anticlimax. Without grace or poise, it deposited him back amid his problems. Along with his troubled home life, he had pieced together the bank's worsening crisis and felt very pessimistic about its immediate future. More convinced than ever, Quentin believed the only way out of the worrying dilemma was to talk to his superiors about early retirement. If he took retirement, it would relieve his stress and enable him to spend more time with Eleanor.

He felt very confident about rebuilding their marriage; maybe they could go on a world cruise and rekindle their relationship.

Gary brought up stocks and shares on the television's Ceefax programme in the day room.

"Here you are, Quent, take a look at this." Patients sat around staring in bewilderment at the financial hieroglyphics displayed on the television, although, for an economist, it made a lot of sense. It confirmed that the investment market world was in a state of flux and would continue to experience volatility for some time to come. It would need consistent sound management from seasoned managers with strength and tenacity to drive it on.

British Petroleum's global share sale had the misfortune of clashing with the dire circumstances of 'Black Friday.' In Quentin's mind, it confirmed that his job was the kind of high-velocity endeavour that, in reality, was for a much younger man. It had all become too much for him, and he was prepared to walk away.

"My word," said Quentin as he stared at the daily stock market trading figures. Pages turned over on the screen. "That's not good... nor that." Convinced he had seen enough market misery, he switched the programme over to afternoon television. Quentin genuinely felt that work was beyond him; it was a huge ask of himself, one he could not fulfil. In reality, the figures helped him confirm the obvious conclusion. Amid the economic gloom, he knew he would take early retirement.

It came as quite a surprise to hear Stan talk at length about economics and his portfolio. Quentin realised he had underestimated Stan, the gee-gee man.

"How's it going, Quent? Stocks and shares, okay?"

"Well, not too well, but it has happened before, so, with government input and the Bank of England's intervention, it will right itself." He didn't believe that an in-depth discussion about finance with Gary would produce a meeting of minds; however, he did have something else on his mind.

"Just like the horses, eh?" confirmed Gary.

"I suppose you could say that – Gary, do you have a moment?"

"Yeah, sure, what is it?"

"Not here. Let's go and talk in the dormitory."

Sitting on a bed, Quentin broke the exclusive news.

"I've got something to tell you."

"Yeah."

"It's happening."

"What's that, Quent?"

"I haven't said anything before now; I wanted to be sure, and now I am. My memory is returning."

"Good one, Quent."

"Well, sort of," Quentin sounded disconcerted. "Since the therapy with Dr Sharif yesterday, I've started to remember; it isn't consistent, in fact, it's still a bit sketchy."

Gary looked around as if making sure they were out of earshot; his actions were designed to give theatrical impetus to his burgeoning joke. Leaning in, he whispered. "It's the vodka."

Quentin's face lit up at the intended fun. It was something he enjoyed about Gary, his sense of humour. In his lifetime, he had never experienced such sustained light-hearted banter from any of his colleagues or acquaintances. Quentin realised that, for far too long, he had been overly concerned with the so-called essential things in life, leaving little time for fun.

"I *am* getting better, if you can call it that; however, I would have to say it isn't all good news."

"Not all good news?"

"No... It's a bit complex, and I need to think it through a bit more, but I am getting there."

"Well, then, that's great. You'll be out of here in no time," said Gary with gusto.

At that stage, Quentin wasn't even thinking about discharge, and his face said as much.

"Well, it's good, isn't it?"

"It is, and it isn't," said Quentin.

Gary looked perplexed; he saw things in black and white and regarded Quentin's remark about 'is and isn't' as odd and confusing.

"Since I've been here," said Quentin. "I have spent a lot of time soul-searching. When I was admitted to the ward, I couldn't remember my past, and then, as the days rolled by, I started remembering odd things here and there. Yet I couldn't quite put my finger on what I needed to remember. It was frustrating me. Thoughts drifted in and out of my mind, driving me to distraction. Then yesterday, thanks to Dr Sharif, I recovered my memory."

Gary looked on quizzically, unsure where the conversation was going. Quentin sensed this and qualified his thoughts. "What I am trying to say is, I now have my memory back and can confirm I am married to Eleanor, the lady you saw, remember?"

"Ah, I know, the one I saw on the ward."

"The very same. I live in Mystic Sands, and I am an investment bank manager."

"Never... Any chance of a loan?"

He smiled again at Gary's wit and continued. "Yes, but it isn't as good as it sounds, Gary. It comes at a price... a considerable price."

"I don't know. All that money and power."

"But that's precisely it. All that money and power came with huge responsibility, and it proved too much for me."

"It fried your brain?"

"Well, you could say that."

"So, what are your plans, then?"

Stuart Roberts

"I don't know." Quentin deliberated for a while. "You see, my life has been so uncertain for the past week; all I craved for was to have my memory and get back to normal. Now I'm not so sure."

"You could always do a disappearing act, like that Lord whatsit," said Gary flippantly.

"Being here has given me peace of mind and... I'm not sure how to say this without embarrassing you, Gary, so I will say it. I have come to appreciate and enjoy your company whilst a patient here. We come from different walks of life, but we help each other in a common goal."

"Oh, eh, Quent, I'm touched; thanks, mate."

"No, really, you're a very genuine down-to-earth person, Gary, and I value your friendship very much."

"Steady on, Quent, you'll have me crying. Shall we cut our thumbs and join as blood brothers?"

Quentin looked on, horrified. "What?"

"Just joking. You should have seen your face then; talk about a Kodak moment." Gary held his hands up as if he were clenching an imaginary camera, and made an audible click with his mouth.

"Well, mate, shall we have a look at the menu and see what we're getting for tea?" said Gary, keen to end the serious, taxing conversation.

"That sounds like a good idea, and then off to the OT. I'm making a hanging basket," said Quentin.

"Wow, good one, Quent. When I first saw it, I thought it was a budgie cage for your tweety bird."

Quentin smiled. "I'm looking forward to tea tonight. I believe it's fish," he salivated at the mere thought.

"Oh, no, fish for tea."

"Don't you like fish?" said Quentin.

"I hate it, ugh," said Gary, pulling a face.

"You obviously have never eaten Cognac Shrimp *Avec Buerre Blanc*?"

"I don't think so, Quent. Do they sell it at the local chippie?"

"No, Gary. I feel certain they don't."

True to her word, Mary didn't visit Gary in the hospital. The mere thought of being in his presence was too much for her to handle. Mentally, she blocked out the attack and busied herself. However, unsettling thoughts of separation and divorce kept popping into her head. The idea of breaking up the family home frightened her, and she hated herself for considering the unthinkable – life without Gary. Most people had tried to convince her to accept him back and to strive to make the marriage work. The strange thing was that, while they were together, she hadn't seen the big picture. Separated for a week, she saw things more clearly and questioned what they had together. The answer was simple – nothing. She kept on running the same question through her mind, like a mantra. Would she be better off without Gary? More to the point, if so, did she have the courage to do anything about it?

Weekdays, Madge stayed over to look after the children, giving Mary the freedom to concentrate on her work and focus on her life unimpeded. For the first time in her married life, she felt unfettered, free to make decisions without having to talk things over with Gary. If she had ever had any ideas for the home, his retort was always the same. 'Why do you want to bother?'

Mary took a day's holiday from work and set to, cleaning the house from top to bottom. As usual, arriving home from school, the children threw their coats and bags on the living room chairs.

"Hang your coats and bags up, please," said Mary.

"Why?"

"Never mind why; just hang them up."

Paisley looked around the living room, unable to find his usual games and toys.

"Mum, where's my games console?"

"Upstairs in your bedroom."

"Why's it up there?"

"Because I want a tidy house."

The two children looked at each other, puzzled and confused, by an unusual departure from their regular, easygoing routine. Undaunted, Paisley headed upstairs to his bedroom, while Kylie investigated an aroma coming from the kitchen.

Busying herself, Mary straightened cushions, moved chairs, polished and stood back. She looked at her handiwork to see if it was presentable. To her surprise, she found herself singing along to the radio and wondered why she had forgotten to do something as simple as singing. On reflection, her life seemed revitalised, and it felt good.

"Mum, why's all that food in the kitchen?" said Kylie.

"Uncle Richard is coming for tea."

"Really?"

"That's what I said."

"Oh, great. Will he bring Rex?"

"I don't know, do I?"

Kylie ran into the hallway to shout upstairs. "Hey, Paisley; Uncle Richard's coming for tea."

"Oh, great, is he bringing the dog?"

"Is that all they think about, the dog?" Mary mimicked a silly childish voice. "Is he bringing the dog?"

With enthusiasm, Kylie dashed back into the living room.

"Mum, what are we having for tea? Is it good?"

"Beef Biryani."

She pulled a face. "Ugh. I don't like that."

"How d'you know, you've never had it?"

"Well, it doesn't sound very nice, does it?"

"Oh, really. And how does sponge and custard sound?"

"Oh, great. I love sponge and custard."

"Well then, you can have sponge and custard if you eat your Biryani," said Mary, with a *fait accompli*.

Kylie gave it a nanosecond's thought. "Okay." She took a few steps towards the hallway and started jumping up and down on the spot.

"What's the matter now?" said Mary.

"I need the toilet."

"Well, go then... Kids, who'd have them?"

In the background, a track played on the radio held Mary's attention: *Little Lies* by Fleetwood Mac. She turned the radio up, took a seat and listened. The song seemed prophetic, a sign of change, an omen for her future. Mary couldn't believe the words she heard, 'lies' and 'better off apart'. The phrase 'better off apart' resonated in her mind. She was lost in a surreal moment. Then a loud bang came from the bathroom, startling Mary.

"Are you all right?" she shouted.

"The toilet seat fell off."

"For God's sake, your dad's supposed to have fixed that." She stopped for a second and realised what she had just said. Mary took a tissue from her pocket and wiped away tears. So far, she had done an excellent job of holding it all together, though it would appear not for much longer. Teetering on the edge, she broke down and sobbed, unleashing a torrent of pent-up emotion.

"Mum, the toilet seat's fallen off," shouted Kylie again, but this time louder.

"Well, sit on your hands, then," said Mary in a raised voice. Her emotions were in turmoil; tears flowed uncontrollably. This was like grief–a loss, and she felt desperately sad. Through his foolishness, Gary had broken up the family home with his selfish ways, and she couldn't forgive him for that. What had it all been about? All that pretence and stupidity. Her overriding thought was of such valuable wasted years.

With a heavy heart and many regrets, Mary seriously questioned if Gary would ever be part of their lives again.

The worm had turned.

TWENTY

Following an unsatisfactory meeting with Quentin on the day of his admission, Eleanor visited infrequently, as advised by Dr Sharif. In his professional opinion, Quentin needed more time for his fragile mind to adjust. He thought it beneficial that he experience as little stress as possible during the early days of the recovery period. This suited Eleanor fine as she always had a full diary.

Talking to her friends about Quentin, she felt uncomfortable and humiliated when she gave an account of his condition. But more so when she explained that he was an inpatient at a National Health Service hospital, not a private one. It seemed evident, even in the upper echelons of society (her pompous friends), that conceit and arrogance were alive and kicking.

Thanks to regression, a return of memory brought relief and an enthusiastic visit from Eleanor. To afford privacy and because it was a pleasant day, Quentin suggested they take a walk. Ambling along in uneasy silence, the beauty and splendour of the hospital grounds did little to ease a frosty atmosphere. Eleanor tried to lift his mood by pointing out small oases of beauty. Even so, he couldn't bring himself to talk; life with her had taken a turn for the worse.

Reaching an area popular with hospital visitors, Quentin pointed to a bench – they sat in silence. However, Eleanor wanted to talk.

"Mr Elwood tells me you're making excellent progress,

darling; I am so incredibly pleased," said Eleanor, trying to breathe life into the awkward silence.

Quentin's mood was strange. The return of memory had ushered in awkward and sensitive issues. He tried to broach the subject of Eleanor's infidelity, but couldn't. He wrestled with his emotions. Pessimism seemed to be winning the fight.

"Frances and Cynthia, do you remember them? Well, they send their best wishes and hope for a jolly good, speedy recovery. Isn't that kind of them?"

Quentin didn't hear her as she droned on. His mind raced. The person he loved and trusted sat beside him, pretended all was well. She had been unfaithful to him. He knew in his heart of hearts that all was far from well. The deep sense of betrayal and humiliation hung heavy with growing belligerence that unsettled him. Yesterday, he wanted to forgive; sat next to Eleanor today; all he felt was antagonism. He was in a dark place and hated himself for feeling that way.

"I rather think it won't be too long before you're discharged and back at work. How wonderful," Eleanor worked hard to prise an answer from him.

"Yes, it would appear."

"So is everything all right now, Quentin? Have you got your memory back and can you remember me, your dearest loving wife?"

He concluded it wasn't a good time to broach the sensitive matter of infidelity, as it could snowball out of control and lead to more misgivings. All the same, he felt hostile towards her because of her flippant and insincere use of the phrase 'your dearest loving wife.' Inaction was the right thing now. He remained tight-lipped, for fear of saying something he might regret. Quentin answered without emotion.

"Mmm... Somewhat."

"Do you remember our home and friends, dear?"

"A little," he felt, frustrated with her silly, inane questions.

"Oh, top-notch, and work, can you remember the bank and the team?"

Quentin appeared vague. He found it all a bit too much to handle. He would have preferred to take his recovery much more slowly, but, as usual, Eleanor was in the fast lane.

Whether her self-assured, quick thinking was hereditary or a product of learnt behaviour, he wasn't sure. Eleanor was an only child and generally got her way. But when things didn't go her way, she threw a tantrum. Displaying questionable parenting skills, they tolerated her demands and paid little attention to their prodigy's selfishness and inability to see things any other way.

Her father, a diplomat at the foreign office, spent most of his time abroad, in the Orient. Mother, a forthright, no-nonsense person, spent her time in the heart of London, where the family owned a penthouse.

For Eleanor, holidays were generally spent with friends. On rare occasions, she flew first class with her mother to join her father in Hong Kong, enjoying all the privileges afforded to a top diplomat.

At the age of twenty-five, Eleanor worked on the board of directors of her uncle's construction company. It was a high-salaried, high-octane job, requiring executive decisions that at times commanded vast sums of money. Nevertheless, Eleanor never faltered; it all came easily to her fine, encompassing mind.

"How about our lovely garden?"

"That is a bit hazy right now," said Quentin. "My memory is returning. Although it would seem I can't rush it. The consultant said to let it emerge at its own pace." He changed the conversation, trying not to appear too negative; "I was able to get hold of my briefcase yesterday and looked at some banking papers."

"How splendid, darling. Oh, talking about work, I nearly forgot," Eleanor dug into her bag. "I have a card for you from the staff at the bank." She handed it over to Quentin. "James sends his best wishes and hopes for a speedy recovery. He said all was well at the bank, and they all miss you terribly."

Quentin gave the card a cursory glance and closed it. "Thank you. That reminds me, it was our twenty-fifth anniversary yesterday, and I have a card for you. I was hoping to do something special for the momentous occasion; however, it wasn't to be."

"Oh, darling, thank you so much, how kind. Maybe when you are discharged, we can have a belated celebration."

"Yes, maybe."

Eleanor looked at her watch. "Goodness, just look at the time, I must fly. I'm supposed to be meeting Joyce. We need to go over the bridge club accounts, and a painter chappie is calling to look at the lounge. It needs decorating desperately before the winter sets in. Well, I won't bore you with all the details." She stood to leave.

Quentin remained seated. "I've got the anniversary card in my locker for you, would you like..."

"Leave it till next time, darling; I am in such a frightful dash." She looked at her watch again.

"In that case, I think I'll just sit here for a little while longer and admire the view." He feigned a smile that went unnoticed.

"All right, darling. Ring me if you need anything." She bent down to offer her cheek. "Terribly good news, getting better. I will contact the bank and pass along your best wishes, and hopefully, it won't be too long before you are home again. Try to get better soon, darling. I miss you awfully." She blew him a kiss.

Despite his negative feelings for Eleanor, he felt terrible for parting in such a way. As she was about to leave, he blurted out something that stopped Eleanor in her tracks.

"When I first met you, I thought you were the most beautiful lady I had ever seen, and our anniversary confirms twenty-five years of love and commitment."

"Of course it does, darling." Eleanor seemed perplexed. Although understanding what he'd said, she wondered why Quentin had voiced something so unusual and entirely out of context with the moment. Confusion showed on her face as she tried to make sense of it all.

Eleanor replayed his words a few times in her mind as she drove to see Joyce. Just as quickly, she dismissed them as the ramblings of her confused husband in a hospital recovering from memory loss. Glory be, she had a lot to put up with.

In no time at all, she was focused on her next appointment and the bridge club accounts. Little did she realise that Quentin's condition would take a turn for the worse; serious consequences were likely to ensue, causing distress and deep soul-searching.

TWENTY-ONE

Following a reasonable night's sleep, Gary sat on the side of his bed in a daze. He was never a morning person and generally found it difficult getting up.

Already awake for some time, Quentin collected his toilet bag and headed to the bathroom. "Are you shaving this morning, Gary?"

"Yeah, there in a minute."

He heard Quentin running water into the sink for a shave. Checking that nobody was around, he sneaked over to Quentin's bedside locker. With caution, he listened for a moment; satisfied that all was well, Gary rifled through Quentin's belongings, finding the prize, his wallet. Working at speed, he acquainted himself with the contents and layout of the wallet, which enabled him to put it all back in the same order. He pocketed five pounds; however, the best was yet to come. Amongst the notes, paper driving licence and bank cards, he found a cheque made out for £2,000. He couldn't believe his eyes. His heart raced, his eyes flickered as he cleared his vision for a second look. This was just like a win on the football coupon. "Oh bloody hell," he said in a whisper. With speed, he put the cheque back into the wallet, placed everything back in the locker, and grabbed his towel. However, a second thought stopped him in his tracks; his mind worked overtime. He threw the towel over his shoulder and returned to Quentin's locker, opened the wallet and took the cheque guarantee bank card.

In a happy mood, he headed to the bathroom for a shave,

humming one of his favourite songs *Can't Buy Me Love*, by the Beatles.

"Someone sounds happy this morning," said Quentin, unaware of the dirty deed.

The hospital's routine continued as usual. After breakfast, Gary and Quentin headed to the OT department. At the craft table, they set up their projects. Gary worked with enthusiasm on his basket weaving. However, Quentin didn't seem to be as adept and nimble-fingered. Coordination and flow suffered because of ruinous thoughts. Eleanor's conversation yesterday held troubling overtones of deceit and pretence. He tried to dismiss her glib, insincere words, consigning the thoughts to the far reaches of his mind, but it did not work. The deceitful scenario bounced back time and time again, persecuting his tormented soul.

He had thought long and hard about Eleanor's disloyalty and lack of obligation. In a forgiving mood, he seemed prepared to overcome their differences and work on a satisfactory solution. Yet, if his mood was on the lower rung of the ladder, he felt pessimistic about the future. Marriage for Quentin was a pledge, a statement that said, 'I want to share the rest of my life with you.' It shouted commitment and explicit trust.

The OT aide, ever vigilant, saw he was struggling with his work and came over to lend a hand. He refocused on basket weaving, thanked her for the help, and tried his hand once more. However, it wasn't right; he seemed to have little control over his errant thoughts, which governed his coordination.

"Are you all right this morning?" said Gary. "You seem a little strange."

"I'm not feeling my best today, Gary. My heart doesn't seem to be in it."

"Why d'you think that is?"

"Between you and me, I'm worried about being discharged. The consultant said he wanted me to consider taking a weekend leave. Despite misgivings, I've agreed to go home Saturday morning. Eleanor is picking me up. But right now it's a big ask, Gary, a very big ask."

"I don't know what to say, Quent."

"Nothing to say, Gary, I will go on weekend leave and give it a try. That's all I can do."

"It's only for a short time, though."

"Only!" Quentin reacted with disquiet.

"But surely your returning memory is the best news ever; it'll help you move on with your life and get you back to normal?"

Quentin took a while to reflect on Gary's point of view. "It seems an incredible thing to say, Gary, but when I didn't know who I was, I felt far happier than I do now."

"Err, you got me there, Quent. I really don't know what you're saying."

"It's easy; as a patient here, I feel safe. Life is so simple. I feel protected from..."

"The big bad world."

"Precisely."

"Yes. But what about your missus? She'll look forward to having you back home, won't she?"

Quentin looked at fellow patients sitting around the craft table. "Not now, Gary, I'll talk to you later."

Elevenses, the great British tradition, continued in hospital, as it did in homes and the workplace. It was that sacred moment when people sat around for fifteen minutes, switched off, drank tea or coffee and talked about things in general.

Quentin had a deep, dark secret that weighed him down, and

he needed to confide in his friend. They took their coffee outside and sat on a bench.

"I was asking you about your missus in there," he pointed to the OT, "and you clammed up." Gary set the scene and waited for the mystery to unfold.

"Yes, darling Eleanor," said Quentin, as he rubbed an imaginary mark on his trousers. He stared ahead, summoning up the courage to speak. "Can you..." he looked around the immediate area. "Can you keep a secret, Gary?" This had his undivided attention. Gary played the game by looking around to scan the area for people eavesdropping. He wasn't bothered if anyone could hear. It was just his way of putting Quentin at ease – acting as a *confidante* – engendering an air of complete privacy.

"Course I can, mate. What's up?"

Quentin's mood was dark. "We don't... get on together."

The reality of his disclosure proved to be a bit of an anti-climax for Gary, who thought it was a standard practice not to get on. Anguish came to the fore, registering on Quentin's face in an uncomfortable, dispiriting moment.

"How d'you mean?"

"We don't get on well if you understand what I'm saying." He rubbed his eyes to try to stem the flow. "You see," he dropped his head in shame. "She... she's seeing somebody else." The floodgates opened. Quentin took a handkerchief out of his pocket and blew his nose noisily.

Gary's reaction was one of annoyance. "The cow! Oh, sorry, Quent. I didn't mean to..."

"No, that's okay, Gary. I thought of something a bit stronger when I first found out." He wiped his eyes and buried the handkerchief in his pocket. The weak sun disappeared behind the clouds, conveying a chill to the troubled atmosphere.

If Gary was intrigued before, he was now positively agog, looking for every gory detail. "But how did you find out? Who was he?"

Quentin couldn't look Gary in the eye; he continued staring at the ground. He had never been the sort of person to bare his soul. The nearest he had ever got to talking about his innermost feelings was work-related. Self-assessment sessions were part of the job appraisal, requiring open and honest discussion about himself and his work. That was nothing compared to his current dilemma. Nevertheless, he must talk and alleviate his troubled mind.

"A few days before I lost my memory, I found a penknife on our bedroom floor. Although it was a peculiar thing to find, I didn't think too much about it. Except, it must have been in the back of my mind. Sometime later, although I couldn't be sure, I thought it might belong to the gardener."

"Got yer," said Gary, already putting two and two together and visualising the sordid scenario.

"So, I thought, a penknife in the bedroom – gardener in the bedroom," Quentin broke down, sobbing.

"Oh, eh, Quent, don't let it get to you," said Gary, with nothing else to offer.

"We haven't been to bed together, if you know what I mean, for a long time... I don't think Eleanor even likes me anymore." Having broached the most troubling aspect of his dark secret, Quentin found the strength to look at Gary, his best friend and confidante. Through his tears, he tried a smile, sensing his momentary breakdown was awkward and embarrassing for Gary.

"So, can you remember everything now, Quent?"

"Since the regression therapy, just about everything," he confirmed.

"Phew! How good is that? From nothing to everything," said Gary, hoping to steer the conversation to one that he could handle.

"Yes, it's all clear and making sense. I'm no psychologist, but I wonder if this had anything to do with my amnesia." Quentin's raw emotion continued. Handkerchief still in hand, he wiped his eyes, blew his nose and tried to put the moment behind him. "It makes me wonder what is left in life, Gary, if I can't even trust my wife. What is left?"

"Oh, eh, Quent, don't be saying that."

"I'm sorry; it's just how I feel, Gary. It's all just a horrible nightmare. I keep thinking I will wake up soon and breathe a sigh of relief because it was all a bad dream."

For once, Gary was lost for words, and it proved challenging. Then he hit upon an idea. As if to add understanding to the problematic moment or merely for something to say, he blurted out a revelation.

"I think mine's been messing about, too."

"What, your wife?" said Quentin.

"Yeah."

"How do you know?"

"Just one of those things, Quent. When my missus isn't interested in me in that department, you know, don't you? I mean, you know?"

"Well... I suppose so."

At that point, the OT aide knocked on the window, pointed to her watch, and gestured for them to come back inside. Gary waved and smiled disingenuously.

"Better get back to the production line," he said sarcastically, "before Tilly Mint throws a wobbly."

"I suppose so," said Quentin.

"I was thinking of going to the library after this; d'you want to come, Quent?"

"No, thanks, Gary. I've got a lot of thinking to do. Probably put my feet up and listen to some music." In that troubled moment, Quentin forgot all about his minder arrangement with the charge nurse.

"Oh, yeah. What music's that, then?" Gary was familiar with Quentin's musical style and believed it wasn't real music.

"Maybe Vivaldi or Bach."

"Oh... do you listen to anything normal?"

"I do happen to like Abba." Quentin stood up and composed himself, ready to continue back in the OT.

"Nice one, Quent. There's hope for you yet."

"Gary, thank you for listening. You've been a great help," said Quentin, feeling relieved to have spoken about his big, dark secret. A weight had been lifted from his shoulders.

To many people, the joy of a library was the peace and tranquillity that enabled them to read or study. Until his hospital admission, Gary had never set foot in a library, believing it to be a place for eggheads. In a limited way, he used the hospital library to work on his secret project. But, before he started his task, Gary cadged writing paper and a pen from Mr Hall. Finding a seat in the corner away from prying eyes, he wrote a letter to Mary. It read in the vein of feelings of sorrow, "won't happen again," "I'm a changed man," etc. A letter was written and put in a hospital envelope. Mr Hall agreed to post it later that day.

Gary took out Quentin's bankcard that he had borrowed earlier. Making sure he was unobserved, he set about copying Quentin's signature repeatedly until he could write it nearly perfectly.

He was happy with the outcome, recalling one of his mates

in the young offenders' prison who had taught him all he needed to know about forgery. Gary and Tommy hit it off from the first moment they met. In particular, one defining moment was when they spoke about forging signatures. Gary was suitably impressed when Tommy asked him to write his name on a scrap of paper; within minutes, Tommy had made a replica of Gary's signature. He recalled looking from one signature to the other and being unable to recognise which was the original and which was the fake. Tommy was good.

Back on the ward, the charge nurse realised that Gary wasn't in the company of Quentin, who in turn explained that he had gone to the library. Within seconds, Mr Elwood was on the phone, confirming that Gary was indeed in the library and, according to Mr Hall, was sitting writing. To his surprise, Gary felt a sense of enjoyment, sitting amongst all the other eggheads. In reality, it was the secret plan formulating in his mind that excited him. His mood was ecstatic, and it showed.

TWENTY-TWO

Ten days spent in the psychiatric unit were pleasant enough if it could be said that being a patient in a hospital was pleasant, but, with an enforced stay, Gary was showing signs of restlessness. Quentin, on the other hand, adjusted well to the hospital's slow, leisurely pace, enjoying the tranquillity and peace of the rural surroundings, where nature still held sway. Like a spiritual retreat, the temporary lifestyle in the hospital gave Quentin ample time to reflect on his perspective on life and humanity. He concluded that banking lacked morality. It was all-encompassing, all-controlling, showing very little or no consideration for people. Joe Public had little choice in how life worked or even in what direction his life travelled. He had to fit in with the system, or he would be left by the wayside. It had taken Quentin a long time to come to this conclusion, but after all those years, he could see it clearly: the minority with power and finance controlled the greater numbers.

Due to modifications to a nearby building, OT was closed for the day. Re-modelling required demolishing a wall to make way for an office and toilet block. With luck, the department was due to re-open for therapy on Monday afternoon.

"Day off today, Quent," said Gary, his words falling on deaf ears. Quentin was wearing headphones and listening to classical music. With his right hand resting on the arm of the chair, his index finger waved back and forth like a conductor's baton.

Gary paced around the day room like a caged animal. Sitting and chilling out had never been his thing; that morning was no exception.

From the age of six at primary school, he had always been in trouble for leaving his desk and disobeying the teacher. His disruptive behaviour spiralled out of control to the point that the teacher, unable to cope, reported it to the headmaster. Despite intervention to help him with his problem, there was little improvement in his unruly behaviour. Consequently, a lot of time was lost in education.

Never regarded as a bright student, Gary left school with reduced reading and writing abilities. Luckily, he found a job in the building industry, where the main requirements were physical strength and minimal cognitive skills. But that was short-lived. Following a questionable accident at work, he continued to complain of lower back pain, saw a general practitioner and the sick notes and painkillers flowed. By talking to his work-shy mates who tutored him, he became adept at controlling the outcomes of the general practitioner's monthly check-ups. With a well-rehearsed 'ooch, ouch' upon examination, the practitioner, it would seem, was fooled. The pills for his imaginary back pain became a nice little earner. He devised a scheme to sell them to others for beer money. Out of work, he mixed with the wrong people and soon became involved in petty crime, finding himself on the wrong side of the law and society.

Gary sauntered into the hospital's quiet room. Comfortable chairs, a coffee table, and bookshelves full of games, books, and magazines created an inviting, relaxed environment. He rummaged on the shelves and found what he thought was a pack of playing cards. Flicking through them, he realised the cards had letters of the alphabet printed on them, not the usual playing card suits. His brow wrinkled with uncertainty; he had never seen cards like them before.

With his usual encyclopaedic brain, Quentin the Oracle threw light on the matter. "Oh, that's the game of Lexicon."

"Wot?"

"Lexicon. You make up words with the cards. It's quite a good game, actually," said Quentin, getting back to his classical music.

Gary sat, giving the Lexicon cards deep thought. "Hang on a minute. I've got an idea here." He interrupted Quentin once more. "Do you fancy a game with these cards, Quent?"

"Maybe later," replied Quentin, wanting to get back to Massenet's *Meditation from Thais*, a masterful, haunting violin solo and Quentin's latest aural delight.

Quentin's nephew, Malcolm, was similar in many ways to Gary. That said, Malcolm's problem was on a different level. He was super-intelligent and always required more and more stimulation to occupy his young, active mind. Like a sponge, his memory absorbed an ever-increasing amount of information. Without it, he became bored, restless and disruptive.

As the music ended, Quentin put the cassette player away; he was curious to see what Gary's great idea could be. The days of Quentin, the authoritarian manager, were changing in favour of a more open-minded, liberal person ready to listen, embrace and share other people's thoughts. However, in Gary's case, it could be mundane, puerile or just plain boring.

On a table in the quiet room, Gary laid the cards out in a circle. In addition, he added two pieces of paper, scribbled with YES and NO.

"What's this, Gary?" He looked at the arrangement of cards with intrigue.

"It's like a game of cards we play at home," said Gary, lying. "Oh, just a minute." He exited the room, returning with a glass tumbler, and placed it upside down on the table, midway between the letters YES and NO. He was ready for the game to begin. "Come on, Quent, grab a seat, then we can start."

Quentin sat down, bemused at the array of cards in front of him, wondering what Gary's intended game was. That said, a niggling doubt crossed his mind.

"Right, put your finger on the glass, like me."

"Just a minute," said Quentin; his thoughts came together. "This looks remarkably like Ouija from where I'm sitting."

"No, it's not, it's called 'Ask the Glass.'"

"I'm not too sure about this, Gary, if..."

"Quentin, trust me. I've done it loads of times, even with the kids," said Gary, lying again, "and they love it, it's a blast. Now put your finger on the glass."

"I'll try it, but I'm not happy. I have a strange feeling about this."

"Quent, you had a strange feeling about going to the pub, and it turned out okay. Be honest; it did, didn't it?"

"Well, yes, but... "

"But nothing, Quent, it's fine. Now put your finger on the glass and concentrate." Gary's tone was persuasive and convincing.

"Are there any ghosts out there?" said Gary.

Hearing the word 'ghost,' Quentin withdrew his hand from the glass with the speed of a magician's hand.

"Just joking, Quent. You fell for that one, didn't you?" Gary gave one of his infectious, cheeky smiles. "Sorry, let's start again."

Quentin placed his finger on the glass.

"Can anyone hear me?" They looked and listened in

anticipation – nothing. "Anyone want to talk to us?" The glass moved for a second, then stopped. Startled by the movement, Quentin removed his finger from the glass again, ready to leave the room.

"Quent, it was just me messing. I pushed the glass," said Gary, lying for the third time. Now come on and sit down, pleeease?"

Taken in by Gary's behaviour, he sat and placed his finger on the glass again.

Why had Quentin engaged in this sort of thing when he was a wise, feet firmly on the ground type of person? He had read about spiritualism and dismissed it as society's obsession with the afterlife. Up to a point, he understood the curiosity. He himself had an enquiring mind, always on a quest for enlightenment. However, the in-depth newspaper articles he had read, although comprehensive, didn't address the bigger picture. What he was witnessing in the quiet room was akin to an Ouija session, yet he felt indecisive about whether it was prudent to continue.

So far, Gary had told him that he had been controlling the glass, thereby lulling Quentin into a false sense of security. However, neither were prepared for what was about to happen.

"Do you want to talk?" The glass moved in circles. It picked up speed as it travelled to the word YES scribbled on the piece of paper. Gary was ecstatic. Quentin sat in stunned silence.

"What's your name?" Nothing materialised.

"Do you have a name?" Nothing. "Do you have a name?" Gary demanded.

Slowly and with purpose, the unseen presence directed the glass to the letters F –L –Y.

"Fly?" He looked to Quentin for input, except Quentin was zoned out, a passive observer unable to speak or move, frozen to the spot.

"Fly? What the hell does that mean?"

Just then, a fly landed on the table. It buzzed around, landed on the cards and settled on Gary's arm. Quick as a flash, he swatted the unsuspecting fly with his free hand. An eerie squeal assaulted their senses. What should have been but a speck of blood grew to a large smear, covering all of his lower arm. Their aching fingers gripped the glass like marine limpets.

Taking on life, the glass moved across the table, spelling out K–I–L–L.

"Gary, let's stop now!" shrieked Quentin, frightened and concerned. A look of desperation framed his face.

Gary had locked them into something far more significant than he could ever have imagined. It was as if the presence had taken exception to the childlike prank and set about teaching them both a lesson. Gary reacted with bravado – a display of defiance. The futility of which soon became disturbingly apparent.

"Are you evil or just a pussy cat?" No response. "Just as I thought a wimp," said Gary, with boastful disregard for the consequences. This was his streetwise response to handle situations bigger than himself – to appear fearless. Nevertheless, Gary was a mere mortal.

The presence, so far relatively subdued, showed its incredible, unequivocal power. Climatic change sent the room into an icy chill. Day-lit windows darkened as if it were dusk, making it difficult for them to see each other clearly, yet a faint glow hovered over the table. Both Gary and Quentin were frightened beyond belief. Adrenalin coursed through their bodies, preparing them for flight, yet neither could run from the scene. Their fingers were stuck in situ, becoming painful and rigid. The supernatural frenzy spun out of control.

"Stop this, Gary! Stop it now!" shouted Quentin. His heart raced so fast it felt as if it was about to leap out of his asthmatic chest.

"I'm not doing anything!"

From behind, Gary heard a ghoulish voice that delivered an unforgettable, bloodcurdling threat.

"I – kill – you." As if the threat wasn't scary enough, in the distance, he heard the odious screams of agonised, tormented souls.

The glass raced from letter to letter, spelling out the word KILL. As if heightened fear weren't enough, a vile, rotten smell permeated the room. It compelled both Gary and Quentin to retch violently, although they didn't vomit. This was their worst nightmare, and they wanted out. Above all, they wanted an end to the unimaginable terror. Their only hope was to flee the room. Yet, that was impossible. The supernatural power held them and continued to taunt their minds and souls. Pictures on the walls swung from side to side. A chair nearby spun on one leg. Mist rising from the floor began to envelop them. In sheer desperation, with his free hand, Gary reached out for the lettered cards and swept them off the table. Their fingers unexpectedly released from the glass. In terrified unison, they bolted for the door. In an instant, time froze.

The familiarity of the quiet room disappeared from view – Gary found himself at home, elevated from a height, looking down upon his family. Held as if by the scruff of his neck, he could not speak, nor move, but was merely fated to watch the unfolding scene. This wasn't a social visit; some dastardly deed was about to unfold. Mary and the children were clearly visible. The family home took on a strange aura as it darkened somewhat. Within seconds, agonising high-pitched screeches emanated from all three of his family in an ear-busting din.

What took place next repulsed Gary to the point that he wanted to retch the whole of his stomach up all over the floor. Their faces underwent transition – hands distorted, turning a glistening black. Short stubble hairs sprouted from their skin. Gary tried to scream, but he had no bodily control; he was impotent, powerless, dangling over the repulsive scene. In what he thought were his dying moments, he focused on Mary, the last visage he would see on earth before he expired. However, the image wasn't pleasant. Her body contracted – legs and arms shortened, taking on a leathery, black hue. Two more legs sprouted from her rib cage, her clothing disintegrated, and wings grew from her back. She was mutating into a variant of an enormous, disgusting fly. In agony, she fell to the floor on all six legs. Her fly-like face, which still had some vestige of human characteristics, looked up at him, grimacing, pleading for help. The inertia of his body in a vicious grip bore heavily on his tormented mind. Above all, he wanted to free himself and leap to his family's defence, yet he could not. He was held captive, witnessing every agonising creak, every stretch of sinew, every painful metamorphosis of their bodies. He dared not look at the children; the image of Mary was traumatic enough without seeing his offspring undergo a vile, satanic experience.

His mind screamed. In the name of God, how can this be? The human fly, once Mary, opened its mouth. Like an African Cichlid fish with its young, Mary spewed maggots, writhing and wriggling across the floor in such a grotesque fashion that it terrified Gary beyond belief.

As if a light switch had been thrown, Gary found himself back in the hospital's quiet room, gripping the handle of the door. "It won't turn!" he yelled. His pained hand matched his expression as he exerted more and more force. But to no avail.

"Open the door, Gary! For God's sake, open the door!" cried Quentin, with intense desperation.

Around them, the *mêlée* continued unabated; bookshelves rocked backwards and forwards with unbelievable ease. Books flew off shelves, crashing to the floor. The cold intensified. Their breath showed up in the sub-zero temperature, as if they were crossing the arctic tundra, except they were in the hospital quiet room.

"I'm trying! I'm trying! It won't turn!"

Desperation engulfed them. All seemed lost. Then miraculously, without warning, the door opened. A fellow patient stood in the doorway, looking on bemused.

"Excuse me. I just wanted a book."

"Don't go in there!" yelled Quentin, fearful for the patient's safety, "there's a..."

Quentin and Gary pushed past the bewildered patient and proceeded at a pace to the dayroom.

Intrigued by the curious warning, the fellow patient popped his head into the room, then looked back at Gary and Quentin as they headed down the corridor. "What are they talking about?" said the patient. He entered the room and looked around – everything was in order. Not a book, a chair or a piece of furniture was out of place. "Huh, I can see why they're in here; they're bloody lunatics," confirmed the patient.

Gary flopped into a chair in the dayroom, his face ashen. He put a hand to his aching stomach and trembled. With sudden urgency, he ran to the toilet to be sick.

Quentin used his inhaler. However, the first attempt was useless. In his rush to seize a much-needed dose, he forgot to prime his inhaler. Desperation turned into panic. With another effort, Quentin bit hard on the mouthpiece. The life-giving inhaler was slow to take effect. Breathing in was reasonable, but breathing out – that was the problem. All the same, begrudgingly, unhurriedly, the attack released its grip. Standing by an open window, he continued to breathe his way out of the worst asthmatic attack he had ever experienced in his life. With enormous relief, Quentin felt the beginnings of normality returning to his beleaguered body.

A good ten minutes later, he made his way to the dormitory to lie on the bed. By a stroke of luck, there was a minimum of staff present in the ward. The strange behaviour went unnoticed, save for one observant member of staff who had seen Quentin using his inhaler. He followed Quentin into the dormitory. "Are you all right?" said the nurse, concerned.

"Yes, I'm fine," he said, unable to divulge what had caused his asthmatic attack. "I think the dust from the building work is getting into my chest."

The nurse took him at his word and closed the dormitory window. "So long as you're okay."

He held his inhaler up in the air and waved it as if to say, 'all was well.' "Yes, I'm fine," said Quentin, not at all happy to have lied.

Gary made his way back into the dormitory. He had retched the contents of his stomach up until his stomach muscles ached.

Earlier thoughts of accommodating Gary's 'idea' had turned to one of annoyance and anger. Quentin knew he had to exercise control over his feelings or else he was in danger of provoking another asthma attack. Even so, it proved challenging to rein in his emotions when anger reigned.

"I told you it wasn't a good idea, Gary, but no, you knew better, didn't you?" He paced around, finding it difficult to control his vexation with what he had to say. "Well, it was unbelievably foolhardy," he stared at Gary, sat on his bed, head in hands. "Don't you *ever* put me in that position again."

"That wasn't meant to happen... "

Quentin cut across him. "I told you I had a bad feeling, and look what happened." In truth, he was annoyed with himself for letting the whole charade happen when he had misgivings.

A chastised Gary knew he had gone too far. "Quent, I'm sorry, it was... "

"But no... You knew better, Mr Clever Gary Lowe." The atmosphere hung thick and heavy with outrage. Neither spoke for a while.

"Quentin, I'm sorry." Their erstwhile friendly relationship was in tatters. Nevertheless, he hoped the feeling of animosity would pass soon.

"And so you should be. I've never been put in such a ridiculous, unbelievable situation as that," he pointed in the general direction of the quiet room, "in my entire life."

Gary shook his head in atonement, not daring to mention the horrific scene he had personally witnessed; that would have pushed the whole sorry saga too far for Quentin.

"This has never happened before... I mean a bunch of stupid cards and... "

"Well, now you know not to engage in things you know nothing about and certainly not the occult."

"I'm sorry. I can't say any more."

Quentin sat in silence. Their relationship had taken a severe tumble; he showed no signs of forgiveness. Another asthmatic attack had begun; he took a much-needed draught from his inhaler to try and arrest it before it started in earnest.

The shocking sight of his wife, Mary, changing into an ugly, grotesque fly continued to dominate Gary's mind. He felt extremely disturbed by the fiendish scene; it was such a surreal, horrific experience, and he didn't know what to think or do. Was it real? Had his family changed into something monstrous?

He had an overwhelming urge to ring Mary, to make sure she was unharmed and not, as he had witnessed at the hands of the entity, a thing, a non-being.

"I don't believe it." Quentin ran his hands over his clothing. "I've lost my crucifix." He took his cardigan off and unbuttoned his shirt, hoping to find that the chain was broken, not lost, but safe, caught up somewhere in his clothing.

Gary looked on, horrified. He pointed. "Quentin, look at your chest."

Running a hand across his upper body, Quentin winced with pain. Three deep red scratches, like raised welts, six inches in length, ran over the area of his chest where the crucifix had hung. Quentin had already voiced his concerns about the occult, but the incident in the quiet room had the potential to blow any scepticism of the supernatural out of the water. This was a genuine phenomenon, and Gary had foolishly dabbled in something he knew nothing about.

They couldn't disguise the look of shock on their faces. It was serious, and neither knew if it was the end or the beginning of evil intent.

TWENTY-THREE

As planned, Eleanor collected Quentin early Saturday afternoon. Although cold, the grey, wet day didn't materialise as forecast. Lunchtime gave rise to sunny spells, which should have made the journey to the St John's home a bit more pleasant. Eleanor listened to the radio, resigned to the fact that Quentin, for some inexplicable reason, didn't want to speak. Apart from the lukewarm greeting she received at the hospital, he sat in stony silence as Eleanor drove. Not, it would appear, a promising start to his leave of absence.

Pulling into their driveway, Quentin decided to stretch his legs and mooch around their garden. He needed time to clear his head and hoped a stroll would put him in a better frame of mind.

The impressive West Country palm had flowered for the first time since planting. Borders shone with colourful late-bedding plants. Spectacular shrubs such as Acer, Mahonia and Berberis took on a striking Autumnal hue. In keeping with good gardening practice, the manicured lawn had been given a longer cut, preparing it for the inevitable frost and snow of the winter months.

As he gazed across the striped lawn, Quentin was reminded of the wonderful time spent at Wimbledon with Eleanor. They met up with friends to watch the enthralling men's singles final – Pat Cash played Ivan Lendl for the coveted title. Although their stay in London was brief owing to work commitments, they promised to do the same the following year.

Testing his newfound memory, Quentin headed to the wine cellar. He cross-checked wine with the stock list, turned bottles of vintage wine, and verified that the corks and labels were satisfactory. As he touched the glass bottles, his mind flashed back to the trauma of yesterday. With vivid recall, he relived the Ouija session and an inability to remove his finger from the glass tumbler. With a feeling of *déjà vu*, he was half expecting his fingers to adhere to the bottles as he touched them, but all was well. Undaunted, he continued to dismiss the mental aberration, knowing that time would help him forget the awful occurrence.

Examining wines, he focused on the country of origin, region, vineyard, vintage, and the best years of wine production, all of which were a testament to his extensive knowledge of the subject. Collecting wines was one of his loves. By and large, he usually took pleasure in his expensive hobby; nevertheless, the day wasn't quite the same as others; he was in an extraordinary mood.

An incomplete return of memory still occupied his questioning mind. Quentin likened amnesia to waking from a dream, remembering only fleeting images. For his sanity, he needed to remember everything; he needed to recover his entire memory. Be that as it may, he found the more he tried to remember events from his past, the more frustratingly distant they became. Added to this, the conundrum he couldn't entirely lay to rest was, if he'd had a period of not knowing who he was because of amnesia, how could he eat, sleep, read and converse in the hospital with people and all without having his memory? Thankfully, his breakthrough came partially through Dr Sharif's intervention. But it was all far from satisfactory. With no answers to satisfy his curiosity, he concluded that the whole sorry saga was 'off the wall.' This was a turn of phrase he had heard his bank staff use. He surprised himself by recalling such an expression, not one he would typically use. When Quentin took a reality check on his progress, as he had done the previous night lying in bed, he felt he wasn't coping with the recovery process very well. Self-doubt reared its ugly head way too often. Dr Sharif had explained that depressive bouts could occur for some people recovering from amnesia, depending on their circumstances. So, he needed to continue seeing the clinical psychologist for help.

Although he hadn't received the news of the weekend leave well, Quentin knew it was the right thing to do. Already, being at home had resurrected deep feelings and posed many searching questions.

Tossing and turning, Gary hadn't slept well; his mind ran and re-ran the horrific scenario of Mary turning into a huge, fly-like monstrosity. He concluded that somehow he had to go home and check for himself, so he hatched a plan. The best way to seek permission for a home visit was on the pretext of needing more clothing and personal items.

"I don't see that being a problem, Gary," said Mr Elwood. "I'll make arrangements for a social worker to accompany you to your house."

"Oh," surprise consumed Gary at the mention of a social worker. This wasn't going according to plan.

"Is that a problem?"

"No, not a problem at all, Mr Elwood. I didn't want to trouble anybody," said Gary.

"No trouble, that's why they're here, I'll ring right now and see if I can get it organised."

Mr Elwood, a true professional, was on to any ruse or con a patient could imagine. He felt certain Gary wanted to go home unaccompanied. That was reason enough to keep an even closer eye on him. Allowing Gary the privilege of being alone in the community would be like letting a child loose in a sweet shop. While Gary was still a hospital patient, he had to be kept under surveillance.

The travelling time to Gary's house was 15 minutes by car in the social worker's pride and joy, a Citroën 2CV. Alternatively, Gary calculated it would take ten minutes or less by taxi, an essential factor if his intended plan was going to work.

As they turned onto the street, Gary pointed. "Can you see the house on the right with the... ?"

The social worker continued to drive, waiting for further directions. Gary had stopped mid-sentence, flabbergasted. His red armchair, customarily situated in the front garden, along with a convenient coffee table for placing a beer or paper upon, was no more. The once small, scruffy front garden had changed in favour of a small levelled area, sown with grass seed. The garden appeared worlds apart from the overgrown monstrosity he remembered. Across the newly planted lawn, newspaper tied like ribbons to string fluttered in the morning breeze, denying birds a free meal. Gary swivelled his head, looking for landmarks to confirm he wasn't losing his mind.

"What number?" said the social worker.

He looked around, bemused. "Err... this one."

"This one?" said Nigel, nodding in the general direction.

"Yep, this is the mansion," said Gary, trying to recover from the shock. "I'll just be a minute," he said, realising he didn't know the social worker's name. "What's your name, pal?"

"Nigel."

"I'll only be a minute, Nige," said Gary, reaching for the door handle.

The social worker had already been briefed about accompanying Gary at all times.

"That's okay, I'll come in with you," said Nigel.

Gary expected him to wait outside in the car, although that wasn't to be. His mind worked overtime on plan B. He might even need a plan C; it all depended on outwitting the social worker, but Nigel was like a shadow.

As usual, Gary put his hand through the letterbox to retrieve the front-door key, much to the social worker's consternation.

"Is that such a good idea, Gary?"

"Oh, aye, not a problem," Gary smiled. "We do things differently here, sort of look after each other." He pointed to his neighbour, Martha, peeping through the curtain. "See, we have our very own early warning system."

"So I can see." The social worker waved to her with a big, cheesy grin.

As they walked into the hallway, Gary called out. "Anybody in?" No answer. They walked into the living room. Little did Gary know that Mr Elwood had phoned Mary earlier to advise her that Gary had been allowed home to collect some personal items. She didn't want the awkwardness of confronting him, so she spent the day with her mum.

Looking around the living room at length, Gary recalled the scene he had experienced during the Ouija session the day before. It came back with such intensity that it shocked him to the core, enough to make Nigel comment.

"Are you all right, Gary? You look as if you've seen a ghost?"

"Yeah, I'm fine," said Gary, relieved not to find any evidence of the nightmarish sight he had witnessed at the hands of the abomination. He moved on with the business in hand, trying to recover his thoughts.

"Take a seat. Can I get you a cuppa?" said Gary. He used his tried-and-tested brand of charm on the social worker to engender an 'I'm an all-right type of guy' persona.

"No, I'm fine, thanks. Where's your wife?"

"Not sure. Must be at her mum's house or out shopping with the kids."

Gary took the opportunity to speak with Nigel. He wanted to take him into his confidence and talk about his troubled marriage.

"Can I ask you something?"

They took a seat on the sofa.

"Fire away."

"Mary hasn't been to see me since I've been in the hospital."

"Okay."

"I was wondering... do you think... ?"

"If it's normal behaviour?" Nigel finished the question.

"Well, yeah."

"Gary, you must remember it's a difficult thing for Mary to overcome – the trauma and all that. When I read your notes, I saw that you had attacked your wife here in the home before admission."

"Yeah, well, I was off my head with drink and speed, you know," said Gary, looking contrite.

"You should stop taking drugs; it can cause mental problems, and speed is very addictive. At its worst, it can kill you."

"Yeah, Dr Sharif told me that, but don't worry, no more, I mean that." Gary sounded like a reformed character. "I wrote to Mary and promised her."

"Good. All I can say is give your wife time. Maybe write to her again and ask her to forgive you. The other thing you must do if you're serious about trying to patch the relationship up is to show her you mean it. The odd bunch of flowers wouldn't go amiss, either. Ladies like to feel loved, wanted and cherished."

Gary held the thought. "You're right."

"Now, do you want a hand with your things?"

"No, I'll be fine. I only need a few clothes and a picture of the family." He pointed to the coffee table. "The local paper's there if you're interested."

As the social worker stood up, showing little interest in the paper, his hospital pager beeped.

"I see you have a phone, Gary; would you mind if I used it? Never know, it could be an emergency."

"Yeah, sure. Help yourself."

That was a stroke of incredible luck for Gary. As the social worker talked on the phone, Gary seized the opportunity and, at a respectable pace, proceeded upstairs to the main bedroom. There, he pulled back a rug, took up a short floorboard to reveal his illegal stash. In a flash, he grabbed a passport and a driving license. He cursed his bad luck having the social worker in tow; even so, he had to work with the situation. Usually, Gary preferred far more time preparing documents to achieve a professional outcome. Despite that, he had to move with alacrity. Placing a passport photograph of himself on the intended page in the blank passport, he grabbed a Foreign Office embossing seal from under the boards and carefully crimped the picture and page. He took a second to admire his work. Later, back at the hospital, away from prying eyes, maybe in the library, he would fix the photograph in place and complete the written portion of the passport.

Pocketing the items, he replaced the board and rug just in time to hear the social worker's footsteps on the stairs. Though

Gary was unaware, in his haste, he had dropped the passport photograph on the floor.

"Will it take much longer, Gary? I need to get back to the office – a bit of an emergency, it seems."

Gary had already made it over to the dressing table, opened a drawer and pretended to rummage.

"No. Just about there, Nige. A few more bits, then we can go." He made great play of searching the drawer for socks and underwear.

"Is that your photograph?" said Nigel, pointing to the floor near Gary.

He turned around from the dressing table to see Nigel making for the photograph. With quick thinking and the speed of an alley cat, he dropped a small travel alarm clock on the floor.

"Let me get that for you," said Nigel. As he picked up the clock, Gary reached for the passport photograph. He knew he had to say something to satisfy Nigel's curiosity.

Holding his thumb over the partially embossed photograph, he held it up. "Yeah, I thought of a little present for Mary. One of the patients in OT can get hold of tiny photo frames, so I thought I would buy one, put my photo in it and give it to Mary as a present, maybe even buy a fancy box and some ribbon." He smiled smugly.

"Now you see, Gary, that's just what I was saying. It's these little things that ladies like. It's a nice, loving gesture that comes from the heart."

The feeling of self-satisfaction in thwarting Nigel pleased him immensely. He had achieved his goal with duplicity and outfoxed Nigel.

The social worker looked around the bedroom, unimpressed. It lacked any sense of organisation. The room was cluttered and uninviting, like the rest of the house, in need of clearance and renovation. Nigel searched his mind for something positive to say, declaring. "They make these houses very... cosy, don't they?" In reality, he thought it was the pits.

Ignoring his remark, Gary held up an away match T-shirt and dropped it into a carrier bag, then added underwear and a picture of the family he had removed from the dressing table. Next, he took a pair of Farah trousers and a corduroy jacket out of the wardrobe.

"I don't think you'll have enough room in that carrier bag," said the social worker, surprised that he didn't have a proper holdall.

"Not a prob." Gary picked up an even bigger carrier bag and, with difficulty, stuffed the remaining clothes into it. "That should do. If I need anything else, maybe we could come back again."

"That's what we're here for, Gary."

They walked out of the bedroom, heading downstairs. Gary stopped.

"Just a minute, almost forgot." Dashing back into the bedroom, he emerged sporting a Liverpool F.C. cap. "I'm dressed proper now. Let's go."

Once every four weeks, Dr Sharif was on call for emergency admissions to his ward. In general, he expected to admit one or two patients in his intake week. Despite that, having worked in many hospitals in his career, he knew admissions didn't pay heed to convention. On-call could be unrelenting, with many patients admitted in one week. The following week, for another consultant psychiatrist, in another area, there might be no emergency admissions at all. Such were the vagaries of mental illness in the community.

A middle-aged man, Samuel, living in sheltered

accommodation, became depressed following the loss of his wife to cancer. His failure to care for himself rang warning bells for a well-intentioned neighbour. Admitted to the unit in an unkempt and confused state, Samuel needed a complete health assessment and involvement with social services. From Gary's perspective, all that Samuel needed was a few tasty meals – that would sort him out.

After the new admission, four patients remained in the ward. The rest had already departed for an extended leave of absence, owing to the temporary closure of the OT department.

Unable to find much to do around the ward, Gary decided a walk would ease his boredom. However, first, he needed permission. Being astute, he knew all was well when in the company of Quentin. Yet to leave the ward alone was a big ask. Only yesterday, he had heard Mr Elwood checking up on him, so he needed to come up with a foolproof idea.

As Samuel sat in the dayroom, Gary chatted and convinced him that a book could help take his mind off his problems. Reminiscent of a child standing outside the headmaster's door, Gary knocked and waited for an answer.

"Come in."

"Would it be okay if I went out for a walk?"

"Umm," said Mr Elwood, unhappy with the request. "Where to?" He wasn't sure if he could trust Gary without a chaperone, and he certainly couldn't spare a member of staff.

"The library's having a sale of books and cassettes, so I thought I'd take a look. I had a chat with the new patient, Sammy, and thought I could get him a book." He tried a smile to see if it helped his cause.

Gary's consideration for the new patient surprised Mr Elwood. That's a turn up for the books, he thought.

At that moment, the office phone rang, upsetting the

smooth running of Gary's near-perfect plan, but in reality, it helped the cause.

"Hello," said Mr Elwood into the phone. "Do you mean now?" It wasn't his usual calm tone. "We've just admitted a patient." He listened, drumming his fingers on the desk, obviously unhappy with the situation. "Well, if it's an emergency... okay, yes, of course, we'll be ready. Sorry, Gary, we've got an emergency coming in, and I must deal with it right away. Okay, you can go to the library. Don't leave the grounds and be back within the hour."

"That's fine, Charge. I'll go to the library and straight back, promise." He thought of adopting the scout's salute as he said promise, but held his weird humour in check.

"Remember what I said." His comment hung in the air as a guarded, woe-betide-you warning.

The plan had worked. "Yes, Charge." Gary smiled with satisfaction. "First, I'll get my jacket. The nurse reckoned it's a bit nippy out there today."

The police brought Arthur in as an emergency admission from town. As cars slowed and stopped to negotiate the traffic junction, they received a blow on their car roofs from Arthur's fist. Dozens of cars had the same treatment before the police became involved. When asked why he had been hitting cars with a hammer-like fist, he replied that they were 'Chariots from Hell' and 'The Devil's Disciples.' Because he was unwilling to go with the police, he was escorted to the admission ward, screaming and shouting obscenities, obviously mentally troubled and in need of help.

SALE
Library books and cassettes today.

The sign, written in bold letters, attracted plenty of interest. Trestle tables laid out with fiction and nonfiction books, along with outdated cassettes, were selling fast. A separate table of free, albeit damaged books, received less interest. Gary was unimpressed, thinking inwardly. What a load of crap.

Unfortunately for Gary, Mr Hall, the librarian, spotted him looking at the books. "Hello, Gary, have you come to take advantage of our wonderful bargains and giveaways?"

"Oh, aye, yeah." Gary flicked through the items, feeling somewhat tetchy. Because of his nerdy nature, Mr Hall always had an irritating effect upon Gary. With this in mind, he wandered off to avoid further contact. Finding a table with used cassettes, he rummaged through the pile and found one by Abba and remembered Quentin's love of the group. Convinced nobody was watching him. He slipped it into his pocket.

"Quentin not with you today?" said Mr Hall, surprising Gary as he appeared from behind a bookcase, almost catching him in the act of thieving.

"Err... no. He's on weekend leave." Gary held up one of the free books. "But I've got a book to keep me company." He gestured to the other side of the library. "Think I'll just take a seat and read."

To appease his boredom, he found computer magazines, took a seat and flicked through them, amazed at the latest innovative ideas from America. In a Walter Mitty mode, he contemplated a thought. Upon discharge, he felt determined to learn more about emerging computer technology – maybe even make it his business to teach. Wow, that would be something; imagine me being a teacher, he thought.

In the background, the library telephone rang. Intuitively, Gary knew that Mr Hall was speaking about him. His telephone voice seemed guarded and at variance with his usual nerdy, befuddled self. The large plate-glass window in front of Gary afforded him a perfect reflection of the librarian as he stood, phone in hand, choosing his words carefully. Mr Elwood was checking up on Gary, and he knew he was right to play it cool. He knew he was extremely smart and could outfox anyone.

"Yes, he is," said the librarian.

Wow, I'm good, thought Gary smugly.

Mr Hall looked over to where he was sitting.

"Yes... Uh-huh... I will... You can rely on me... yes, thank you. Goodbye."

Prepared to prove the charge nurse wrong, Gary took his jacket off and settled down to read his computer magazines. Later, he would practise Quentin's signature and return to the ward within the hour as promised, in time for lunch. "Maybe this will show him I can be trusted," thought Gary, in a happy and more contented frame of mind.

With an uneventful first day at home, Quentin satisfied himself pottering and catching up on household finances. He settled into a comfortable chair to watch the evening news. Eleanor had noticed a relenting of antagonism towards her, but an unsettling atmosphere still hung in the air. Although distressing, she put his behaviour down to the frustrations of recovery from amnesia. All the same, she felt ill at ease.

He did indeed feel hostile towards Eleanor, even more so since he had reacquainted himself with the home. He found it hard to believe she had jeopardised their marriage and social standing with an appalling act of disgusting self-indulgence. He couldn't blame the gardener entirely. In Quentin's estimation, he found Eleanor culpable. The gardener was polite and thorough. She had led *him* on; of this, he had no doubt.

Some of his colleagues at work spoke about romantic affairs outside of their marriages. When hearing of such outrageous goings-on, Quentin had regarded himself as lucky, convinced that he had a happy, trusting relationship with Eleanor. How wrong he was. The trust had gone.

Earlier, he had paused at the main bedroom door, having slept in the spare room for the night. He dwelt on what might have happened between Eleanor and the gardener and felt repulsed, betrayed, and disillusioned by her behaviour. He felt helpless and forlorn. Their marital discord kept bouncing back, overwhelming him. He couldn't bring himself to talk about her behaviour, so he locked it away in his mind.

Similarly, Quentin had noticed with concern that he thought of Eleanor as 'her' or 'she', realising that his implicit love and affection for her were slipping away. Maybe it had gone completely? He wasn't sure. But what to do about it, that was the big question?

"Would you like a drink, darling? Oh, maybe you shouldn't drink whilst taking your medication?" said Eleanor, standing by the drinks cabinet.

"Whether I can or not, I'll have a very large malt," said Quentin with an edge to his voice.

She handed him his malt whisky, which he took without the usual 'thank you, darling.' Shaking his head in disgust at the television, he switched it off as Eleanor sat down with her gin and tonic.

"Damn, depressing news."

"That's not like you to swear, darling. I hope it's not the company you have been keeping in the hospital."

For Quentin, this was too much. He reacted with uncharacteristic anger. All their married life, he had conducted himself in a civilised, courteous manner, which at that moment highlighted the degree of hostility he really felt towards her.

"What do you know about people I've met in the hospital, or anybody, come to think of it?"

"Darling, I was only saying..."

"Well, don't. You say too much. You don't think, Eleanor, that's your problem. You blurt it out and to hell with everybody and anybody."

"But..."

"Just leave it there, Eleanor; for God's sake, just leave it!"

The atmosphere was frosty. Quentin's mood was foul. Eleanor vowed to herself never to mention the hospital again. She picked up a magazine and leafed through the pages at speed. Trying not to let the tiff dominate, she put the magazine back down and tried to push on with routine matters.

"What would you like to do about an evening meal, darling?"

Unconcerned with such matters, he chose to ignore her.

"If you felt up to it, we could meet up with..."

Quentin cut across her with unfettered abruptness. "No! For God's sake, no!"

"Oh!" Eleanor visibly jumped, frightened by Quentin's thunderous response. The evening was destined to produce the very first row ever in the St John's household.

With incredible timing, the front doorbell rang. The welcome caller had unknowingly broken the spiralling tension.

"Joyce, darling. How lovely to see you. How are you this evening?"

"I'm fine. Just thought I'd pop round to see the patient."

She had always admired Quentin for his courteous, polite manner. Maybe in another time, they could have been husband and wife, such were her feelings for him.

"We are in the living room, come through." Eleanor showed

no sign of the heated discord she had encountered just minutes ago.

Joyce bounced into the room looking and sounding bright and breezy, irritating Quentin, although he kept his polite composure.

"Quentin, darling, how are you?" said Joyce. She kissed him on the cheek.

"Take a seat, Joyce. Can I get you a drink?"

"Just a little one, Eleanor, I'm driving," she turned her attention to Quentin. "So, how is the patient?"

"Fine, thank you, Joyce. If you'll excuse me." He stood up to leave the room.

"But darling, Joyce has called to see you."

"Sorry, Joyce. I've got a headache; I'm going to have a lie-down." He held his head to feign discomfort.

Quentin slept in the spare bedroom Friday and Saturday night, returning from his weekend leave of absence Sunday lunchtime.

"Hello, Quentin, you're back early, everything all right?" said Mr Elwood as he tried to gauge his mood.

"Well, I found it a difficult weekend."

"That's okay. It's to be expected. Maybe next weekend will be a bit better," said Mr Elwood, with encouragement.

The prospect of another weekend off filled him with dread. However, the relief he felt at being back in the protected environment of the psychiatric ward, with the people he knew and respected, was palpable.

"Well, put your things away. We've just had lunch, but if you're hungry, I can send up to the kitchen."

"No, I'm fine."

"Oh, there is something I must ask you." Mr Elwood opened

his desk drawer and took something out of an envelope. "The cleaner found this gold chain in the quiet room." He held it up for Quentin to see. "Is it by any chance yours?"

Overwhelming delight engulfed Quentin's face. "Oh, thank heaven for that; it belonged to my mother. I was so upset at the thought of losing such a precious keepsake." On closer inspection, he noticed the crucifix was inexplicably different; it hung upside down on the chain, not delicately suspended but welded to it. He knew this was something that suggested irreverence towards Christianity by some Satanists, Agnostics and cult groups. Reading about it in a newspaper article, he remembered feeling quite shocked at the time.

"That's strange," said Quentin, "it wasn't like that before." He accepted the chain and cross, knowing they were his, yet remained puzzled as to why they should have undergone such a transformation. "Maybe it's been near hot water pipes," said Quentin, looking for a simple answer.

For all that, what he didn't know was that it took 1,064 degrees centigrade for gold to melt. There was no way the heat from a radiator could have melted the gold crucifix and chain.

Walking through the day room, Quentin acknowledged other patients already back from leave. He wondered if their weekends had been as disastrous as his. On the ward's television, sports were playing. Members of the nursing staff showed a polite interest in his return. Quentin found the welcome uplifting and gave an account of his weekend, omitting the unsettling anguish. That said, he confirmed it had been a difficult leave. Staff Nurse Gwyneth Jones came over and made a fuss of him. She insisted on carrying his belongings into the dormitory and helped him lay things out on the bed, painstakingly tidying them away. Hearing the conversation, Gary sauntered into the dormitory.

"Hello, Quent, how's it going?" said Gary, hoping that any animosity towards him from the Ouija incident had subsided.

"Don't ask."

"That bad, eh?"

"Worse than that, Gary."

Quentin looked around the dormitory as if he had been away for weeks, instead of just two days. "Do you know, it's so good to be back?"

"I know. It's been dead here. Oh, I've got something for you," said Gary. Opening his locker, he found the Abba cassette and handed it to Quentin with ceremony. "Err, this is just a little something, and I'm sorry for the other day."

"For me?" said Quentin.

"Sure. It's just one they were selling off in the library. I knew you liked the group, so..."

"Thank you, Gary. It's the nicest thing anybody has done for me in a long time." Quentin hugged Gary, patting him on the back.

He pointed to a track on the cassette with pride. "There's your favourite *Knowing me knowing you* by Abba."

"Thank you so much. When I've put my things away, shall we go for a walk?"

Before he had time to reply, Gwyneth called out.

"Gary, you've got a visitor."

Expecting a visit from Mary in response to his letter, he walked eagerly into the day room to see Madge by herself.

"Hello, Gary."

"Hi, Madge. Where is she?"

They took a seat.

"Mary wanted to come, Gary, but... well... " she struggled for words.

Gary let fly. "I wrote to her. What's the bloody problem

now, for God's sake?"

Hearing a commotion, Mr Elwood left his office to check. With uncompromising authority like a headmaster addressing his pupils, he enquired. "Everything all right, Gary?"

The transformation was immediate; Gary checked his overt behaviour.

"Sorry, Charge... just bad news... I'm okay."

"If you're sure you're all right," repeated Mr Elwood, with authority.

"Yes, I'm okay, fine, thank you."

Madge was grateful for the charge nurse's intervention. Deciding enough was enough, she made her excuses and departed, aware that the worst was yet to come. As Gary walked Madge to the door, she stopped, turned and handed him an envelope.

"What's this, Madge?"

"It's a letter from Mary. She wanted you to understand how she felt, so she wrote you a letter."

"Oh," he looked inquisitively at the letter.

"Well, bye, Gary. I hope everything works out well for you."

"Yeah, see you, Madge." Only then did he focus on her parting remark and wondered what she meant by 'I hope everything works out well for you.'

Gary walked into the dormitory to read the letter as Quentin relaxed on his bed, listening to the Abba cassette on his portable player.

Gary, I've tried so hard to forget what you did to me, but I can't. Even now, I have nightmares thinking about that day. It could happen again, and I can't take that chance.

Because you are never there for us and because I can't take a chance you might harm us again, it would be better if we parted were divorced.

Please try to see it from our point of view and agree so that we can all move on with our lives. Mary.

"The fuckin' cow!" In a rage, he screwed the letter up and threw it across the room. Quentin looked up, aware that out of the corner of his eye, something had flown past him.

"Everything all right?" Quentin pulled his headphones off, resting them around his neck. Gary closed the dormitory door, making sure they couldn't be overheard.

"Well, that's it, the stupid little bitch!" He was so wound up that he found it difficult to speak coherently. He kicked the bedside locker in anger.

"Let's go for a drink." His comment turned out to be an instruction more than an invitation, and one that Quentin felt obliged to go along with.

Mr Elwood had sanctioned walking in the grounds because Quentin, the sensible one, could be trusted to look after Gary and report any problems. Therefore, going out for a walk wasn't a problem. They walked quickly to the pub. Quentin found it challenging to keep up as Gary stormed ahead like the devil possessed, ready to kill anybody who looked at him the wrong way.

Despite it being a chilly Sunday afternoon, trade was brisk. Children played in the enclosed park area at the back of the pub as families ate lunch or watched football on the big screen in the bar. Gary and Quentin found themselves a quiet spot in the beer garden, drinking vodka shots.

"Do you know what that bitch is doing?"

"Sorry," said Quentin, as he tried to follow the drift of Gary's bluster.

"That bitch, Mary."

"Your wife?" said Quentin.

"Yes, her. She wrote to me – wants a divorce. The cow. What about the years when I provided and done my best for her?"

"Oh, dear," said Quentin.

Gary knocked his vodka back. Still agitated, he repeated himself. "Gave her and the kids the best years of my life, and look at what she does."

"Gary. I'm so sorry."

"That's all right, Quent. I'm just so pissed off with the little bitch."

"Anything I can do to help?"

"Yeah, there is something. Buy a quarter bottle from the off-licence, and we'll go for a walk; too many people here earwigging." He looked around the garden in a quarrelsome frame of mind.

The vodka shots worked on Gary's foul mood, mellowing his mind, to the relief of Quentin. They sat in solitude on a bench in the hospital grounds where Quentin and Eleanor had sat three days before. Then, to the annoyance of Quentin, she had declared that she was his 'loving wife.' How incredibly crass it had sounded.

Off in the distance, barges coasted effortlessly along the canal, disappearing out of sight as the water level in the lock fell, allowing barges to negotiate the next lock.

Gary held his alcohol well as he swigged from the bottle. "So, do you reckon your missus loves you if she was doing a line with the gardener?"

"I'm sorry to say, no. It seems she was thinking of herself and nobody else."

"No, same here. Mine's just taken me for all she can get. Selfish little cow." The phrase resonated with Gary, describing his contempt for Mary.

"So what are you going to do about it?" said Gary, as he handed the bottle over.

"Do about it?" said Quentin, worse for wear from vodka.

"Yeah. Do about it?"

"I don't know," said Quentin.

"Well, I've had enough with the whole damn lot. I'm going to end it all." He gave Quentin a look and waited for the imminent reaction.

"Do you know what you've just said?"

"Yeah, end it all." He took the bottle from Quentin for another slug.

"Oh..."

"Sometimes it all becomes too much," he said, handing the bottle back. "It all becomes too much for any man to bear."

Quentin wrestled with the enormity of it. He was easy prey.

"Shall we then?" said Gary, picking up the conversation.

"What, end it all?"

"Yeah, damn right. End it all."

"I'm just astounded that you are thinking like this and would want to," was Quentin's retort. "At times I've considered it, but just as quickly dismissed it."

"Really," a moment elapsed. "Can you swim?" said Gary, hatching a plan.

"No."

"Me neither," said Gary, as he closed in for the kill. "There's a big, deep canal over there," Gary pointed. "Let's walk up to it, stand together as mates and step off. Let's show them how we really feel."

In his alcoholic stupor, Quentin was easy prey. "Well... I... I have nothing else to live for. If Eleanor doesn't love me, then what is there?"

"We'll teach them, Quent, really shove it up them, mate. Show them they can't mess with us."

Five paces from the canal, Gary and Quentin looked intently at each other and then embraced. Seconds passed in contemplative silence. Side by side, they walked with solemnity to the edge of the canal. Like soldiers before the impending battle, they stood and waited, knowing the next few seconds would be their last here on earth.

"Well, mate. It's now or never."

An almighty splash, intensified by the canal's acoustics, resonated around the cottages.

Gary stood alone on the canal side, motionless. He looked around, fearful that the splash might have alerted someone. It hadn't. Showing no signs of remorse, he turned on his heel and walked away. Looking around, he made sure nobody had witnessed the assisted suicide. Even so, if they had, Gary would have broken down in tears and blamed Quentin for talking him into it, declaring that he had stopped at the last minute because of religious feelings. He was smart like that – always ready with an answer, always ready to fool the unsuspecting, whatever the situation.

Back on the ward, Gary headed to Quentin's locker and pocketed the cheque and some banknotes. Cunningly, he left a little money in the wallet to allay any suspicion from falling upon him. He then freshened up, used some of Quentin's mouthwash, and headed to the ward dining room for tea, aware he had to act in his usual manner.

Partway through his meal, Mr Elwood approached. "Have you seen Quentin?"

"No, not for a while, Charge. We went for a walk, and when

we were just outside the ward, Quent stopped and said he had some thinking to do, so he went off by himself."

"I see. It's not like him to be late for a meal. He's usually so punctual."

Gary kept the conversation to a minimum. He didn't want Mr Elwood to suspect he'd been drinking.

"Check the ward for Quentin," was the instruction to the staff. "If you don't find him here, go outside and check the immediate area. He might have had an asthmatic attack."

"Can I help?" said Gary, sounding concerned.

"No, thank you, Gary. You stay here; one patient missing is enough for one day."

TWENTY-FOUR

The night was interminable for Gary. Asleep, he dreamt of Quentin. Awake, his mind re-ran the scenario in which Quentin fell to his death. Moreover, that splash, that odious splash when he fell into the water. Gary couldn't erase the sound from his memory. Whether he perceived himself to be a hardened criminal or not, the thought of Quentin's death played heavily on his mind. It skittered around his brain, popping up time and time again.

At one point during the night, he woke with a start, conscious of someone or something close to his face. Intense fear paralysed him. Hairs stood up on the back of his neck; waves of chilling shivers ran down his spine. Gary lay in a state of heightened fear, not daring to move. He had no knowledge of time but wished for the morning, for people and normality. Minutes passed. Unaware of the eerie presence, he opened his eyes – nothing. He raised his head off the pillow and looked around – nothing. Yet he felt edgy – ill at ease. Was that something moving in the shadows by Quentin's bed? With one swift action, he pulled the covers back, leapt out of bed and ran to the bathroom.

Standing in front of the sink, mind in a whirl, he splashed water over his face, waited and listened. The night light gave little comfort to his bogeyman fear. He held his right hand out as if to confirm what he already knew; it quivered uncontrollably.

Gary caught sight of himself in the mirror. A nebulous,

blurred image of his face moved in waves, as if underwater. The reflection held his gaze. It transmogrified into Quentin's face. The mouth moved in slow time, out of sync with the angry voice.

"You lied to me," protested the aura. "You deceived me, you cheating, good-for-nothing, miscreant wretch. Your turn will come; see if it doesn't."

Gary's blood ran cold. His throat tightened. Terror gripped him. Wild emanations in his mind built to a crescendo. Instead of screaming, which would have brought the night staff running, he was rendered speechless. Grabbing a towel, he rubbed his face vigorously. In essence, he tried to erase the very being of Quentin from his mind. Glancing in the mirror, ready to run, he saw his own visage.

Minutes later, trudging back to bed, he cautiously looked around – all was well. He flopped into bed, exhausted. There were no answers to the questions firing in his troubled mind. How could there be? None of it made any sense. To calm his mind, he focused on the following day's business. From sheer exhaustion, he fell asleep, oblivious to the day's events.

At seven o'clock in the morning, the night staff shook Gary from his slumber. With effort, he sat on the side of his bed, head in hands, feeling like the personification of death. On autopilot, he trudged his way to the bathroom, tentatively looking around, just in case something odd or untoward was about to happen. Twenty-five minutes later, with the benefit of a shave and shower, he felt nearly normal; however, the bags under his eyes told a different story. All he needed was a cup of coffee to prepare him for the day's event, and what an event it would be if all went well.

Following a light breakfast, he changed into his Farah trousers, polished shoes and shirt and put a tie in his pocket. In case staff thought he was overdressed for the OT department, he put his old zip-up cagoule over his corduroy jacket, zipped it up, and checked into Mr Elwood's office. "Any news of Quentin, Charge?"

"No, sorry, Gary, nothing."

"Do you think he might have gone home?" said Gary, as he played a cunning game to deflect any thought of personal guilt.

"Not sure, Gary, but the police are involved now, and I'm sure we will get to the bottom of it pretty soon."

The OT department was sombre. An outpouring of empathy and unease was evident, reflecting the staff's concern over Quentin's bizarre disappearance.

"Still no news of Quentin?" said Sara.

"No, nothing," Gary's subdued voice was befitting the moment. His demeanour screamed worry and concern, but, in reality, his thoughts were working overtime on another agenda, to the point that he found it difficult to control his emotions.

There was just one hour from the end of OT until lunch on the ward. Sometimes he and Quentin had walked before lunch or visited the hospital shop for mints or a paper. He knew that he had just one hour to accomplish his goal before he was missed. If Gary were to succeed, he had to be precise with no room for error, and he knew he had to give a stunning performance. With one chance to get it right, he risked everything.

As he stood in the bank queue, a ten-minute taxi drive away from the hospital in the town centre, Gary did his best to look composed. Adrenaline coursed through his body, creating a mild euphoria. Unbuttoning his corduroy jacket, he made sure his tie, which he had appropriated from Quentin's locker, was straight. Earlier, he had screwed his cagoule up, put it in a carrier bag and stuffed it into a waste paper bin. He hoped the cagoule would still be there later for his return journey to the hospital.

With time on his side, he stood in the queue and mentally practised what he had to say.

Hi, love. Nooo, that's no good, you stupid bastard. Try to talk posh. I would like to cash a cheque. Not bad but a little posher, Gaz. Good afternoon. Yes, that's it. I want to cash a cheque, please. He was beginning to relax. The mark of a good con, according to Gary, was to believe it himself. He felt pretty convinced that he was Mr Quentin St John. This was a branch of his personal bank, and he was confident he could withdraw money. Why shouldn't he make a withdrawal? It was his money when all was said and done.

What if she asks why I want the money? Don't be stupid; she won't. But if she does...? I know, say... say it's for an 'oliday. No... You stupid bastard, a holiday. His challenging thoughts were slowly coming together.

Gary looked around the bank and focused on a list of currency rates. For some reason, Spain registered in his mind. In reality, he knew nothing about travelling abroad; he had never left Merseyside, although he recalled his cousin had been to Fuerteventura years ago with his mates for a stag party. 'Great piss up,' according to him.

"Next... Next!" called the teller, raising her voice.

Gary was thrust back into reality; he focused his mind. This was his moment; a first-rate performance was essential.

"Good afternoon." He pushed the £2,000 cheque towards the cashier. "I would like to cash this cheque, please."

She looked at the cheque and appraised Gary.

"Have you any identification, please, Mr St John?"

Gary's work on a forged driving licence and passport would

be under scrutiny; he hoped his work was good enough. The paper driving licence was easy to copy, but the passport demanded much more time and skill, and he had put in the time to make it look good. He hoped all that time spent on the ward and in the library would pay off. His proficiency was about to be tested.

Although he felt very confident, luck also played a part. His mate, Tricky Ricky, caught out by bad luck, was in the process of cashing somebody else's Giro. Regrettably, for him, the cashier at the post office recognised the person whose cheque it was; with rapidity, she alerted her manager, who in turn contacted the police. He was quickly arrested.

"Driving licence okay?"

"Anything else?" queried the teller.

"Yes, I have my passport with me."

"Thank you. I'll look at both."

As she scrutinised the passport and compared the photograph with Gary, he engaged her in conversation, trying to break down barriers using well-honed street psychology.

"You can't be too careful."

She looked at him and smiled. "I wish everybody were as understanding."

"No, I really understand. You've got a job to do, and you're looking after my interests," said Gary. He complimented himself on such a nice touch.

She handed the cheque back to him. "Can you sign the back, please, Mr St John?"

If he could hold his nerve and offer a good signature, he was home and dry. "Yes, of course," he chattered away like a long-lost friend.

"We're all going on vacation." He felt particularly pleased using the word 'vacation,' a word he'd heard from one of his mates at the club. Maybe the thought of getting away with the family for a holiday was, in reality, a conscious desire.

"Anywhere nice?"

"Yes, Spain."

"Oh, how lovely. Do you need any Spanish Pesetas or travel insurance?"

"Umm. No, thanks. I leave that to the wife."

"Very good. Would tens be okay, Mr St John?"

"That's fine."

"We've had a run on the twenties this morning. If you needed larger notes and could come back later."

"No, tens are fine," he smiled, through gritted teeth. In reality, he was thinking, just give me the money, you silly bitch. Do your job and give me the money.

She handed the envelope over.

"Thank you," said Gary, tucking the envelope into his jacket pocket. He turned to walk away, aware he had to move with haste if he were to complete his deadline and get back to the ward. Travelling to the bank, he had already worked on the story to tell his mates in the pub. He knew they would be intrigued to hear all the details, particularly Gary speaking posh. His street credibility was about to go through the roof. He reached the door and was about to grab the handle.

"Just a minute, Mr St John!"

People in the queue stared. Gary froze, suspecting the worst. Looking at the door, he wondered if he should make a dash for it; however, he had second thoughts. Turning around, he smiled.

"You nearly forgot your passport and licence," said the teller.

"Silly me, I really *do* need that holiday, don't I?" He felt incredibly smug with his quick retort and made a mental note of the line to impress his buddies.

Aware that time was tight, he took a taxi to his local bank to complete the business. Elated with his achievement, he glanced heavenwards. "Thanks, Quent, my old mate. I couldn't have done it without you. Although five thousand would have been better."

One final taxi ride to the hospital would mean Gary had pulled off his finest coup, and with ten minutes to spare. He felt euphoric, a far cry from the early hours of the morning, when he woke from a nightmare, experiencing all kinds of weird happenings. With a positive outlook on life, thanks to £2,000, he believed that last night wasn't anything other than an overindulgence in alcohol mixed with hospital medication that had led to an atrocious dream. In recent years, Gary had experienced many weird dreams and many hallucinatory happenings connected with drug abuse. That being the case, he rationalised that maybe last night was just a flashback. Yes, that's it, he thought.

With the dastardly deed done, he headed back through the hospital grounds in the direction of the ward. Putting his hands in his pockets, realisation dawned. He still had the incriminating evidence and had to get rid of it, and fast. In the distance, he saw the industrial side of the hospital. An idea formed in his mind. Boilerhouse – maintenance – porters – incinerator. At the entrance to the boiler house, he saw a locked door with INCINERATOR written on it. Nearby were plastic bags in a huge wheelie bin, on which was written FOR INCINERATION.

"You little ripper," said Gary. If he had been better educated, he might have thanked the Roman goddess *Fortuna* for her intervention in the crime and cited, 'Fortune favours the bold.' Gary, without a doubt, had been bold and very fortunate.

He opened a bag, at once recoiling from the putrid smell. He retched. Unperturbed and determined to press on, he took the passport and driving licence, ripped them and tried to push them into the bag. With effort, he managed to hold the bag open for a second or two before he retched again. Next was the cheque guarantee card. He tried to snap it in half, but it merely bent. "Oh, what the hell." He threw the card in the bag, resealed it and buried the bag in the bin for incineration.

Passing the fishpond, he stopped to wash his stinking hands in the pond. However, a passing, overzealous porter saw Gary with his hands in the water.

"Hey, you! Get out of that pond!"

With lightning speed, Gary fired back a rejoinder. "No, it's okay, mate, I saw a bit of plastic in the pond and wanted to get it out. Not good for the fish, you know."

"Oh... okay. Sorry, I thought you were messing about."

How ironic it all seemed to Gary to have completed his mission in skulduggery, maybe to have fallen at the final hurdle. He mused on his earlier thoughts about a well-planned job and smiled at the near-lousy luck.

Making sure his cagoule was zipped up, concealing his smart clothing, Gary wandered back onto the ward. He would change into something more comfortable before lunch.

Mr Elwood caught Gary's attention. "A minute of your time before you have lunch, Gary? I was beginning to think you weren't coming back."

"Oh, I didn't know you wanted me, Mr Elwood. I went for a walk and got some mints from the shop." He took a packet of mints out of his pocket, which he'd bought days before. As if to prove a point, he held them up, feeling pleased with himself.

Entering the office, Gary looked around to see two police officers. He froze on the spot. Blood drained from his face. He recalled the first time he was arrested at the age of sixteen for handling stolen goods. Then he was young and foolish, thinking he was invincible and above the law. Watching The Sweeney on TV, he believed only the big crims were ever apprehended.

Mr Elwood looked solemn. A strange sense of foreboding hung in the air.

"I know you're an acquaintance of Quentin, and I'm sorry to have to tell you this, Gary... Quentin has been found dead."

The Royal Academy of Dramatic Arts (RADA) would have been enthralled with his performance. Gary drew on many encounters from the past where he played the fool or became Mr Charming or Mr Sincere. He was proud of his ability to squirm out of the most impossible situations and hoodwink anyone. After all, Gary had served his apprenticeship. He was a successful professional.

"Oh my God, no, not Quent," he flopped into a vacant chair. "What happened?" As he queried the circumstances of the death, his face took on an intense look of solemnity.

"We don't know the full details right now, but I can tell you, he was found in the canal."

"I can't believe it, poor Quent dead," he shook his head in disbelief, feigning a moment of agonised shock. "But he was getting better, wasn't he?"

Mr Elwood saw a side of Gary he didn't think possible. "The police would like to have a word with you, as you could have been the last person to see him alive. Is that all right?"

Gary looked to the policeman sitting by him. "No probs – poor Quent. What a shock. I can hardly believe it," said Gary, thinking about his criminal record. Bollocks, I hope they don't check me out. The shit'll really hit the fan. Time to turn on the charm, he thought.

With Mr Elwood present, the police officially interviewed

Gary.

"You'll understand, Mr Lowe, nobody is being accused of anything. We just want to establish the last movements of Mr St John in the hospital."

"Yeah, sure, anything I can do to help," said Gary, never suspecting he would ever be asked to assist the police. He quite enjoyed the Mr Nice Guy persona. Added to his performance at the bank, this was turning out to be a phenomenal day.

"How long had you known Mr St John?"

Gary's answer was nicely paced; he took a few seconds for effect before he answered. "Well, me and Quent..."

"Quent?" queried the officer.

"Quentin," affirmed Gary. "Me and Quent met on the ward for the first time about two weeks ago."

"Did he ever talk to you about his personal life or circumstances?"

"No... Not really," his mood changed, befitting the gravity of the moment. "I knew he was married and worked in Southport, but that's about all he said on that matter. He had a memory problem, you know."

The officer smiled. "And did Mr St John ever talk to you about suicide?"

"Who, Quent, suicide?" he shook his head once again in disbelief. "No, certainly not," Gary showed mild indignation at the suggestion. "He was getting better... suicide? No, never." He gave it a moment. "Are you saying he committed suicide?"

The officer ignored the question and continued. "So, can you tell me what you and he did on the day Mr St John went missing?"

Gary enjoyed his performance; he took a moment to add theatre. "Let me see," he put a hand to his chin, taking a few more seconds. "Well... Quent came back on Sunday after dinner. I had a visitor, and after that, we went for a walk in the grounds."

"What time would that be?"

He pondered. "About three o'clock, ish. I remember it well because I had a visitor; bad news, you know."

The officer cut his rambling short. "How did he appear at that time?"

"He was a little quiet, but Quent was a deep thinker and was often quiet. I don't think his weekend leave went too well, but he was okay." Gary dropped in a possible cause for suicide when he mentioned the troubled leave of absence; Mr Elwood would confirm this to the officer later.

"You became very good friends in the hospital, Mr Elwood tells me?"

"Yes, I suppose so... I never thought about it like that, but yes, I suppose we were friends."

With the office door closed, Gary felt hot and a little faint due to the extra clothing. He realised that if the interview didn't finish soon, he might collapse and, in so doing, be found wearing extra clothing that would appear inappropriate for the OT. Searching questions would be asked, and who knows where it would all lead.

"And that afternoon?"

"Well, as I said, we went for a stroll. After about ten minutes, we..." he pretended to search his mind. "Oh yes, that was it; we sat by the pond and looked at the fish. I'd had enough and wanted to get back to the ward, so Quent walked part of the way with me and then decided to walk on further so he could do some more thinking. He even said, 'See you later.'"

"And was that the last time you saw him?"

Gary stared at the wall. In keeping with the clever act, he rubbed his eyes and held back tears.

At school, he had joined the drama club, more to avoid lessons than for the love of dramatics, although, surprisingly, he enjoyed the theatrical bit, learning many skills. If ever he needed a focus for sorrow, Gary concentrated on his mum's death. She died tragically in a car accident. When he thought deeply about her death, he became emotional.

"I'm sorry... It's terrible... No more Quent." His chin quivered, tears welled, and his head dropped.

The policeman looked at Mr Elwood, who nodded with reassurance.

"Okay, just one final question, Mr Lowe. Do you know if Mr St John drank while he was a patient in the hospital?"

Gary accepted a tissue from Mr Elwood, wiped his eyes and focused on the question. "Who, Quent... drinking? No... I don't see how he could; he was a patient here in the hospital like me, here for treatment."

"Well, thank you, Mr Lowe, you've been most helpful. I'm sorry if this has distressed you, but we have to investigate such matters thoroughly. This is a very serious matter."

"Yes, I understand that, officer." He looked at Mr Elwood. "Charge, could I skip OT this afternoon? I don't quite feel up to it with the news of Quentin and all that. I need to sit quietly and think about things."

Gary rubbed his eyes again. "Poor Quentin, I can hardly believe it."

TWENTY-FIVE

The staff changeover at eight o'clock saw a new staff nurse, Carmel O'Shaughnessy, along with Tony Holmes, a permanent member of the night staff. As usual, the ward routine ran its course without any problems. Patients watched television, read, chatted or played cards. Concluding supper and medication, they drifted off to bed, with one or two night owls encouraged to retire. At eleven o'clock, lights were dimmed, and silence descended upon the ward.

Sitting in the dayroom with a cup of coffee, Tony explained the ward layout and ran through the day report, standard ward procedures, and patients' case notes. This prompted a conversation about the recent death of Quentin.

Tony referred to the ward records. "Quentin St John was admitted from Southport General Hospital with amnesia. Investment bank manager – slightly overweight – suffered from asthma. We never had a minute's problem with him, and he was making reasonable progress, especially after regression therapy. He made great inroads into his physical health by walking in the hospital grounds with a fellow patient. He went home on weekend leave, returned just after lunch on Sunday, went for a walk in the hospital grounds and then went missing. Sadly, the police found his body in the canal. Gary, a fellow patient who walked with Quentin, was the last person to see him alive on Sunday."

"I'll bet that was a shock for him to hear of Quentin's death," said Carmel.

"Certainly was, and I don't think he's coping with it too well. We'll check in on him later – last night he was very restless."

"And how about Quentin's family?" enquired Carmel.

"He had a wife but no children; according to Mr Elwood, she was completely devastated... Okay, and now for the ward routine."

The second night following Quentin's death didn't come any easier for Gary; he tossed, turned and mumbled in his sleep. At one point, he sat up in bed in a cold sweat, looked around and put his head back down on the pillow.

Unable to sleep, he got up an hour before breakfast and decided to shave and wash. The morning's routine helped divert his troubled mind. With a burgeoning hunger, he considered egg and bacon for breakfast.

Shaving equipment on the sink, towel around his neck, Gary splashed his face with hot water. Standing in his underpants and vest, he wasn't a pretty sight, as Mary, his wife, had often commented, though, on an all-male ward, it was acceptable. Still bleary-eyed from his poor night, he found it difficult to focus on the mirror; his reflection was indistinct. Paying little attention and in automatic mode, he squirted shaving foam in his hand and applied it to his face. Unknown to Gary, all hell was about to break loose.

A lone fly landed on the mirror, which was unusual, given that, in the cold of late October, flies wouldn't usually be around in numbers. He continued his shave. A second and a third fly settled on the mirror, gaining Gary's attention. Unperturbed, yet curious, he continued his shave. Even so, he paid more heed when flies continued to appear out of nowhere, landing on the mirror. The seething mass swathed the mirror in a black murkiness. The *en suite* took on a disturbing depth of repulsiveness. He jumped back from the basin in shock, repelled by the horrific, black swarm.

The writhing mass buzzed and moved around the mirror with a sense of purpose. Incredibly, they began forming into three distinct areas on the mirror. The surreal spectacle, although abhorrent, was mesmerising; he couldn't break his gaze. In what seemed a lifetime and yet mere seconds, the flies formed to spell the word *DIE*. Gary stood transfixed, unable to break his gaze, spellbound by the flitting beat of their wings. They flapped in unison, producing a hypnotic, pulsating sound that entered the deepest recesses of his mind, like an endless mantra, a hypnotic, primordial sound. He seemed incapable of movement – rooted to the spot. The rhythm increased in volume to a thunderous crescendo. Protecting his ears with his hands, he closed his eyes tight shut and stepped back, stopping when his back met the shower cabinet. His heart raced out of control. His breathing escalated violently. He felt giddy – close to collapse. As if that wasn't bad enough, in his mind, he felt a sudden hatred, anger and rage. In that instant, he was ready to kill. He saw rivers of blood, heard screams and smelt the most putrid of smells. A hand gripped his shoulder. He squealed with fright.

"Are you all right?" said Tony.

"Erm... it..." Gary's mind was blank, as if brought out of a hypnotic trance prematurely. He looked around, trying to make sense of his surroundings.

Tony didn't spot the malevolent, black shadow, skulking in the corner of the *en suite*.

Gary got his wish: egg and bacon, served up with coffee and toast. It all looked very appetising; even so, after the morning's shaving experience, his earlier enthusiasm for breakfast had waned. Fellow patients in the dining room ate and chatted. Gary sat alone with his thoughts.

Impassively, he buttered toast. With his knife and fork, he placed the fried egg on the toast and coated it with tomato sauce. Stan and his friend, Harry, had finished their breakfasts, cleared the table and came over to talk.

"Terrible business about Quentin," said Stan.

"I know. For the life of me, I don't know how he ended up in the canal. Poor Quent," said Gary.

Harry, who hadn't known Quentin at all well, commiserated with Gary. "You were quite close, weren't you, Gaz?"

"Suppose so. Just goes to show, Harry. As my mate from the club always says, 'Here today, gone tomorrow.'"

"He's not wrong there, Gaz."

Exhausting the correct and proper platitudes, Stan and Harry moved on.

"See you later in the OT, Gaz."

"Yeah, see you later," said Gary. He took a sip of his coffee and wondered what Mary and the children were doing at that moment.

"Nearly finished, Gary?" Gwyneth broke his daydream. "I need to take the dishes to the kitchen."

"Yeah, just about there. Tell you what, take the other dishes, and I'll bring mine when I've finished."

He sliced his egg on toast and, with a bit of runny yolk, took a mouthful. Then something strange happened. Without warning, his left hand that held the fork became tremulous. He stared at his errant hand as if it were in some way disconnected from his body – acting independently. His wrist was bent, the fork pointed towards his face, moving closer and closer. Dropping his knife, he grasped his left hand to hold the fork at bay. It was becoming a battle of wills. A reddened and contorted face registered the physical effort required to maintain the impasse. He stood up to gain purchase over the errant hand. It inched closer and closer. Gary saw the tomato and egg-covered tines of the fork up close, about to kebab his eyeball. At the moment when the unthinkable was about to happen, a mere two inches from his eye, the hand relaxed, became normal, and was back under his control. Whether it was because of elevated blood pressure with the effort of exertion or a mere coincidence wasn't certain; however, blood trickled from his nose. He grabbed a serviette to stem the flow. That was enough for Gary. Like the devil possessed, he raced out of the dining room into the *en suite* to splash his bloodied nose and face with cold water.

Making a final sweep of the dining room, Gwyneth found Gary's dishes still on the table. She rolled her eyes. "Typical."

Gary's disturbing behaviour in the en suite that morning was brought to the consultant's attention.

"Staff tell me you had a strange experience this morning in the bathroom. Would you like to tell me what happened?"

"It's nothing; I just had a bad night," said Gary, conscious that Dr Sharif wasn't aware of the fork incident at breakfast. He would not divulge any strange happenings, for fear of racking up more trouble for himself.

"Horrible dreams, that's all."

At all costs, Gary wanted to work towards his discharge. He needed to be viewed favourably for discharge soon; otherwise, he may not be released this side of Christmas. He did not want to be pulling crackers or singing carols in the hospital.

"Have you been hearing voices or seeing things?"

"No, I'm just tired. I had a bad night," said Gary, visibly bothered and fidgety.

"It's okay if you have; you can tell me about it, and then I can help you."

"I just had a bad night," insisted Gary.

He sat in silence while the consultant recorded his findings in the notes. "Okay, Gary, I'll see you tomorrow. If you have any more problems, please talk to the staff or me. We are here to help you. Do you understand that?"

"Yes," said Gary, reluctant to talk. Above all, he was keen to exit the office and forget the incident.

Attendance in the OT department was in body, not in mind. Hours later, Gary ate very little for lunch. In fear of a knife or fork attack that might exact revenge upon him, he opted for soup and bread floats. The spoon he used to eat his soup and bread could not cause him any damage, could it? Lunch over, he sat in a dream in front of the television, oblivious to any of the programmes. At the consultant's instruction, the staff kept a wary eye on him. Therefore, it seemed entirely innocent when a fellow patient asked him if he wanted to play dominoes. Although a little quiet and withdrawn, Gary entered into the spirit of the game, requiring the occasional prompt to play his domino. Staff relaxed and chatted with other patients, unaware of the growing evil that was unfolding.

The patient sat opposite Gary, had just made a move when a fly landed on a domino, flitting and circling most bizarrely. Waving it away, the patient waited for Gary to play his next domino.

"What?" said Gary, staring at the patient.

"I didn't say anything."

"Yes, you did. You said, 'Give it back.'"

"No, I didn't; what are you talking about, idiot?"

Gary stood. "You said give it back, I heard you, you fuckin' evil moron!"

Staff nearby looked on at the unfolding kerfuffle, ready to intervene. It was quickly becoming a volatile situation, critical enough to spark violence.

"I haven't opened my mouth, Psycho." The patient stared at Gary in disbelief.

Nurses tried to intervene and gain Gary's attention to talk him down. However, in his fury, he didn't hear anybody but continued to eye the patient with contempt, knowing he was as guilty as sin of lying. The confrontation grew as his domino partner stood to face up to Gary. A most bizarre event accompanied the patient's following few words. As he ranted, a cloud of flies emerged from his mouth. The room became jarringly silent – distant. The movement continued, yet all sound ceased, as if watching a black-and-white silent movie. Flies in their hundreds took flight, forming the equivalent of a dust devil, circling, soaring. Gary, compelled by the phenomenon, looked in different directions as he followed the mini-tornado's path. However, he became aware of one solitary fly buzzing around his head, freaking him out. The buzzing stopped. Then a strange and frightening squeaky voice echoed in his ear. "Die a painful death."

With shock and fear, he screamed. "The fly... The fly spoke to me!" Looking around in a panic, he saw flies covering the domino table in a thick, writhing, black mass. Without a second's thought, Gary upturned the table in a rage. It flew through the air, missing fellow patients by a whisker and smashed into a display cabinet. Shards of glass and ornaments littered the floor.

Nurses leapt into action, subduing Gary with incredible difficulty. A repeat of his hostile admission was unfolding.

Dr Sharif excused himself from an interview and hurried out

of his room to witness bedlam in the dayroom. Gary continued to scream as he was carried bodily to the emergency side room.

"It was Quentin. He's a fly. I heard him. He's a fly," said Gary, letting his overt behaviour rip unabated for all to see and hear.

"Okay, Gary," said Dr Sharif with patience. "It will be okay. We'll help you."

"No, really, it's Quentin. He's here. He spoke to me. I heard him."

Following the commotion, all that was necessary was for the staff to calm the other patients and tidy up the mess. Stan's take on the uproar was that 'Gary should be in a bloody madhouse.'

With time, Gary settled in the side room, following a tranquilising injection.

"Keep a close eye on him. He should start to settle soon," said Dr Sharif, having seen such outbursts many times before in his career. Except that sometimes the outcome wasn't always as imagined.

Four days of increased medication and confinement to the side room brought about a state of calm in Gary's mental condition. In that time, he made very little sense. Being confused and disoriented, he rambled frequently and required assistance with eating and personal hygiene. Then, on the fourth day, he asked one of the nurses, "Where am I?" From then on, he rallied and took an interest in life and his surroundings.

Gary's mind pushed to the extremes of normality, bounced back to overcome the recent traumatic episode, much to the surprise of everyone. With Gary feeling much better, Dr Sharif interviewed him in the consulting room. He glanced through the notes. "Well, Gary, are you feeling any better today?"

"Much better, thanks, Doc, but I don't really know what happened."

"To put it simply, you had a breakdown. It's difficult to say how or why. Suffice to say, the medication helped, and here you are back again in the real world, feeling and looking a good bit better."

"Yeah," said Gary, glad to be out of the side room, "I do feel a lot better. Can I sit in the day room with the others, err, sorry, what's your name?" Dr Shariff looked to the charge nurse and nodded.

"Yes, I think that would be good for you to be in the dayroom and chat with other patients. My name is Dr Sharif. Try not to worry about your memory. It's just the effect of the medication. It will come back. Now, let's look ahead and be positive."

Gary stood up, walked to the door and turned. "Is Quentin really dead?"

"I'm sorry to say he is."

"Oh... I wasn't sure," said Gary, as he left the office, accompanied by a nurse.

"It would seem Quentin's death has had a huge impact on him," said Dr Sharif.

"I'll say it has. I feel quite sorry for him," said Mr Elwood, "but I still don't understand why Quentin took his life; he was making such good progress."

"I know what you are saying, but in the world of psychiatry, Mr Elwood, anything can happen, and often it does. However, the causative factor for Quentin's death, I believe, will remain a mystery to us all," said Dr Sharif, shaking his head, struggling with the inexplicable question.

TWENTY-SIX

A week after Quentin's death and following four days' confinement to the ward, Gary's condition improved to the point where he was transferred back into the four-bedded dormitory. He mingled with other patients, cracked the occasional joke and joined in with the ward routine. Treatment had worked. If his current progress continued, he would attend OT in a few days. Eating and interacting well, talkative and responsive, he showed renewed interest in life, which didn't go unnoticed.

At about eleven o'clock, one of the ward nurses, Oliver, accompanied Gary for a walk in the hospital grounds. It was thought beneficial for him to take light exercise before lunch and engage in some mental and physical stimulation. Dressed in warm, comfortable clothes, sporting his beloved red Liverpool cap, all indications for Gary's recovery were positive.

"Sure, you don't mind walking me around like this, Olly?"

"Not at all; besides, it's nice to get off the ward for a bit of a break and stretch the legs."

"Quent liked walking around like this."

"Did he?"

"Yeah, we'd talk about all sorts – his life, my life, work, music, everything."

As they headed to the hospital shop to buy Gary a sports paper and some mints, he nodded to people he knew and to some he didn't. With a mint in his mouth and one for Oliver, paper rolled up in his back pocket, they walked in the fresh morning air. The pace was slow yet steady. Gardeners busied themselves, sweeping up leaves and tending the garden borders. Gary acknowledged them as he walked. There was a noticeable brightness in his demeanour as he trudged through autumnal leaves strewn across the footpaths. He kicked the occasional pine cone for good measure. Life went on at its usual pace, and he felt good to be out strolling. Two grey squirrels scampered up a tree trunk and across branches, with the agility of young athletes. The walk was a tonic, and it showed in Gary's face.

As they meandered further on past the office block, in sight of the canal, the conversation changed once again to that of Quentin.

"One of the patients said Quentin committed suicide. How crazy is that, Olly?"

"Doesn't seem to make sense, does it?" said Oliver, tactfully. He hoped to avoid any more conversation on the subject that sent Gary over the top.

"No, doesn't make any sense. I mean, he was getting better, wasn't he?"

"He was," confirmed Oliver.

Sauntering along a narrow lane in the hospital grounds, bordered by lawns and shrubs, they approached a T-junction. Gary pointed to the canal lane leading to staff cottages.

"Can we walk down there, Olly?"

This was a difficult call for Oliver; he would have preferred to avoid the area at all costs. Likewise, he didn't want to make it appear to be a big deal – a forbidden area. Had Gary forgotten that this was the area where Quentin took his final steps? Whatever Gary's thinking, Oliver thought it prudent to avoid the vicinity if possible. The aim of the walk was to take light exercise, not to confront his past demons.

"Let's just take a few minutes here." Oliver pointed to the

seat where Quentin had sat with Eleanor. "Just for a few minutes," he reiterated. "And then I think we should be getting back to the ward."

"They should call this 'Quentin's place,'" said Gary in a strange, profound mood. "He loved the hospital grounds and often talked about gardening stuff."

Oliver steered him away from the subject. "How about you, Gary? You have family, I believe."

"Oh, yeah, big style, I've got two great kids – lovely little monsters." A moment of reflection followed. "Hasn't been too good with Mary, my wife, though; can't say I blame her. I can be a snaggy bastard at times, although I don't mean to be; it's just..."

About to regale Oliver with more about his family, he noticed something strange. The shoulder pad of his jacket, without explanation, bulked up. Gary continued to stare at his shoulder.

Although it hadn't happened in a while, he thought he might have been hallucinating – encountering a 'flashback.'

Abusing illegal drugs in the past, he had experienced many hallucinations, some incredibly mind-blowing, some comical with shapes, colours and hues that drifted in and out of his crazy mind. Even so, hallucinations could be nasty, evil and disturbing, an undesired effect of some illegal drugs.

Sitting next to him, Oliver was unaware of anything untoward. He was about to call time and head back when Gary was wrenched from his seat, leaping forward by four feet and landing in an upright position. Mistakenly, Oliver thought he was acting the fool.

"Gary, stop messing. Come on now, it's time for us to get back to the ward."

"I'm not doing anything. Help me? Help?" shrieked Gary,

having no control over what was happening to him. With immense unseen power, Gary's body careered down the lane towards the canal, a few feet at a time, in short, jerking motions.

Despite shock and fear, Oliver's first consideration as a nurse was to his patient. He chased after him along the lane. "Gary, stop!"

"Help me; I can't," he shrieked.

With effort, Oliver caught up, grabbed him by his arm and held on tight. One hundred and fifty yards from the canal on the approach road to the cottages, they stood in confused horror at the inexplicable, crazy experience.

"What was that?" said Oliver, shaking uncontrollably. No answer was forthcoming because no one could have explained such an unbelievable phenomenon. "Gary, are you okay?"

Without warning and before he could reply, a powerful force hit Oliver midway in the chest. He flew back, hitting the ground with a sickening thud, stretched out where he fell, motionless.

As before, the unthinkable happened. Gary flew forward a few feet at a time toward the canal; he screamed and implored whatever it was to stop. Nevertheless, the power was uncompromising; it was out to get Gary.

"Hhhhelp?" screamed Gary.

Merely a week ago, he had walked this very same path to the canal with Quentin, farewelled his friend, and it seemed, prepared for a double suicide. But then he watched on as Quentin fell to his death. Thereafter, he walked away, leaving his one-time pal for dead. He had lied, cheated and forsaken a fellow human being simply for self gain.

A sense of impending doom permeated Gary's mind; it was becoming apparent. "Noooo! Please don't. I'm sorry, it was all a mistake. I didn't know what I..."

Day turned into darkness. The green of the grass and shrubs, the blue of the sky, and the contours of the cottages changed in a flash. In its place, a dark cathedral-like immenseness stretched about him as far as the eye could see. Pitiful light seeped from cavities, arches and passageways, giving a mere impression of size, form and structure of the colossal cavern. Underfoot, a well-trodden path, littered with debris and bones, led in and downwards to a vast emptiness. In the distance, screams pervaded the stench-laden air. He made an instant neural connection with the Ouija session days ago when he had heard the self-same screams.

A creature the size of a Yeti mercilessly carried Gary by the scruff of his neck. With his feet, some distance from the ground, Gary's legs swung from side to side, like the pendulum of a clock. At times, the rhythm was broken, as his feet or legs hit a protruding jagged rock along the pathway, which only added to the already unbelievable pain. He squealed in agony, only to be punished by a violent shake from the abomination. With increasing pain, he learnt to keep quiet and pray that the nightmare would end soon. The thing changed its grip. Gary felt the pincer holding the back of his collar and the skin of his neck tightening. It inflicted untold agony as he bounced along at the mercy of his captor. The putrid stench of rotting corpses became unbearable.

Onward the creature loped, striding towards a glimmer of greenish light in the distance. With gravity, the weight of Gary's body caused the skin, muscles and collar around his neck to tighten, compromising his oxygen levels. He panicked, fighting for breath; his eyes felt as if they were about to pop out of their sockets. In the distance, he heard the sound of running water. The air grew heavy with moisture. Cold droplets from above landed on his face and head, reviving him somewhat. After a moment's hesitation, without movement, the monstrosity shuffled on a downward path and turned to the right and then left. With every step, the reverberation of water became louder until the noise became unbearable; even so, bear it he must.

His thoughts were with Mary and the children. Oh, how he wished he could be with them. He wanted so much to put his arms around them, to hear them talk, to love his family. But, it was out of the question. In that moment of realisation, he knew he had thoughtlessly played life according to *his* rules. All he wanted was just one more chance to show he could change. Yet the hope, the love, the wanting, came to an abrupt end as the abomination stopped and turned Gary around to face his grotesque countenance. If fear could kill, then the sight of this monster would surely end Gary's life. The huge compound, mosaic-like eyes with a multiplicity of mini prisms scrutinised Gary's fear-riven face. Antennae projecting from the fly-like head brushed Gary's face; he grimaced with horror. The sucking proboscis, the mouthpart of the abomination, extended forward, covering the whole of Gary's face, closing off his airway. He struggled for breath, went limp and unconscious. The grotesque monster was playing with the insignificant, pathetic being held before him in his pincers. It viewed the weak, lifeless body with contempt. The depraved, sadistic mind searched for more entertainment. Proboscis retracted, it shook life back into Gary, ready to continue the suffering. A jagged, pointed rock nearby made a perfect, sharp protrusion to hang Gary, just like meat in a slaughterhouse. The back of his collar proved ideal for suspending his entire body. Thankfully, it eased the pressure on his throat; his clothing took most of the strain, enabling him to suck in deep gulps of life-giving air. Even so, presumably because of rough handling, he felt a searing pain down his back. Most probably, the jagged rock had gouged his skin as he was almost skewered on the sharp, rocky projection.

The enormous, inhuman eyes bore deep into Gary's soul, unleashing a profound, unimaginable terror. It gratified the creature who emitted high-pitched whines of pleasure. I – Kill – You constantly played in Gary's mind, like a needle reaching the end of a vinyl record. I – Kill –You, I – Kill –You, I – Kill – You. It permeated his soul with such intensity and force that he shrieked in sheer terror. "Nooo, stop." His voice trailed off as he blathered and wept. The evil entity knew he had crushed Gary. His will had been broken.

A quiet moment gave way to searing pain. He looked down from his rocky entrapment to witness a grotesque, hairy claw dragged across his chest. Blood oozed from the deep gouges. In agony, Gary remembered the scratches on Quentin's chest after their Ouija session. Presumably, the missing crucifix, ripped from Quentin's neck, thrown away with vile hatred, was a symbol that enraged the entity. This confirmed it; the creature must, without a doubt, be the anti-Christ, the devil from the depths of Hell.

Then all became clear to Gary. When his mother died, he had a crucifix and the date of his mother's death tattooed across his chest, representing his depth of feeling and loss. Tears rolled down his cheeks as maternal love flooded his mind, resurrecting deep emotions. As if mocking, the monstrosity touched his face with a hairy pincer and rubbed. The sensation was unbearable. Gary screamed again, but screaming could not help him; he was fated.

Unhooked from the rocky pinnacle, Gary fell into a heap on a flat, rocky promontory. With impatience, the entity prodded him to stand. Like a newborn lamb, his trembling legs barely supported him.

For a moment, he thought it was all over; maybe he would

be set free. Nevertheless, the entity had other appalling ideas. A thud in his back propelled Gary forward. He kept moving, just to put distance between him and the ungodly being. Another step, and Gary was in free fall. His body hurtled downward, hitting the occasional protruding rock, causing him more agony, then a lifeline. By sheer reaction, he had thrown out a hand and mysteriously caught onto something flexible – substantial. Had his brush with the dark and disturbing evil come to an end?

A suspended tyre hugging a damp, slimy wall – protection for barges as they travelled along narrow canals- became his lifeline. Gary's vision cleared. He was hanging, gripping hold of a tyre in the canal. His very existence hung in the balance on the integrity of a balding car tyre. He screamed for all he was worth. A single hand thrust over the side of the canal could save him. However, he experienced a downward pull on his body. He was losing his grip. The sensation of hands clamped around his ankles – pulling – determined.

"Please! Quickly! I can't hold on!" bellowed Gary, for all he was worth. His fingers, one by one, lost their grip. "Please, someone, anyone, save me."

He lost the battle; his fingers slipped from the tyre, his body plummeted, hitting the water with a resounding splash. Rooks lifted out of the nearby trees, giving their caw of approval. His time was at hand; within seconds, his light would be turned out, never to shine on his loved ones ever again—Gary was no more.

Oliver began to regain consciousness. With luck, an off-duty porter driving along the track to his cottage saw him lying in the road. He rushed to his aid, kneeling by the semi-conscious nurse. Although the porter didn't recognise Oliver, the fact that he wore a white coat and badge designated him as nursing staff.

"Are you all right, nurse? What happened?"

Although dazed, Oliver's mind began to clear. He came around. "Where... where am I?"

"The hospital. You're in the hospital. I just found you lying here in the lane. Do you know what happened?"

"No," he said, sitting up, cradling his shoulder. His mind cleared some more. In extreme pain, unsure which was worse, the pain in his chest or his shoulder, he tried to piece together the mystifying events. However, shoch was confusing him.

"Can you make it to that seat?" The porter pointed to a bench about ten yards away.

"I think so."

With help, accompanied by cries of agony, Oliver lurched towards the seat.

"Phew," said Oliver, as he sat, pale-faced, trembling and still holding his shoulder. Although he was convinced his shoulder was fractured in the fall, his primary concern was for his patient. "Where's Gary?"

"Who's Gary?" said the porter.

"My patient. I was out walking with him." He faltered. The pain was becoming intense, clouding his thoughts. "I can't quite remember what happened. I felt a pain in my chest. I think I took a punch and then flew through the air."

"Flew through the air?" questioned the porter. "That must have been some punch." However, he believed the nurse's words were inexact and may have been slightly scrambled by his confusion from the effects of the trauma.

Oliver's sense of duty came to the fore. "What am I thinking. Quickly, can you go to the new psychiatric unit and raise the alarm?"

"Sure, you stay here, I'll get help. What did you say the patient's name was?"

The staff couldn't understand Oliver's garbled account of walking in the grounds with Gary or, moreover, how and why he had received a blow to the chest. They presumed, incorrectly, that Gary had punched the nurse and made off.

With Oliver in A&E, there was little information to go on except his sketchy account of events. Staff combed the area, looking for Gary, calling out his name in case he lay injured somewhere. More staff arrived to join in with the hunt. They had little to go on and so organised themselves into groups, checking obvious possibilities – the mystery deepened.

"I found the nurse on the path here and helped him to that seat over there," said the porter, trying to be helpful. In reality, he added nothing tangible to the growing uncertainty.

Mr Elwood looked around, scratched his head, and looked around some more; he was puzzled. Then, out of the blue, a loud cry came from the canal area; it hung in the air, conveying urgency.

"Over here, quick! I think we've found him!"

With speed, staff raced to the canal-side; a nurse waved them over. He pointed into the deep canal. Gary's Liverpool F.C. cap floated around in the canal's murkiness. Just below the surface of the water, clothing came into view, indicating the gravity of the find.

"Quickly, run back to the ward and ring the police," ordered the charge nurse to one of his staff. "I can't believe this, another death. Oh, my Lord."

TWENTY-SEVEN

One Week Later.

Two patients dead in a week.
Alarmingly, the new Department of Psychiatry has clocked up two deaths in a week. Hospital management have issued a statement.

Mary threw the newspaper to the floor in disgust. She had just read the paper's account, 'A second suicide in a week,' and she was livid. Mary took an angry sip of her coffee, plonked the mug down on the coffee table and seethed. She hadn't coped with Gary's death very well. In part, her disquiet was because she hadn't seen him since his enforced removal from the house by the police on that determinative day. Mary felt guilty for not seeing him before he died. She hadn't said goodbye. It had left a big hole of regret in her life. A mixture of raw emotion and disbelief dominated her mind. She needed to deal with the grief, but that would take time. Her anger with the press had stirred up her feelings all over again. They had insensitively turned personal pain into cheap, trivialised news, just for the sake of selling papers. How dare they? She thought.

Gary had gone from her life. With difficulty, she grappled with the enormity of the devastating news. Never again would she see him, touch him, or shout at him. The intrinsic substance of a partnership, taken for granted by many in life, had unexpectedly ceased. She had become an emotional wreck, vulnerable, sensitive and disbelieving.

Uncharacteristically for Mary, amid mourning, she experienced an angry phase. "Why didn't the staff look after him properly? If they'd done their job, he would still be alive," she said to Mum.

For her part, Madge sat and empathised with Mary. However, being there had started to pay off. In stages, Mary responded to the attention. Nevertheless, she still found it hard to accept that Gary was no more.

But, for Mary, the grey cloud of uncertainty was about to worsen. As next of kin, she was required to identify Gary's body. Nothing was more certain to confirm and reinforce death than seeing the cold, lifeless form lying in the mortuary. Maybe then, she could accept his passing and move on with her life.

In keeping with legal requirements, Dr Sharif had notified the coroner of the unusual circumstances surrounding Gary's death. That being the case, the first step was to identify the body; the rest of the legal requirements would then ensue. A police investigation or possible inquest in the coroner's court might follow. Dressed in black, Mary attended the mortuary. The absolute horror of the proceedings impacted her as she stood in the anteroom, waiting to view the body. Even with mum's support, Mary felt nervous enough to avoid her responsibility.

In the cold, clinical area of the morgue, Mary's breathing became stilted and shallow. Stomach cramps ratcheted up another notch, adding to her discomfort. Looking around nervously, she prayed it was all just a horrible nightmare, but it was for real. A brief look at Mum confirmed all was far from well. The ordeal, *if* she didn't run like crazy, would resurrect deep-seated feelings of grief and anguish in her tormented soul.

The attendant reached for a large metal cabinet drawer; Mary read the label on the front. Gary Lowe – 10/11/87. She took a handkerchief out of her pocket, which held the odour of her perfume. It was a temporary, welcome distraction. Madge stepped in to take her arm. The cold, clinical mortuary was unquestionably the worst place Mary had ever been in her life.

With great sensitivity, the attendant looked over and waited a few seconds.

"Are you ready?" she said. With a nod from Mary, the metal drawer slid out on rollers, exposing the form of a body covered in a white sheet. Mary froze, rooted to the spot. At that moment, an image of happier times at Halloween came to mind. As a child, Mary recalled wearing a white sheet over her head and body, with her arms outstretched, pretending to be a ghost. Then it was a bit of fun. However, the identification formality was deadly serious. She held her breath, trying to block out the queasiness. She swallowed hard. The sheet was pulled back, revealing a very dead, very blue Gary. Her horrified expression spoke volumes. "This isn't Gary; it's a dummy," she said. "It isn't my Gary; he must be alive. It's a mistake." All at once, her world changed; she became giddy, her vision blurred, and sounds became distant.

Mary recovered in A&E. She had collapsed at the sight of Gary's body. Luckily, the quick-thinking attendant, who was standing nearby, caught Mary before she fell to the floor. In the event, Madge, a tower of strength, identified the corpse, negating the need for Mary to subject herself to such trauma again. The sight of Gary would haunt them for a long time to come. In particular, the blue appearance of his skin, typical of drowning victims, would dominate their minds and cast horrific images for many weeks.

The following day, Nigel, the social worker, drove Mary to the psychiatric unit. Primarily, her visit was to collect Gary's personal possessions. That said, she wanted to thank the staff for their kindness and help afforded to Gary while he was a patient in the hospital. Earlier thoughts of 'the staff should have done better' or 'they killed my Gary' had abated in favour of a more balanced view, thanks to Madge's significant involvement.

Maybe the charge nurse could throw some light on why Gary had committed suicide, Mary thought. Be that as it may, she wasn't sure if her limited emotional strength could hold out long enough to talk about death; only time would tell.

As they entered the main door of the psychiatric unit, a lady dressed in a smart black dress and jacket walked past them. Nigel, the social worker, acknowledged her. "Hello, Mrs St John." No response. She was in a world of her own.

It took a few seconds before Mary realised that this was the wife of the other suicide patient in the same ward as Gary. In an instant, she turned in the doorway and caught up with Eleanor.

"Excuse me, Mrs St John?"

"Yes," she said, surprised that a stranger knew her and had called for her attention.

"You don't know me, but I just wanted to say how deeply sorry I was to hear about your tragic loss," said Mary, with heartfelt sympathy.

"Thank you," said Eleanor, not wanting to talk, merely being polite to someone who offered their condolences.

"I know how you feel," Mary welled up. "My husband, Gary, died here as well; he knew your husband, Quentin. They were friends and..."

Without further ado, Eleanor turned on her heel and walked away, much to the dismay of Mary.

Nigel introduced Mary to the charge nurse. Forever the gentleman, he stood. "Please come in, Mrs Lowe?" he said, shaking her hand and offering her a seat. "Can I get you some tea?"

"No, thank you," said Mary; her voice, thin and tremulous, suggested vulnerability. Eye contact was minimal. How strange it had all seemed to her that the last weeks of Gary's life had sadly played out on this very ward. Guilt feelings had washed over her since his death in ever-changing intensity. Remorse bounced back time and time again. She wondered if it could have turned out differently had she visited Gary or even tried to patch the relationship up for the sake of the children.

"I'm sorry for your sad loss, Mrs Lowe," said the charge nurse.

"Thank you." She reached into her bag for a handkerchief.

"And now the reason for your visit," he pushed a brown envelope towards Mary. "Here are your husband's possessions. We also have some of his clothes," he pointed to a bag nearby.

She looked at the envelope and began to sob. Through tears, she tried to speak. "Do you know, Mr Elwood, we didn't get on well, and Gary was never really there for us. People might even say he wasn't a good father. But, if I could change it to how it was before, even with all his faults, I would have him back in an instant." The mention of 'have him back' opened the floodgates.

With consideration, both left the office, allowing Mary time to compose herself. Later, a female nurse entered the office with a cup of tea and a sympathetic smile.

Mr Elwood had seen a lot of grief in his lifetime; nevertheless, Mary's anguish played on his mind. She reminded him very much of his daughter, Jane, of similar age, looks and disposition.

Feeling calmer and more composed, Mary attended to the matter at hand.

"So, if you're feeling better?" said Mr Elwood.

"Yes, much better. Thank you." Mary took a deep breath, looked at the envelope still sitting on the desk and gave an assuring half-smile. "The clothes... could you dispose of them? I can't." She was teetering on the edge and in danger of breaking down again.

Nigel reacted to defuse the situation. "Yes, of course. That won't be a problem. If we can help in any way, for example, with his remaining clothes at home, contact us. Somebody will collect them from your house and take them to a charity shop."

She smiled again, "Thank you; you are so kind." She took another deep breath to hold back the persistent weeping.

Recovery from grief was particularly difficult for Mary. Usually, talking about the trauma amidst floods of tears and heartache was the first step on the road to dealing with a tragic loss. Nevertheless, of late, Mary's emotional symptoms were spiralling out of control. Talking about Gary brought the emotional pain flooding back with great intensity. Crying stressed her to the point where she became fearful. If she started to cry, she might not be able to stop – she may have a breakdown.

It all came to a head recently when she stood at the supermarket checkout; she experienced the weirdest of feelings. Mary was just about to pay for her shopping when she lost control of reality. It was as if she were in a dream, detached from the outside world. Mary could see her purse and the cashier as she paid, but her mind was blank. The best way to describe it, as she did to mum, was like an out-of-body experience. She was scared and, at all costs, didn't want to repeat *that* ever again.

On the ward, she talked about Gary's death to the staff and, as such, she felt desperately ill for doing so.

"There are some personal belongings in the envelope – a ring, a photograph and some keys and papers that you might need," said the charge nurse. He placed a form in front of Mary. "If you could sign this, Mrs Lowe? It's just to let you know you've received his personal belongings. I've added his clothes and noted that they would be donated to a charity. Is that okay with you?"

"Of course," said Mary, signing the form. She took a moment, mustering up the courage for a final, compelling thought. "I would just like to thank you and the staff, Mr Elwood, for all you did for my..." At that point, she sobbed bitterly, picked up the envelope and fled the office in an undignified dash.

In a moment of untold grief, Mary broke the news of Gary's death to the children the night before the funeral, although even more upsetting and heart-rending was Kylie's question as she tried to grapple with the reality of her dad's passing.

Midst tears, she said. "If Dad is living in heaven now, will he call in some time to see us, Mum?" Those few words resonated with Madge and Mary, leading to many more moments of heartache and anguish.

With a few friends and relatives, the funeral service was held at a crematorium near Anfield. As a final gesture to his memory, Mary draped a Liverpool FC scarf over the coffin as the congregation sang *You'll Never Walk Alone* by Rodgers and Hammerstein. In that melancholy, stirring moment, there was an indescribable, all-powerful feeling of oneness with a higher presence. Maybe it was the culmination of emotions, the stirring song or the acknowledgement of their mortality.

Whatever the phenomenon, Mary felt it, just like everyone else. Although no one spoke about the moment, there was a sense that something unique had happened. There wasn't a dry eye at the service. Even some of Gary's rough-and-ready mates wiped away tears as they sang.

In many ways, the funeral seemed even more poignant, given that most people present had attended the wedding a few short weeks earlier. No one could have predicted that a funeral would follow the marriage so closely. Even Gary wouldn't have taken odds on that bet.

Following Gary's death, Madge offered to stay over and give much-needed support. Both tried to concentrate on household routine, shopping, cleaning and organising. Nevertheless, tearful moments weren't far away. Mary found constant reminders about the house that became the catalyst for sadness and pain.

Madge offered guidance when needed and looked out for moments when her daughter could slip into the depths of despair. That said, she couldn't shake off the sadness she felt for her one and only daughter and grandchildren, all traumatised by the death of Gary.

Bit by bit, the sadness and tears changed to missing and remembering. They moved on, in due course, until thinking about Gary was relatively pain-free.

For ten days, the envelope had sat alongside the wedding photographs on the living room sideboard. In light of the funeral and cremation two days prior, for Mary, the envelope held little importance. Her motherly feelings of responsibility towards the children took precedence; she was single-minded in ensuring they didn't suffer any more trauma. They gave her the strength to carry on and, as such, she woke every morning determined to keep the family routine ticking over, come what may.

The envelope gathered dust on the sideboard. Mary stared at it several times, then dismissed it. For all that and feeling a bit better, one day she summoned up the courage and tore the envelope open. Sliding the contents out onto the coffee table, she instantly recognised his watch, ring and the picture. Then she focused on something quite odd. Along with the personal belongings were a bank receipt and a key, both with the bank's insignia stamped on their tags. Mary held the key up, looking on quizzically.

"Bank key? Why would Gary have a bank key?" She shook her head, put the items back in the envelope, and waited a few more days.

Dressed in black, Mary sat in the bank manager's office. She spoke quietly but with confidence. "Thank you for seeing me at such short notice."

"Not a problem, Mrs Lowe. How can I help you?"

"My husband..." Her voice faltered. She started again, determined to get through it. "My husband, who died recently, had this bank key and receipt." She handed them to the manager for his perusal.

"First, Mrs Lowe, let me offer my condolences for your regrettable loss."

"Thank you." Even in her grief, Mary was genuinely surprised by how kind people had been in recognising her suffering. With empathy, the bank manager helped to smooth out what could have been an awkward situation.

He examined the key and the receipt. "Yes, this is undoubtedly one of our safe deposit box keys."

"Safe deposit?" said Mary, even more perplexed.

The manager keyed the number into his computer system. "Yes, here we are... Mr Gary Lowe, safe deposit box began the twentieth of this month." He handed the key and receipt back to Mary. "Of course, we have to follow protocol. For the bank to release the secure box to you as next of kin, we need a death certificate and proof of identification."

Mary wasn't sure where this was going; nevertheless, she felt determined to see it through. Her curiosity was aroused. Gary, the person she knew inside out and, in all probability, better than he did himself, had a safe deposit box.

"I have what you need with me." She rummaged through her bag and handed over the documents.

He perused the paperwork at length, checking and cross-checking with his computer.

"All appears to be in order, although I must say your personal account isn't looking too healthy, Mrs Lowe."

"Yes, I know, but I will make sure it is sorted as soon as possible." She gave a reassuring smile.

"Well, not a problem right now, Mrs Lowe. I'm sure you have more pressing matters to attend to. If you want to come back in and see me at your convenience, maybe I can help you sort the account, so to speak," he held Mary's paperwork up in the air. "Can I take a copy of these?"

Full of foreboding, Mary looked around the windowless, cold bank vault. It was functional, not intended to be aesthetically pleasing, merely safe and secure. Over the table, a fluorescent tube flickered. The surroundings reminded her too much of the mortuary. She dismissed the distressing thought with a start and focused on the security box as the assistant placed it on the table before her.

"Just press this bell when you've finished," said the assistant, trying to be helpful.

"Could you wait just outside the door? I'll only be a minute?" She needed to know that help was at hand in case she felt ill or needed assistance. Being alone in the room was freaking her out.

Apart from a quizzical look, he agreed. "I'll just be on the other side of the door then," he pointed to the heavy security door as if to confirm her strange request.

"Could you just pull the door to a bit?" Mary shook so much, her voice quivered.

"Well, if you're sure, but we normally close it for customer privacy."

"No!" She hadn't meant to shout; her nerves got the better of her. Mary moderated her voice. "I understand that, but can you, please?"

The assistant saw her fragile state; she clutched her bag tightly and swallowed deeply. A look of anxiety framed her face.

"Yes, of course. I'm just..." he pointed to the door, "just there if you need me."

It had all come down to this. Gary was dead, she was a widow, the children were without a father, and finally, there was an answer to the mystery of her late husband's safe deposit bank key. She stared at the box, frightened to touch it, nevertheless curious. Minutes passed. She experienced an irrational thought: when she opened the box, Gary would pop out and say, *'fooled ya.'* That was stupid, she knew. Still, she was apprehensive and needed time. Except that she didn't have time; the assistant was waiting for her outside.

He knocked on the door. "Hello, Mrs Lowe. Are you okay in there?"

"Yes... Yes, I'm fine, nearly finished." The knock on the

door, instead of reassuring her, had startled Mary. All the same, it was good to know he was close at hand.

"Come on; it won't bite," she muttered to herself, trying to boost her confidence, but mounting pressure dominated her mind, probably because the assistant was waiting outside. She moved towards the security box, trying to control the tremor in her hand. Mary focused on the keyhole, but it wasn't proving easy to perform even such a simple act as putting the key in it. After the third attempt, the key found its place. Momentum absorbed her; Mary unlocked it in a rush, in case she changed her mind. She lifted the lid. Inside was an envelope. Then it happened. Her eyebrows furrowed in disbelief as she peeped inside the manila envelope. "Oh... my... God." It was stuffed with money, more than she had ever held before in her life, except for the money that punters won and lost at the casino where she worked. She flicked through the notes in disbelief, struggling to assimilate the reality of it all.

Then out of the blue, she heard a faint voice. It was somewhere, yet nowhere. "Miiiine bitch." Mary looked around the vault, wondering if she had imagined it. She stopped and listened, trying to pinpoint the location of the strange sound.

Her frail voice, directed towards the door, looked for reassurance. "Did you say something?"

"No," was the reply from the assistant.

"Oh. Maybe it was just a noise coming through the wall vent or a squeaky pipe."

Whatever it was, it spooked her. Hearing no more, she dismissed the voice with a shrug of the shoulders, yet her mind was troubled. Mary stuffed the envelope into her shoulder bag. With no idea how much was in the envelope, she formulated a plan. Later, in the privacy of her home, she would count it and decide what to do. With considerable disquiet, she had to get out of the creepy, disturbing vault – fast.

Instead of answering the mystery bank query, finding the money raised more questions than it answered. Foremost in her mind was, where had Gary got the money from? And if it were legitimately hers, what should she do with it?

As she stood outside the bank, her feelings were all awry; Mary was unsure what to do next. A worrying lightheadedness took hold. Her left hand covered her forehead as she put her right hand to the wall to steady herself.

"Are you alright, Mary?" The odd voice reverberated in her mind, appearing unreal. Seconds elapsed. Unknown to her, a customer who frequented the casino saw her looking pale and weak and in a state of shock. His concern for her well-being was paramount.

"Shall I call an ambulance? Or... maybe I could give you a lift home if that would help."

TWENTY-EIGHT

15th May 1988 – Hotel Poolside.

Mary lay unconscious, lifeless, infested by damnable flies, intent on doing their worst, sapping every ounce of life from her body. Like a protective oscillating black wall, the aggressive flies circled the body just like a swarm of angry wasps. They waited for Mary's demise, hell-bent on wreaking havoc with anybody who dared to come near. It was an impasse; the flies were winning.

Then, out of nowhere, a saint stepped forward. Sweeping Mary up in his firm, muscular arms, he hurried her away to the children's paddling pool and stepped in. Pestilent, angry flies covered him, but his demeanour showed a brave disregard. Shaking his head to clear flies away from his vision, he laid Mary down in the pool and supported her head. Flies floated away from her lifeless body. The crowd, shaken by the spectacle, applauded with relief. Flies covered his face and body; still, he gave little thought to personal discomfort. The muscular hero was single-minded, unstoppable. Even so, the flies hadn't given up yet. They launched a second wave that gave the battle impetus. Sheer numbers arrived covering Mary's face, suffocating all life from her. The flies acted in unison, on a mission to block off her airway, a sure means of snuffing the very life from her. The hero shouted for a towel. Wanting to help, yet not wanting to get too close, a bystander bundled a towel and threw it in the paddling pool. With speed and immense care, he wet the towel and set about wiping Mary's face, clearing away the insistent flies. A faint flicker of life, probably due to the cold water on her face; she coughed and spluttered. Only then did the hero bob his head under the water to free himself from the annoying crawling mass. It appears that chlorine in the pool water was acting as an insecticide. Although weak, Mary regained consciousness. She looked into the eyes of her saviour.

"Hello, handsome."

"Hello yourself, cutie," said the man.

In the face of defeat, the remaining flies lifted into the palms. But as fast as Mary gained consciousness, she slipped back into unconsciousness. Still holding her head out of the water, the hero looked around, shouting. "I need help; is there a doctor or a medic here—anybody?"

With incredible luck, a fellow holidaymaker stepped forward. "Yes, I'm a paramedic; I work on the ambulances in the UK. Quick, get her out of the water and lay her on that sunbed." He adjusted a sun lounger into its flat mode. With speed, muscles lifted Mary gently on the lounger. The medic made a quick assessment. He inspected her mouth and nose, looked into her eyes and took her pulse. Flies in the back of her throat threatened to close off and choke the very life from her. Only quick action could stop her airway from being blocked by the dead and dying kamikaze flies. He swivelled Mary onto her side in the recovery position just in time. As he did so, she vomited the contents of her stomach over the side of the lounger, along with dozens of dead flies. He rechecked her mouth; this time, it was clear. Mary took a shallow, wheezing breath through painful, swollen lips. The signs were encouraging, but she was experiencing difficulty breathing. Her blue lips and extremities were concerning. She needed oxygen and urgent medical help.

"We need to get her to the hospital," shouted the medic to the hotel staff who stood nearby. In the background, a siren could be heard. Someone had already phoned.

The ambulance drove at breakneck speed, hurtling through red lights and heavy traffic to the local hospital. Mary was immediately admitted as an emergency patient suffering from Anaphylaxis (allergic reaction). Life-giving oxygen was administered, and fluids via a drip hydrated her shocked body. Adrenaline, intended to reverse the allergic reaction, was administered promptly.

Lying on the A&E examination bed, unconscious with hundreds of bites that covered her body, she looked a sorry sight. A nurse hooked Mary up to a heart monitor. In the hands of the A&E team, she stood a good chance of recovery. Regular monitor beeps gave the hero a sense of reassurance as he stepped back from the scene.

Dr Garcia checked her vital signs. "Blood pressure low, heart rate slow," he looked around. "You are Mary's husband?" said the doctor, speaking in excellent English.

"Yes, I am Richard Lowe."

"She is doing very well, Meester Lowe," continued Dr Garcia, "she is young and strong; we give an injection to help her body recover from bites. You call it Anaphylaxis. The man in the ambulance he say flies bite her mucho."

"Yes, hundreds of them. I don't know how or why, but yes, crazy flies."

"We treat her now," said the doctor, "she is getting good help. We know more when she is conscious. Now, Mary is safe. We keep close eye on her. But you have many bites on your face," he looked Richard over as if making a clinical assessment.

"No, don't worry about me; I'm fine." Moreover, he did seem fine, apart from the unsightly bites.

"If you are sure, Meester Lowe."

"Yes, I'm okay," said Richard, with confidence.

"Would you like to go back to otel for some time to yourself to shower and change clothes?"

The concern on Richard's face conveyed his answer.

"She will be okay; we take good care of her."

As they spoke, Mary mumbled. With relief, she was regaining consciousness.

Richard moved close to her and took her hand.

"Are you okay?"

Mary moved her tongue, trying to moisten her lips. She coughed a little to clear her throat. Wincing with pain, she croaked a few words. "I'm like a pincushion."

"Well, you still have your sense of humour; that's something," said Richard.

Doctor Garcia glanced at her vital signs on the monitor and smiled assuredly. With a friendly hand on Richard's shoulder, he and the team stepped out of the cubicle, leaving them to talk. The frenzied activity during Mary's admission, a sign of urgency, had abated. Richard gently kissed her sore, blistered lips. "Do you remember what happened?"

"Sort of. I remember being by the pool; I think you went back to the hotel for sunglasses. I talked to the waiter, and it's a bit vague, but then I seem to recall hundreds of flies swooping down on me, biting me. At least I think they were flies and the rest..."

"And then I arrived just in the nick of time."

"Maybe. I don't know. The last thing I remember was flies biting, then choking, and everything went black, and now here I am looking like a..."

"Like somebody from the village of the dammed," said Richard, happy to see Mary over the worst of the trauma. His reassuring smile and contact comforted her. "Whatever crazy thing it was, it's all over now, and here you are back on the mend. But you might have to stay in the hospital for a day or two." Richard waited for her objection – no comment. Mary was just happy to be alive; staying in the hospital seemed to be the least of her problems.

She moved her body to find a comfortable spot, wincing with the slightest movement. Raising her head, Richard fluffed the mini pillow under her head.

Her sore lips needed moistening. "Can you give me some of that water?" She looked towards the small trolley situated nearby.

Attending to routine matters, a nurse bobbed into the emergency cubicle and gave Mary a cursory glance. Richard looked, catching her eye. He pointed to the water. She nodded, holding her thumb and finger half an inch apart to signify a little. With care, he offered her the water with a straw.

She sipped slowly. "Wow, that feels good." Her thirst sated, Mary shrank back on the pillow and emitted an agreeable sigh.

"Hey, I just remembered, there was something else," said Mary. "When I was at the poolside before the flies, I heard a strange voice."

Richard looked on quizzically. "Strange voice?"

"No, really. I can even remember what it said. It was spooky. 'Give me my money back, Mary,' that's what the voice said."

Richard shook his head in disbelief. "That's a bit wacky, isn't it?"

"I'm telling you, it did," said Mary.

He knew she wasn't prone to exaggeration and thought the voice could have been a result of the traumatic shock. "Maybe it's..." his diplomacy failed him, "maybe it's just the shock of it all playing tricks on your mind." He drew on a convincing thought. "It's not every day you get bitten by six thousand flies on steroids, is it?"

The things that endeared her to Richard were his good looks, kindness and fun-loving manner. He always saw the humorous side of life, and in her eyes, it was this that set him apart from others.

After Gary's death, Mary didn't consider another relationship. Despite that, Richard was different. He was kind, considerate and good to be with. Of course, his captivating looks played a part in the overall scheme of things.

Mary took a moment and reflected on the trauma hypothesis. "But I heard it, I really did, 'give me my money back,' that's what I heard. It sounded so real."

Richard became aware that the monitor beeps were increasing. Her blood pressure and heart rate rose, indicating a warning. He sensed she was becoming uptight and uneasy. Intuitively, he ended the conversation. There would be plenty of time to have the 'voices' conversation again sometime. "Well, in that case, it must have been real if you feel so sure about it." In reality, he didn't honestly believe she had heard a voice. When Mary was feeling better, they would look back upon the events and have a good laugh. She settled. His instinct was right; Mary had become edgy, which, in turn, had raised her heart rate and blood pressure. Thankfully, she was settling again.

"Why don't you go and have a break, Richard? You look shattered."

"I wouldn't say no to that. I think I'll grab a bite to eat and maybe a beer," he said, savouring the thought.

"Good. Go on, then. I'll be fine."

He kissed her gently on the head. "If you're sure."

Through painful lips, she smiled. "I'm sure, now go and have a beer for me and no flirting with those sexy señoritas, or else."

The beef burger and beer from the hospital cafe hit the spot; a cigarette would complete the delectation. Maybe he would buy an English newspaper and see how things were back home. With the emergency over, logical thought took place. He considered phoning Madge and the children back in the UK. Though just as quickly, he dismissed the notion. Mary was on the mend, and the doctor had told him the bites would fade in about a week. Why worry the family unduly when we have another 9 days of holiday and relaxation? Maybe there isn't even a need to trouble them, he concluded.

Deep in contemplation, he took a cigarette out of the packet, popped it in his mouth and searched his pockets for a lighter. A Spanish lady nearby, clearing the tables, pointed to a no-smoking sign. With a smile, she gestured to the window. "Outside, you smoke."

Earlier, at the hotel, following Mary's trauma, the ambulance driver had refused to take Richard with them in the ambulance. That being the case, Richard ran at top speed to the hotel room, dressed, picked up a few belongings, threw them into a bag, and made his way to the hotel entrance. There, he found a taxi driver parked up reading the daily newspaper. Ever ready for a Formula One dash, the driver headed at breakneck speed to the hospital when he heard the word 'emergency'. In retrospect, the whole sorry saga turned out to be a blessing in disguise. Richard had changed his clothes and picked up a few personal items. He hadn't realised then that he would be at Mary's side for some time.

Richard wandered outside and took a seat by the hospital's main entrance. There, he witnessed the comings and goings of hospital life.

Built in the centre of town, the emergency hospital treated patients twenty-four hours a day. As well as the usual emergencies, it took care of tourists with a variety of conditions – sunburn, dehydration, sprains, strains, alcohol abuse and adverse reactions to illegal drugs, to name but a few conditions witnessed in the emergency department.

Sitting at a vantage point, he observed holidaymakers leaving A&E with arms or legs in plaster, some in slings, and some with stitches to their faces or heads. As he watched the world go by, it made for an entertaining ten minutes or so. If the constant flow of injuries sustained by holidaymakers weren't so serious, they could have been funny. Richard imagined people saving their hard-earned money for a year, only to end up in A&E in Spain. The irony of it all amused his fertile imagination.

He looked up at the blue sky, feeling happy and secure in the knowledge that Mary was improving. Upon her discharge, they would be able to pick up where they left off and enjoy the rest of their honeymoon.

Energised and eager to see Mary again, he looked at bunches of flowers just inside the shop entrance and considered a bunch of carnations, her favourite flowers. But, before he could give it any more consideration, a nurse in a white uniform ran up to him. "You are Meester Lowee?"

"Yes, I am." Richard resisted the urge to correct her mispronunciation of his name. He had a bad feeling. Her intense communication signalled urgency.

"Come quickly; it is Mary!"

He threw his cigarette to the floor, forgetting all about the flowers and chased after the nurse.

Joy and happiness turned to shock and despair. Richard stood back in a daze as doctors and nurses worked urgently to resuscitate Mary. He made a quick assessment of the desperate situation before him. Doctor Garcia stood with paddles in each hand, ready to place them on Mary's chest. It all seemed so surreal. Only twenty minutes ago, she was in recovery. However, here she was now fighting for her life. With all the might he could muster, Richard willed Mary to recover. Right now, he would make a pact with the devil to save her life; such was his profound love for her.

The doctor's urgent instructions hung in the air. "200 joules – clear!" Mary's lifeless body rose and fell as the paddles on her chest passed an electric current through her heart. Doctor Garcia glanced at the monitor in anticipation. A nurse continued heart massage (CPR) on Mary's chest.

Richard's mind was in turmoil. It seemed horrific to brutalise her body, but he knew the medical staff were doing all that they could to save her, and for this, he was so grateful. Members of the team looked at the monitor; however, the signs weren't good.

"She's in VF," shouted the doctor, with urgency. "300 joules – clear!" The team stood back, allowing the life-giving machine to do its work. As before, her body rose abruptly and fell in response to the shock. Still, there was no change in Mary's condition. They were running out of options. Desperation showed on their faces—time ticked by – more jolts from the defibrillator. Heart massage and a will to revive Mary had no effect.

The monitor's dreaded monotone sound filled the room. She had flatlined. Richard knew what this meant – no life – no hope – the end. Doctor Garcia gazed at the monitor to confirm what he already knew. All was lost. Even so, a nurse continued with cardiac massage. There were no more medical options for a lifeless Mary.

"How long has it been now?" said Doctor Garcia.

"Fifteen minutes," was the reply. Time had passed quickly in the fight to save Mary's life. Cardiac massage, oxygen, drugs, and modern technology in the hands of experienced medics that had the potential to save life had sadly failed. With no other choice, Dr Garcia instructed the nurse to stop the cardiac massage. He placed a stethoscope on her chest and listened for a heartbeat. He checked for a pulse and looked into her eyes – nothing.

With no vital signs, the doctor had no alternative but to cease any further attempt at resuscitation.

Richard surged forward between the despondent medical staff who stood around. "No, don't stop; you can save her! Please, carry on." He looked to Doctor Garcia, who shook his head.

"I am sorry; we can do no more."

In tears, Richard took Mary in his arms. He held her lifeless body close to him, the way he had done so many times before. "No, Mary, please don't go, don't go; I need you." He caressed her head and held it close to his chest. He sobbed uncontrollably.

With respect for his grief, the staff left Richard alone with his wife. Later, a nurse would look in on him to help with the formal death process. At that moment, it was more important for him to have time to grieve.

He lay her head gently back on the bed, held her hand and kissed it. Like an angel, quiet and at peace, Mary lay motionless, an image, a lifeless shell.

Richard didn't witness the ball of white light emerging from her body. Her spirit, in the form of white light, hovered above the bed, as if uncertain about what should happen next. Maybe her love for Richard and the children held her spirit earthbound. Finally, the ball floated higher and disappeared through the ceiling of the A&E department. Her soul was somewhere else.

Richard knew she was in a world without pain, without suffering. Yet, he so desperately wanted her to be with him, right here. She was his love, his partner, his joy; he couldn't go on without her. Richard looked at her longingly. In death, she seemed serene, otherworldly.

He lay his head on her chest, stroking her brow. We should have continued on together for many years to come, with lots of memories, he thought. Tears trickled down his cheeks onto her motionless chest.

He often thought about his brother, Gary, and his stupid disregard for Mary and the children. She was such a lovely, willing partner, full of fun and joy. He recalled how their relationship blossomed. It was slow at first. On occasions, they went to the cinema; sometimes, they had a meal out. Money permitting, the whole family would go for days out in his van. Then, one night, Mary asked him if he wanted to stay. From then on, their love blossomed, and they became as one, inseparable, happy lovers. Richard put the council house in order and attended to all the annoying little jobs. He painted, decorated and transformed the house to its present-day delight.

Once she knew life with Richard was certain, Mary didn't dwell upon Gary's parting. She thought about the future and made plans for a new life.

However, it was all over; their honeymoon was abruptly ended. Richard would never be the same again. His life would end without her love, his soul mate, his *raison d'être*.

He ran his fingers through her hair, holding the last moment that would shortly end as the warmth left her body. Her life form on earth would be transformed like a butterfly into a chrysalis.

Bump. He needed to ring Madge and the children to break the devastating news.

Bump, bump. Richard felt so grateful that the children were at home with Madge and not here to witness the horrors that befell their loving mum.

Bump, bump. His train of thought was interrupted.

Bump, bump. "There it is again?" said Richard as he raised his head to look at Mary. In the background, the cardiac monitor started up, emitting an unmistakable *beep*. He put his head back on her chest to listen. Dare he believe what he was hearing? His own heart skipped a beat. Richard raised his head again and looked at the monitor. Before, where there had been a flat line on the monitor, there were now spikes and numbers.

Looking at Mary, her colour improved. The audible sound took on a regular, rhythmical *beep*. "How can this be?" His mind was in a whirl. He scanned her face and body to confirm what the monitor sound was telling him. Curiously, her right hand was clenched. Uncertain what to do, he took her hand and kissed it. Instantly, her fingers unfurled like the petals of a spring flower. Enclosed within was a single white feather. "What?" said Richard out loud, not at all sure why this should be happening. It was entirely out of context with the moment. He shook his head in disbelief. Then, the unbelievable happened. Mary blinked and moved her head. She looked at Richard through bleary eyes and smiled the most enchanting smile.

EPILOGUE

Richard and Rex, the dog, moved in with Mary, much to the children's delight. The unexpected cash windfall spent on a wedding – a honeymoon to Spain – a van deposit – new garden tools and business cards - was very welcome.

With a new van and business 'Weedum~Feedum' and married to a lady he had secretly admired for years, Richard felt a renewed sense of purpose in life. He had a loving partner, two lovely children and a flourishing garden business. His life was complete. He advertised in the local rag and found new customers, adding to his growing *clientele*, which also included Eleanor.

The voices Mary encountered initially didn't abate. Looking for answers, she sought help from a local spiritualist, who believed the voices were from an earthbound negative spirit. At a planned séance in Mary's home, the medium encountered wild and frightening emanations. Realising she was out of her depth, she ended the séance abruptly and advised Mary to seek help from the church.

Her parish priest, Father Godfrey, made numerous house calls to talk to Mary. He concluded that she wasn't possessed, thus negating the need to collect evidence to apply to the diocese for an exorcism. Instead, the father agreed to bless the house in the presence of Mary and Richard. The unusual occurrences did abate for some time.

The pest controller made numerous visits to the Lowe

household; however, he could not completely eliminate the nuisance flies.

Mary kept the strange, troubling secret to herself, for fear of being branded a lunatic.

The white feather found clenched in Mary's hand following her recovery was inexplicable. Neither could make sense of the occurrence until they returned home and spoke to Mary's mum. She confirmed that the feather was the sign of an angel's presence. It symbolised love and protection, and in Madge's estimation, it was a blessed manifestation. When Mary was in the Spanish Hospital's A&E, where she died, it wasn't deemed to be her time.

Mary and Richard became regular attendees at the local parish church and also enrolled in a local psychic interest group.

Solicitors acting for the estate of Quentin St John failed to understand how £2,000 had left Quentin's account after his death. They could not trace the money after it was withdrawn from the bank. With no further evidence, the investigation was wound down.

In the wake of a second death that week in the new Department of Psychiatry, the hospital management held crisis talks. Behind closed doors, the board met and concluded unanimously that, although there had been no infringement of any rules or practices on the psychiatric ward where two suicides occurred, somebody had to be seen to take responsibility for the deaths. In media parlance, someone had to fall on their sword. After lengthy negotiations, the charge nurse of the psychiatric unit took early retirement on health grounds. To the satisfaction of the management team and the public at large, managerial action was swift and uncompromising. Mr Elwood was considered the perfect scapegoat for the 'unfortunate' events. His departure from the National Health Service would allow the hospital to move on, putting the lamentable deaths behind them.

In reality, Mr Elwood had just three years to work before his official retirement. Therefore, the offer of a full pension and release from work in the stressful psychiatric environment was an opportunity too good to miss. Following a no-brainer discussion with his wife, he gladly accepted early retirement.

A final farewell by nursing staff, friends and medical staff, including Dr Sharif and Dr Reece, took the form of a leaving party at a local hotel. It celebrated his many years of service and loyalty.

For a retirement present from hospital staff, he was given a classical guitar. Not many people knew that he was an accomplished classical player. For many years, he had taken guitar lessons and improved to a very impressive standard. Overwhelmed with his retirement present and the love shown to him, amidst tears of joy and sorrow, his friends asked him to play something special to recall the moment. Guitar on the lap, he played his favourite piece, *Recuerdos de la Alhambra* by Francisco Tárrega.

Although he felt fulfilled in his working life, his later years in the health service proved very challenging and stressful. His departure from the hospital was tinged with sadness and yet relief.

With both children having fled the nest, he and his wife moved to the Canary Islands for peace, tranquillity and an agreeable climate. There he learnt Spanish, took up Flamenco guitar, joined a camera club, pottered in his garden, made new friends, and lived out the remainder of his years in peace and contentment.

ABOUT THE AUTHOR

Stuart Roberts was born in Neston, Cheshire, England. He qualified as a psychiatric nurse (RMN) in the historic city of Chester and went on to work in other hospitals in Cheshire. Later, he qualified in community psychiatry (CPN cert) and continued working on the Wirral Peninsula as a team leader in community psychiatry.

Since retirement, Stuart has enthusiastically pursued his ambition to write and publish fiction (Psychological Thrillers).

Two of his great loves are reading and listening to music. He also writes screenplays, one of which was the basis for this, his first novel.